PRAISE FOR PAPER TIGERS

"*Paper Tigers* is full of hauntings of every sort, a modern ghost story of the very best kind, combining the delicate mania of Charlotte Perkins Gilman, the subtlety of Shirley Jackson and the raw dynamism of Joyce Carol Oates. But what Walters delivers here is thoroughly her own creation: a starkly beautiful tale of what it means to survive."

HELEN MARSHALL, World Fantasy Award-winning author of
Gifts for the One Who Comes After

"*Paper Tigers* gathers the best from every childhood scary story—creepy antiques, haunted houses, seemingly friendly ghosts—and repackages them with the worst and most isolating of adult fears. Walters' prose is vivid and gripping, luring you in, feeding you images that will leave you comforted by the light of your bedside nightstand; horror nostalgia at its finest."

REBECCA JONES-HOWE, author of *Vile Men*

"With *Paper Tigers*, Damien Angelica Walters has created a hauntingly elegant portrait of loneliness and longing for healing. But where she confronts real terror is in answering the question of what it costs the wounded to be whole again. This book is at once as beautiful and frightening as a scar on smooth skin or a scream with perfect pitch."

BRACKEN MACLEOD, author of *Mountain Home* and *Stranded*

"Damien Angelica Walters pulls you into the heart of her characters and traps you there until you're not sure if the story is haunting you, or you're haunting it. Wonderfully creepy and heartwarming, fear and sadness alternate and blend throughout in a story that's packed with atmosphere. Keep the lights on and the tissues close."

PAPER TIGERS

DAMIEN ANGELICA WALTERS.

DARK HOUSE PRESS

PUBLISHED BY DARK HOUSE PRESS,
AN IMPRINT OF CURBSIDE SPLENDOR PUBLISHING, INC., CHICAGO, ILLINOIS IN 2016.

FIRST EDITION
COPYRIGHT © 2016 BY DAMIEN ANGELICA WALTERS
LIBRARY OF CONGRESS CONTROL NUMBER: 2015957759
ISBN 978-1940430577

EDITED BY RICHARD THOMAS
INTERIOR ARTWORK BY GEORGE C. COTRONIS
DESIGNED BY ALBAN FISCHER

MANUFACTURED IN THE UNITED STATES OF AMERICA.
WWW.THEDARKHOUSEPRESS.COM

FOR MY FATHER,

who took me to the library

"I am like a small creature swallowed whole by a monster, she thought, and the monster feels my tiny little movements inside."

SHIRLEY JACKSON, *The Haunting of Hill House*

"In another moment down went Alice after it, never once considering how in the world she was to get out again."

LEWIS CARROLL, *Alice's Adventures in Wonderland*

PART I

OLD HURTS

Please don't look at the Monstergirl.
Please, don't look.

CHAPTER 1

Alison Reese tugged the scarf on her head, pulling the fabric down to cover most of her forehead, and shoved her gloved hands deep in the pockets of her jacket. The soles of her shoes marked each step away from her front door with a thump, then a pause, then a heavier thump.

A woman's voice, high-pitched and nasal, broke the 3 a.m. stillness—"Get outta here!"—and Alison froze, a rabbit in disaster's headlights. Ten feet away, a man stumbled from a house with his shoes untied and the tails of his shirt flapping around his hips. The door slammed behind him, and he let out a string of mumbled curses. Alison tucked her chin toward her chest, willing herself into an insignificant shape, another shadow in the night, and only when the man crossed the street and disappeared did she move again.

Once she reached the street sign at the corner, marking the point of no return, her steps quickened. Her first rule: if one tiny sliver of shoe went past the edge of the sign she had to go on and, of course, tonight it had. Her second rule: she couldn't alter her steps approaching the sign to prevent such an occurrence.

She paused. If she turned left, she'd pass by the elementary school, and although it used to be her favorite route, she hadn't been that way in months. Not since the night she'd stumbled upon a few teenagers lingering in the playground. If she'd seen them first, she never would've entered the playground and she never would've heard their words. Alison blinked twice, forcing the memory away. Decision made, she turned right.

She passed more houses, all nestled next to each other. Narrow brick boxes, some with painted screens covering the basement windows, others with awnings over windows and doors, and all with a marble stoop, a Baltimore trademark.

The original residents of Hampden, a triangular shaped area in northwestern Baltimore, were mostly millworkers. Now, artists, college students, and families took their place.

The late September air held a promise of rain underneath the scent of old exhaust. Alison turned onto 36th Street and a quick gust of wind ruffled the scarf covering her head. Shops and restaurants with darkened windows lined both sides. Traffic lights cast arcs of red, yellow, and green on the asphalt. An empty plastic bag spiraled on the pavement and bounced across the street. Alison peered into the windows and saw cloth-covered tables in one, shelves of handmade jewelry in another, and racks of women's shoes in the next, teasing her with their proximity, taunting with their inaccessibility. When she neared the last store at the end of the block, her pace slowed and she smiled. The skin on her right cheek twisted and tugged, turning the side of her face into something closer to a grimace than a grin.

A small hand-lettered sign in the corner of the window read Elena's Antiques in careful print. Antiques, maybe. Junk, definitely. Until a month ago, the building housed an art gallery. Not the sort with champagne openings for brilliant young artists selling work for six figures, but the type featuring art heavy with barbed wire and faces contorted in misery and torment. All prices negotiable, of course.

The streetlamps cast a pale glow on the items on display: an old tricycle with faded plastic streamers hanging from the handle grips, a lamp with a multicolored glass shade, several small stone dragon statues, a hand mirror with a gilded handle, the reflective side facing away, and a photo album with a worn, ash grey cover. A large split in the leather ran from one corner down to the center, and the bloated shape of the page edges gave proof of the photos within.

Over the past three weeks the shop had filled up with old furniture and other odds and ends, but the sign and the items in the front window were new additions. She bent close to the glass, turning slightly to see everything with her one good eye. A quick succession of footsteps heading in her direction pierced the silence. She exhaled and stood, leaving behind a circle of breathy fog on the window. The steps drew closer.

A short, round woman with a bright scarf wrapped around her hair emerged from the shadows. Alison backed away from the window, blinking in disbelief and dismay. 3 a.m. on a weeknight was normally safe; she never ran into anyone. And twice in one night? She hunched her shoulders.

The woman unlocked the door, turned, and jingled a large ring of keys in her hand.

"You want come in?" she asked.

"No thank you," Alison said, angling her face away from the glare of the streetlamps.

"Is okay."

She glanced at the photo album. She could call her mother tomorrow and ask her to pick it up. But what if someone else bought it? A ridiculous thought. But what if?

"Aren't you closed? It's the middle of the night."

"Sometime close, sometime open. If you want something, I let you come in anyway."

Alison worried her lower lip between her teeth. The woman gave the keys another shake. Why was she so willing to open her door, so unconcerned at this time of the morning?

Alison whirled around, moving away from the store. Red flared inside her, a deep shade of crimson shot through with scarlet, and she tightened her hands into fists, hating the way the right curled in, misshapen and smaller than the left. The red swirled in and around, twisting her every cell into a grim reminder of what she had, what she remembered, and what she lost. Her vision blurred.

Go away, Monstergirl, a voice said.

How she wished she didn't know that voice so well. The voice, sharp of teeth and cruel with contempt, bit down hard. The woman remained at the door, her eyes narrowed.

Alison closed the distance between them with several short steps that helped hide her ungainly walk, ignoring the ache in her right hip.

"The photo album in the window. I want." She cleared her throat. "I'd like to buy it. Please."

"Okay, you come in."

The woman held the door open with one hand and gestured with the other. Alison paused, her mouth dry. How long since she'd been inside any building other than her house or the hospital? She couldn't even bring herself to cross the threshold of the house in which she'd grown up, in spite of her mother's assurances that she'd taken down all the old photographs.

Her mother's words came to mind: *Babygirl, you have to try.*

Alison kept her chin down and when the woman turned on the lights, she turned her face away.

Leave, leave, leave. She hasn't seen you yet, a voice said, not the voice of the red, but of the sharpest yellow. Alison swallowed hard. Shoved the voice away.

The walls still retained the previous tenant's paint, a steely shade of grey, complete with unpatched gouges in the plaster. Some of the ceiling tiles in the long, rectangular space had been replaced, but others, stained and bowed in the middle, hung from the framework. A fluorescent tube near the window flickered.

"You want look around some, is okay," the woman said as she headed to a counter in the corner, her scarf, a vibrant fuchsia with dark flowery swirls, bobbing up and down the entire way. "I here for little while."

"Thank you," Alison said.

She nudged the hand mirror in the window out of the way, and grabbed the photo album. It slipped from her grasp, sliding back with a heavy thud and a puff of dust. She cast a glance toward the counter, but the woman (maybe Elena?) muttered to herself and crouched down, leaving only a curve of her scarf visible. Alison wrapped her

old scars, old hurts

gloved fingers around each side of the album, breathing in the passage of time and a hint of tobacco as she pulled it free and held it close against her chest.

Despite the bright lights, the shop called out with a siren's song, and after another check to make sure maybe-Elena wasn't watching, she let her feet answer the call. The smell of old boxes, yellowed paper curling at the edges, and unwanted clothing hung in the air, musty and thick. And beneath, a trace of artificial rose, reminiscent of the squares of decorative soap her grandmother had kept in a porcelain tray in the bathroom. From a large bookcase set against the far wall, she removed a volume of Poe's works, but a dark stain covered more than half the pages and rendered the text illegible.

She traced a set of initials—JSJ—carved into one corner of the desk, and her fingers left three trails behind in the fine layer of dust covering the scuffed mahogany. A brass-handled drawer gave a tiny squeal of protest, and the carved legs ended with well-worn lion's feet. The sort of desk designed for a master wordsmith's time and tales. Alison's own poetry, all random, chaotic outpourings of battered emotions, did not warrant such a masterpiece.

If a writer didn't purchase the desk, Alison hoped a teacher would. The kind of teacher students gave gifts to; the kind of teacher students remembered long after they left the classroom. She could almost see a stack of test papers on one corner, an open lesson plan in the other, a collection of pens off to the side. She closed the drawer a little harder than she intended, picked up the photo album, and made for the counter.

"How much please?" she asked, keeping her chin down.

"Five dollar."

When she handed the money over, their fingertips touched, glove against skin, and she held her breath. Maybe-Elena said something low, something soft and not in English, but Alison recognized the tone. Oh yes, she did. Yellow raced in, a huge wave (so young, so ugly) crashing down, too fast and too hard to hold still, and she stumbled back, grabbing the album, refusing to lift her gaze, refusing to see everything she hated—feared—in maybe-Elena's eyes. Without another word, she fled back into the safe anonymity of the shadows, her heart a steady beat of hurt.

● ● ●

It took three tries before Alison could hold the key still enough to slide it into the lock. She rushed in, flipped the dead-bolt latch, and stood with her back against the door, the album clutched to her chest.

Red and Yellow, two of the Muses of Disfigurement accompanying Alison on her journey through the land of scars, still fought within her. She envisioned them as women in flowing robes, their faces hidden behind swathes of fabric. Red carried anger in her fists; Yellow bore the weight of pity upon her shoulders. Both had voices far too strong and sharp to ignore. Both were bound to Alison with unbreakable chains stronger than steel.

Alison's eyelids fluttered shut and she willed herself to a blank slate. Emptiness flowed in, leaving her still, silent, and colorless—the absence of self, the absence of everything. Her pulse slowed, and her breathing turned even.

She slipped off her gloves (plain thin gloves, not the hateful pressure garments meant to tame the scars into submission), shifting the weight of the album from side to side. The spaces where pinkie and ring fingers on her right hand should be cried out with a familiar phantom itch, familiar enough to ignore. As she kicked off her shoes, her hip gave a small thank you. The reinforced heel of the right shoe kept her hips properly aligned and turned her limping gait into something less awkward, but like braces on teeth, the forcing of crooked into straight held a price.

She shrugged out of her jacket and sat on the end of the sofa, closest to the light, with the album on her lap. She'd done it. She'd gone into the store and braved the woman's stares. Sure, she'd hightailed it out of the shop, but that was okay. She'd faced a stranger. That had to mean something.

Baby steps, babygirl. Baby steps.

Tracing her fingers along the cover, she imagined the feel of the old leather. Rough, yet smooth, perhaps cool to the touch. The tip of her forefinger caught on one jagged edge of the long split, hard enough to leave a small mark, a raised line of white against the pinkish skin glove of scar tissue, but not sharp enough to draw blood.

She opened the album, smiling at the scent of tobacco. They never smelled the same. Another odd smell conjured images of old furniture and empty animal cages.

Faint smears of indigo marred the stiff, heavy paper of the first page. Traces of old ink? She tilted the page. Yes, definitely. Old words too faded to read, but still there nonetheless. She angled the album a little further, almost able to make out the handwritten words. An inscription? The name of a family? One line stood out at the bottom, a little darker than the rest, the handwriting old-fashioned and spidery. Not a name, though. Too many words for a name. She held the album even higher, and the words came into focus. Alison read them twice to make sure.

A paper tiger to swallow you whole.

A snippet of poetry perhaps. Oddly compelling.

"Here there be paper tigers," she said and turned the page.

The yellowed paper crackled and a small corner crumbled off into her hand. The first page contained one photo, a sepia-toned, somber faced man in a dark suit, a dark stain obscuring the bottom half of the picture. Alison traced the man's face with her finger, willing it to memory. Dark hair, bushy moustache, stern eyes, small spectacles balanced on a strong nose, thin lips pressed into a narrow line.

"George, I think. You look like a George."

A bachelor with a penchant for strong drink. A banker or a businessman. The fantasy spilled out and took shape. His voice deep and raspy, yet eloquent. Educated. A haze of pipe smoke floated around his head, illuminated by the glow of candlelight. A journal, ornate script on its pages, lay open on the table. The sharp bite of liquor. Brandy.

"A good year. Only the best," he said, lifting his glass in a toast. "Only the best."

A predatory smile and quick shift of the eyes. He slammed his fist down. Glass shattered and liquor pooled onto the journal, blurring the ink. Blood seeped between his fingers and mixed with the alcohol and the ink.

Alison pulled her hand back from the page and the images drifted away. The tips of her fingers tingled again, the disconnect between brain and dead nerve endings teasing her with the memory of sensation. She dropped her hand onto the sofa, and her breath caught in her throat. Smooth fabric played beneath her skin, soft and real and warm, not phantom. She pushed harder; the sensation melted away, leaving her with the familiar nothingness and tears burning in her left eye. But she knew she felt it.

The red coiled tight. *Liar*, it said. *Fool.*

It wasn't the first time it had happened, nor would it be the last. It could happen for years, her doctor had said. When she asked how many years, he'd glanced away. Obviously, more than two. Then he resumed his pep talk about living in the here and now. Easy to say, and even easier to do, for a man with all ten fingers, two eyes, a full head of hair, and unscarred skin.

A dull, uncomfortable ache nestled in the pit of her stomach.

Let me out, Monstergirl, Red said.

She closed her eyes, counted to five, and let it all go. Nothing more than spilled milk. Not worth the tears. Not worth the hope.

She grabbed the next page in the photo album. A triangular piece of the paper ripped, disintegrated to parchment confetti between her fingers, and spiraled down to the sofa. She slid her finger under the opposite corner of the page and lifted. The corner split; she gave a small growl.

Flipping the album on its side, she fanned the page edges with her fingernail. A brittle yet musical rustle danced up, but all the pages, save the first, held fast together despite no visible sign of water damage darkening the thick paper. She tried sliding her finger between two pages. They wouldn't budge. At least George's photo, his face, made the album interesting enough to keep. Behind the spectacles, his eyes gleamed with an intense light, like the look of a caged animal with dusky stripes pacing past the walls of its prison, waiting for a chance to be free.

Or to attack.

CHAPTER 2

Three quick little raps of knuckles against wood announced her mother's arrival, and Alison closed her laptop before opening the door. Her mother bustled through, wrapped in a comforting cloud of gardenias, all smiles and shopping bags. She set down the latter before she pressed her lips to Alison's unscarred left cheek.

"Wait until you see the sweater I bought you," she said, stepping back. "It might convince you to change out of your pajamas once in a while."

"Please. You don't have to buy me something every time you step foot in the mall," Alison said. "And my pajamas are perfectly fine. You're the one who bought them for me anyway."

"Hush. I can buy my daughter a present if I want to. Are you sure I bought those?"

"Yes, I'm sure. Remember? I asked you to after I saw them online."

"Hmm," she muttered. "Monkey pajamas. What every well-dressed twenty-four year old woman is wearing these days." She glanced over at the laptop. "How are your friends?"

"They're fine," Alison said.

A shred of guilt wormed its way in, turning the words bitter. For a few months after her release from the hospital, she belonged to an online forum for survivors, but once her friends started discussing their reintroduction to society, she deleted her account and all the subsequent emails. And in the year since then, she'd avoided any website that even hinted at human interaction.

They never spoke of the other friends, the old friends and coworkers

pushed away

long gone.

Her mother stopped in the middle of the living room and sniffed. "What is that smell?"

"What smell?"

"It's dreadful. Can't you smell it?"

"I can only smell your perfume. Too much, like always." She let out a fake cough, hiding a smile behind her hand.

"Hush."

Her mother pointed at the album. "It's that, I think." She fanned the air in front of her face. "Oh, Alison, it's horrible. It smells like dead, wet leaves. How can you stand it?"

Alison shrugged. "It doesn't smell that bad to me. A little musty, but it's old. I bought it last night."

"Last night?"

"Well, technically this morning, but yes, I got it from a new shop on 36th Street, one of those places with a handful of antiques and a lot of junk. This was in the window."

Her mother stopped with her hand in mid-air. "You went in the shop?"

"I did."

"Oh babygirl, I'm so proud of you," she said, taking Alison's hands in hers.

"It was no big deal. I was out walking, and the woman was going in. She saw me looking at the album and said I could come in. She wasn't open, though. There weren't any other customers, I mean. Just me."

"But you went in?"

"Yes, I did." Tears glittered in her mother's eyes. Alison gave her hand a small squeeze. "It doesn't mean I'm going to go out in the middle of the day. I wanted the album."

"But it's a step in the right direction. The next time you go out will be easier and soon—"

"Enough, okay?"

"Okay. Well, show it to me."

"You don't even like them."

"I've never said that. I just think it's morbid. All those dead strangers. Of all the things you could possibly collect…"

Alison rolled her eyes but flipped the front cover open. "You've said that too, more than once. What can I say? I like them. This one isn't much, though. The pages are all stuck together. You can only see one picture."

Her mother fanned the air again. "From the smell, I can believe it. It's like someone dipped it in manure and rolled it in mud."

"It's not that bad."

"Sorry dear, but it is. I think you have so many of them you've become immune. I wish you would collect something…more aromatic."

"Like perfume? Sorry, you have the market on that one. Do you want something to drink? I can make some tea."

"Tea would be wonderful, but I can—"

"Nope, you stay put. I'm not crippled."

In the kitchen, Alison filled the teapot and set it on the burner before she turned the knob, hiding the tiny blue flames from her sight. She normally used the microwave to make tea for herself but it made her mother happy when she used the stove. Another check mark on her "Alison is making progress sheet."

Alison clenched her jaw. It was hard enough to make progress; knowing her mother was always taking notes made it harder still.

"Mom, are you hungry?" she called out. "If you want, I can make something."

Her mother came into the kitchen and fetched the sugar bowl. "No, I'm fine. I had a little something before I came over."

"You couldn't sit and wait, could you?"

"Oh you know me. I get itchy feet when someone else is in the kitchen. Maybe I'll come over next Sunday and make you dinner."

"You don't have to do that. Why don't you come over, and I'll make you dinner."

"But I like doing things for you."

Of course she did, but did she have to try so damn hard? Alison wasn't going to shatter into pieces. She'd made it this far, hadn't she? She held her tongue, said only, "I know you do."

"I've been thinking. I can add a cell phone to my plan at any time and since you go out walking now, I'd like to get you one."

"I don't want one. I'm fine with the phone here."

"But what if something happens? What if you fall—"

"Mom. Please? If I decide I want one, I'll let you know."

Her mother held up both hands. "Okay, okay." Her nose wrinkled. "You're not really going to keep that album, are you?"

"Sure, why not? I might be able to get the pages unstuck and get to the other photos."

"I think you should throw it away. The man in the picture is horrible."

Alison turned away so her mother wouldn't see her smile. "It's just an old photo, and he's just an old dead guy. He's perfectly harmless."

"Still, it's unsettling. Please, don't keep this one."

Alison turned back. "Okay, fine. I'll throw it out."

The tea kettle rang out with a high-pitched whistle, and they jumped in unison.

• • •

After her mother left, Alison took a butter knife into the living room and sat on the floor beside the coffee table. She slid the blade between two of the photo album's back pages and wiggled it from side to side, wincing at the sound of tearing paper and pulling it out when it met resistance.

She flipped it to George's photo. Despite her odd daydream of broken glass in a slammed fist, his gaze held only a middle-aged man, dark of eyes and hair, from a forgotten time, his name lost everywhere but her own imagination. Nothing visible anchored the photo in place, and the edge of one corner bent out. She tapped the knife against her palm, set it aside, and slid her finger under the tiny separation. The paper crackled in protest, but the photo stayed intact. When the edge came up a little more, she poked and prodded the opposite corner until it lifted as well. The third corner wouldn't budge, so she traced the edge of her fingernail around the last one, and with a tiny, brittle creak, it gave way. As her fingertip slipped under the picture, a white crack appeared at the edge, breaking through the sepia tones in the shape of a lightning bolt. She pulled her hand back, and two drops of blood dripped onto George's shoulder.

"Damn," she muttered. "Sorry, George."

She cleaned off the blood from the photo with her thumb, leaving behind a small smear. Crimson welled from the small gash on her finger, a wet mouth within scarred lips, and she pressed her thumb on the cut, longing for the sharp sting. This wound would scab over and gift her construct of ruined flesh with yet another mark. As if she didn't have enough.

Yellow rushed in, sunshine bright belying the ugliness it contained. It spoke of Monstergirls and broken things, useless fingers (and not quite enough because two little finger-piggies went away and never came home) and fractured images in a mirror, wrapping her in a blanket of familiar hurt. She closed her eyes, and tried to find the nothing-place, but the scars crisscrossing her palms and fingers and the back of her right hand didn't care about closed eyes.

They all stare at the Monstergirl. They stare and point and make faces because you're the sideshow freak, and they can't resist the horror. Come, give up a tear or two, you poor, poor thing. So young, so trapped in your unmistakable destruction. Save your prayers, your hopes, swallow everything you ever thought you wanted. This is all you have now. Take it, choke it down, drown in it—

A heady scent of tobacco pushed through the voice, and her eyes snapped open. A grey wisp of ribbon-thin smoke hung in the air. Then it vanished. She held out one hand, touching the space where the smoke had been.

She wiped the blood smear again. Tingles raced up and down her thumb and she hissed in a breath. Under the pins and needles, the exterior of the photo changed from a dull pressure to rough against her skin, not the slick, slippery feel of a new photograph, but parchment, textured and warm. She traced the outline of George's face; when she slid her thumb from the picture to the surrounding paper, a cool heat like icemelt on a hot pavement radiated from its pebbled surface. Spreading her fingers wide, she set her hand down, half-covering George's photo, half on the paper, but the coldhotcold touched only her thumb. The rest of her skin remained an insensate landscape of alternately ridged and smooth scars. The tingle intensified, a creeping, insectile buzz beneath the skin. She blinked and the sensation ceased, like the phantom smoke. With a sigh, she stuck her finger in her mouth, tasting the metallic tang of blood.

A paper cut from a paper tiger.

CHAPTER 3

"Remember, Alison. Breathe."

Tiger teeth bit into her right shoulder, and agony lanced down to the small of her back. Alison inhaled, shut her eyes, and turned her head to the side. The teeth gnawed again, a whole pack of beasts taking their time, savoring every moment.

Meredith's hands stopped. "Are you okay?"

Alison nodded. Meredith smiled, and in spite of the lines feathering the corners of her eyes, she appeared little older than Alison. She was tall and broad shouldered, her arms wiry with muscle. The first time they'd met, Meredith had crossed those arms, cocked one eyebrow, and said, with her slight Southern accent, "You're not going to give me any trouble now are you?" Alison had said no, but she didn't think she'd said another word to her for months. The silence didn't deter her, though. As both a physical therapist and masseuse who worked exclusively with people with traumatic injuries, and had for over fifteen years, she was accustomed to nearly every emotion brought to her table.

"I'm going to move a little lower."

"Okay." Alison said. She took another deep breath, trying to clear her mind, but it didn't work didn't work, so she thought of George in his study, recounting the day's events in his journal. Dipping his pen into the ink—

Meredith reached the scar tissue near the base of Alison's spine, where it twisted thick and knotted, and the tigers ripped into her skin with a frenzy, all claws and teeth, and the thoughts of George vanished.

"Alison, stop holding your breath. You know it makes it worse when you do."

"I know."

"So why do I have to remind you every time?"

Alison opened her eyes and took a few deep breaths. "Better?"

"Yes, now don't stop."

Meredith's hands pressed again, and hot tears blurred Alison's vision. The pain didn't compare to debridement, the savage slicing away of unhealthy flesh, but the sweet anesthetic of drugs had dulled that torment. Meredith's massages and the stretching exercises came with no such mercy. Alison breathed in and out, long and slow, and stared at the bookcases lining the walls. The one directly in her line of sight held photo albums, including George's, all containing stranger's faces and lives captured, kept, and then discarded. She'd found most of them on online auction sites, sold for trivial amounts by people who'd discovered them tucked away in attics or basements. George's album sat on the top shelf, next to her favorite, an old one she called The Lions because everyone in its sepia world had thick, unruly hair. She thought it fitting the cats kept company.

Meredith's hands pushed at a spot above her tailbone where the results of three skin grafts overlapped and tucked into each other, a basket weave of skin harvested from other parts of her body, and Alison sucked air through her teeth.

"Okay, let's turn you over. Almost done now."

Alison did, keeping her eyes closed, hating the way it felt to have Meredith's eyes on the scar tissue on her chest, where her right breast should be, the underlying muscle too damaged to support reconstruction. Not even her nipple survived. Once, she half-joked to her mother that they should've removed the other breast in the interest of symmetry, and the wild, panicked look on her mother's face, like that of a snake-startled horse, was something she'd never forget. Her mother didn't understand that the removal would have made little difference; Alison's entire right side, from head to heel, was damaged.

Blinking back tears, she focused on the photo albums. Her first album, purchased on a whim not long after her release from the hospital, sat on the other side of George's, its cover a dull shade of twilight sky as viewed through a camera lens spotted with grime. She'd been compelled to buy it after seeing the auction photo of the first page, a photo of a young woman in a lace wedding dress, holding a bouquet of flowers. A woman who would've been pretty, save for the large kidney-shaped birthmark on her cheek. In spite of the mark, someone found her pretty enough, or at least suitable enough, to marry, but the wistful look in her eyes struck a deep chord.

Before Alison gave it too much thought, she'd placed a bid, tapping her fingers on the table while the minutes wound down. No one else bid. Once she received the album a few days later, the small smile on the woman's face, a detail not visible on the auction site photos, told a story of hope and happiness far more compelling than the wedding dress, the flowers, or the mark on her cheek.

The rest of the album contained more photos of the woman and her husband, a sharp-jawed, handsome man. In the last photo, the woman held a baby in her arms. Regardless of the birthmark staining her cheek dark, she glowed with a halo of contentment and secret beauty.

The second time Alison viewed the album, she left it open on the last page and let her mind wander. She gave them all names, breathing imaginary life into their snapshot stillness by inventing more children, happy smiles, days filled with laughter, and nights filled with love. All the things she'd never have.

If only she'd—

"Done," Meredith said, lifting her hands away. "Ready for some stretching?"

Alison sat, wiping her cheek. Her back tingled, as though a mild electric current ran under the skin, a sensation that would last for hours before fading. The stretches would leave her sore for days, but they allowed her to bend over and put her shoes on without pain. And they helped take away the fear of her skin splitting apart at the scarred seams, turning her into a broken doll of disfigurement all the reconstruction in the world couldn't stitch back together.

● ● ●

Alison slid George's album off the shelf and carried it into the living room with slow, limping steps, her hip crying out the entire time. She balanced it on her knees and ran her fingers over the front page, yearning for a tiny flash of sensation, whether tease or phantom.

Not fair.

The words hovered deep inside, urging sorrow, urging her to curl in a tiny ball and bury—hide—the right side of her face in the cushion. She took a deep breath, then another, but *notfair* lingered, a sweet darkness asking her to put on her victim shoes and dance into its warmth. To keep company with thoughts of small, slippery pills chased with wine, or the sharp edge of a razor sliding across skin dead to the sting of the metal kiss. The words found shape and substance.

Why do you even fight it, Monstergirl?

"Go away."

Never, the voice said, trailing soft laughter as it slipped back under her skin.

A chill raced up her spine, and she closed her eyes, searching for a blank slate, but the steady throb in her back and the numbness of her fingers wanted a voice of their own. She would give anything at all to feel again, to be something close to normal, something less than a Monstergirl.

She pushed the photo album off her lap onto the cushion beside her, and the front page flipped over, covering George's face with ink-smudge writing, the paper tiger swallowing his image whole. She steepled her fingers under her chin and caught a whiff of tobacco. Unless it was a phantom smell. Like the heavy smoke and the roasting—

"Stop," she said.

She closed her eyes and took another deep breath. George's face appeared in her mind. He bent over his journal, smiled around the pipe jutting from the corner of his mouth, and scratched black words onto the paper with a gold-nibbed fountain pen. He caught her gaze and turned the journal around.

Lonely in isolation.

He tapped the page with his pen and new words took shape.

Lonely, scarred, and alone.

"Yes, that's me," she said.

He nodded and took the pipe from his mouth. "Perhaps we can do something about that," he said, his voice timbrous and heavy with inflection, not accent.

"I don't think so."

"Many things are possible, if you want them enough. The real question is, how much do you want the things of which you dare not speak?"

Smoke curled from the end of his pipe and spiraled around his head in a dark blur. It swirled and expanded, obscuring his face. A heavy rush of wind, cold and biting, pulled the smoke up and out and when it vanished, so too did George.

She blinked awake. Aware. The setting sun bathed the room in shadows and grey, a cobwebby veil of solitary confinement. She transferred the photo album to the coffee table, and stretched out on the sofa, groaning under her breath. From the back of her neck to her tailbone, her muscles cried out. The tingle of almost-feeling beneath her skin was gone, leaving behind the dead space of ruined flesh, but she tucked her hands under her cheek and smiled.

CHAPTER 4

Using the back of her left hand, Alison gauged the temperature in her shower, turning the knob until the water ran lukewarm. The rings rattled across the bar as she pulled the curtain closed, closing herself off in a dark cocoon, untouchable by either the sunlight, blocked by a window darkening blind, or the room's solitary 25-watt bulb. She put her face into the spray, turning so the water ran down her left side, and kept still for a long time with her palms pressed against the tiled wall. Dark hair hung over her forehead and clung to her cheek, the one-sided ripples mimicking the folds of the shower curtain. A few wispy strands partially concealed the reconstructed ear on her right side. When she was

whole

younger, she wore it halfway down her back; now the hair on her left side barely skimmed the top of her shoulder. Moving out of the spray, she grabbed for the shampoo, her skin pulling uncomfortably with the movement. A dark image of her slippery red insides coiled on the white of the tub played through her mind then danced away, a grim little fairy tale of illusory horror. After she turned off the water, she parted her hair on the left with her fingers and flipped it over, hiding some of the scar tissue on the right side of her scalp. A grim comb-over trick a nurse once showed her. A trick used by many, she'd said. Alison tugged a few of the strands forward in Veronica Lake fashion and slid the shower curtain open, neither a Hollywood starlet exiting a limousine nor a butterfly escaping the chrysalis in a drapery of color, but a morbid grotesquerie climbing up from the depths of hell. An open set of shelves hung on the wall in place of a mirror, sparing her the sight.

Maybe it was time to replace the mirror; maybe it would help. She ran her finger across scar tissue and exhaled softly. No, she wasn't ready for that yet.

She patted her skin dry, applied lotion, slipped on a pair of pajamas and exited the bathroom in a wreath of steam.

Thump.

She stood immobile. Heard the thump again. Cold droplets ran from her hair down onto her forehead and the back of her neck, cold until they met scar tissue, but she made no move to wipe them away. She stood with her arms slack and her head tilted to one side. A neighbor's voice, muffled through the walls, filtered through the quiet then dwindled away.

She crept to the top of the stairs on tiptoe. The furnace kicked on, sending out a whoosh of warm air through the vents, and she squeaked in surprise.

"Mom?"

The furnace responded with another push of air. With slow steps, she descended the staircase, her breath a tight knot inside her chest; when she hit the landing, she stopped and sniffed the air. Tobacco?

"George?"

Laughter spilled from her lips. George, long dead and captured in a photographic capsule of time, was merely a paper man in a paper world, tigers not included. The living room appeared as it always did—sofa with a fleece throw draped across one arm, two standing lamps, a coffee table made of dark wood, a small television in one corner, and in the opposite, half-hiding the slate hearth from the walled-up fireplace, a bookcase with various hardcover and paperback novels. Next to that, a fire extinguisher, one of four in the house, hung from a waist-high bracket on the wall. Her eyes flickered over everything once, twice, and snapped back to the coffee table, occupied by a half-empty glass of water. Before her shower, the photo album sat next to the mug with its cover closed. Now the album rested on the floor next to the table, its cover open and George's picture exposed.

She checked the front door lock, but the dead bolt held fast and secure. The front windows were also locked; same for the back windows, the kitchen door, and the door leading into the basement. She remembered setting the album down on the corner of the table, far enough from the edge to keep it from toppling over. She picked up the album, resting her right palm flat on George's face. One of his eyes peeked out from the space where her pinkie and ring finger should be. Sudden pins and needles tingled from her palm to the tips of her fingers, and she dropped the album on the table, waving her hand in the air until the feeling vanished.

She headed for the kitchen, water glass in hand, pajama pants swishing around her ankles. Ice cubes clinked and splashed as she dropped them into her glass one by one. Slivers of melting ice stuck to her fingertips, cold and stinging; she wiped them away on a dishtowel softened to the texture of a baby blanket by many tumbles in the dryer and turned the faucet on. Stepping back from the sink, she picked up the towel again. Underneath the skin of her left hand (all finger-piggies present and accounted for, as useless as the three on her right hand), the blanket was a not-thing, held but not felt; in her right, the velvety fabric, far too real and smooth for an illusion of memory, slipped and slid across her patchwork skin.

She tossed the towel on the counter, stuck her right hand under the faucet, and shivered. Laughing out loud, she trailed her wet fingers along the edge of the sink, the stainless steel cool beneath her touch. Forgotten, the water rushed and splashed from the tap, sending droplets up and out. She extended her arms and ran both hands along the counter; one hand met nothing at all, the other met old tile and rough grout. At counter's end, she slid her hands back up and down again, the scars on her face tugging as her lips stretched into a distorted smile. Her hands crept back up and the sensation stopped. No pins and needles, no fading away, but an abrupt cessation, all the feeling severed as sure as a limb cut off by an axe-wielding movie villain. Minus the theatrical screaming and fake blood, of course.

She turned the water off, her movements clumsy.

Phantom, phantom, it fooled you again. Stupid, gullible, ruined girl.

● ● ●

The children ran in circles in the yard, the summer sky bright and clear overhead. Helen watched them with a smile on her face, one hand up to cover the birthmark. She didn't even know she did it and he couldn't bring himself to tell her. He liked the birthmark. It made her a little more real, a little more human—

The phone rang with a shrill pitch, shattering Alison's daydream into pieces.

After their hellos, her mother said, "I'm getting ready to run out to the store to get some Do you need anything?"

"No, I'm good. I have a delivery coming tomorrow."

"Are you sure?"

Alison flipped open George's album and picked at the corner of his photo with her thumbnail hard enough to make a tiny *snick-snick* sound, but not hard enough to tear the paper. "Yes, I'm sure."

"I was thinking of stopping by the bakery, too."

Alison rested her hand on George's face. "You are evil. You know that?" Pins and needles radiated through her hand. She gave it a shake.

Her mother laughed. "Sugar cookies, maybe?"

The sensation receded. Alison lowered her hand again. "The last time you brought me those, I ate them all in a day."

And sat in a sugar-induced stupor, afraid to move, afraid the ex-

panding fat, albeit imaginary, would push the scars to their breaking point.

"So is that a no?"

The paper warmed underneath the skin of her hand. She frowned
and pressed her palm flat, splaying her fingers. Warmth spread to her
fingertips. She took her hand off the album and turned it palm-up.

"Alison?"

The skin, with its crisscross pattern of pink and red flesh—a macabre pie crust holding in the bones and gore—tingled. She held it
against her left cheek and gasped at the heat.

"Alison?"

"Uh-huh?"

"Is everything okay?"

"Yes, everything's fine. I, I almost dropped the phone, that's all."

"Okay, so do you want me to pick some up for you?"

Alison ran her hand against her sleeve. The fleece of her pajama
top rubbed smooth against her skin. "Sure, that sounds good." She
traced her fingers over the sofa cushion; the pattern in the fabric
sprang to life beneath her fingertips.

It was real, not phantom. She didn't care what the doctor said.
This was real.

"Okay, then. I'll bring them over when I'm done shopping."

She ran a throw pillow's silken tassel between her index finger
and thumb. "Okay, thank you."

"Then I'll see you in a bit. I love you, babygirl."

"Love you, too."

She tossed the phone aside and set George's album on the table. Ignoring the strange heat still pulsing in her palm, she circled
the room, trailing her fingers across everything she came in contact
with—the bead fringe on the lampshade, which gave off a musical
tinkle, the hard edges of her television, the smooth screen with a
thin layer of dust that came off on her skin in streaks of grey, the pit-

ted plaster walls, the many small holes filled in with putty and painted over again and again by the previous owners. When she touched the blinds covering the window, outlining the honeycomb shape designed to hold out the light and keep in the shade, tears burned in her eye.

She ran her right hand across the photo albums' spines. The textures mixed and mingled—slick vinyl, velvet worn smooth, rough burlap with its crosshatch pattern, leather torn with time and many hands, and then nothing at all. She shook her hand. No pins and needles. No heat. A corpse hand, dead and lifeless, the blood inside little more than a lie.

Did you think it would stay? It's your imagination anyway.

"It was real," she said.

Lie to yourself all you want, but touch something now. Go ahead and tell me what you feel.

Alison cupped hands over ears, but the voice wouldn't stop.

You want to be whole, you want to be real, but you're not. Even if your stupid hands learned to feel again, it wouldn't make you anything but what you are, Monstergirl.

Alison paced back and forth, her breath slow and even as she searched for the white calm buried under the hurt. Inside her private war, time slipped and slid away, and when her mother knocked on the door, she forced a half-smile.

In addition to the bag with the bakery's swirling logo, her mother carried a shopping bag and two plastic grocery bags nearly filled to bursting. Alison nudged the photo album aside to make room for the bags, and as her right hand whisked George's picture, pins and needles crawled under the skin again. She curled her fingers in then out, gave them a quick shake, and the tingle diminished.

"Mom, I told you, my groceries are coming tomorrow. You didn't need to get anything for me."

Her mother shrugged. "I picked up a few things I thought you might like. Here, this one has perishables. The other bag doesn't. The shopping bag has books in it I've been meaning to bring over."

Alison took the bag from her mother and held it with both hands. The handle slid across the skin of her right hand with a cold kiss of plastic; on the left, the expected nothing. She tipped her head to one side. Her mother's voice lifted in the air, the words a gentle susurration. Alison shifted the bag to her left hand and ran her fingers over the surface, shivering at the chill from the contents within.

"Alison," her mother said, touching her shoulder. "Is something wrong?"

Alison blinked, and smiled again, wider than the careful and not quite grotesque half-smile. "No, not exactly. In the past few days, I've had some feeling come and go in my right hand, and it happened again. I can feel the bag. And the ice cream inside."

Her mother smiled back, but the tiny lines at the corners of her eyes didn't crease. She opened her mouth, clamped it shut, and tucked Alison's hair behind her ear.

"I know you don't believe me," Alison said. "It's okay. But I know what I feel. It isn't my imagination. Not this time."

"I know it's all still hard for you. Maybe you could come over this weekend or next weekend and stay for a few days at the house. A change of scenery might do you some good."

Alison's fingers dug into the bag.

"I have plenty of room at the house, you know. You could stay in the guest room and you could even bring some of your photo albums." Her mother laughed. "Except for the smelly one."

"No. I appreciate the offer, Mom, but I'd rather stay here in my house."

"If it's the, the mirrors you're worried about, I can easily cover them up."

"It's not the mirrors. I want to stay here, okay?" She hoisted the bag. "I should put this stuff away."

Her mother gave her a quick kiss on the cheek. "I didn't mean to upset you. I wish I could stay and talk more, but I'm going over to Nancy's house tonight. You remember her, right?"

Alison ran her finger along the bag. "Sure. Miss Nancy from the neighborhood. The one who used to yell at us if we stepped one foot on her lawn."

"Yes, she did, didn't she?" She patted Alison's arm. "You would call me if you needed something right? Even if you just wanted to talk. You know I'm here whenever you need me."

Alison bit the inside of her left cheek. "Mm-hmm, I know."

The sensation faded from her fingertips as soon as her mother left the house. Alison unpacked the bags, slamming both the freezer and cabinet doors. Then she stalked back into the living room and gathered the photo albums. Halfway into the dining room, her sock slipped on the wood. She let out a shout and lost her grip on the albums. They cascaded to the floor with a rattle-thud of old paper and heavy covers. She grabbed for something, for anything, her body jerking forward like a ballerina with lead feet attempting a pirouette. The heel of her foot came down on the corner of an album, sending it across the floor in a slow spiral. She cried out, and knees buckled. The right landed atop a cushion of photos and thick paper; the left slammed into the hard wood, and all the air rushed out with a loud gasp. Both palms struck the closest album with a dull thump.

Breathing heavy, she held still, eyes closed, while the hurt in her knee sang a lullaby of pain. Once it subsided to a soft hum, she lifted her head. George's photo album rested beneath her hands, the cover flipped open, his face covered by her palms. She shifted her weight back on her heels and lifted her hands. George's eyes glared from the photo. The intensity of his paper gaze sent a cold chill down her spine.

"Stop looking at me," she muttered and closed the cover.

The long crack in the worn leather ran sharp beneath the skin of her left hand. The chill returned. She raised her hands to her face, her fingers trembling. Warmth kissed her skin. Under her right palm, the scars nestled against the ridges of scar tissue on her cheek, a rough map of almost-matching lines. Under her left, the skin a smooth, unmarked canvas, pulled the heat in. She took her hands away, held them out, and tipped them from side to side. Scarred and ruined, as always.

She stood, keeping her weight on her right leg, picked up the albums one by one, and slid them back onto the shelf. Spirals of pale rose filled her. Pink held only a handful of hope in the palm of her hand, hope as light as dandelion fluff and equally as prone to shifts in the wind. She was as fragile as spun glass, and battered and chipped at the edges. The others banished her to the far corners of Alison's mind and did their best to keep her there.

When Alison's skin turned to nothing again, she hooked her finger around the spine of George's album and carried it with both hands as she limped into the kitchen.

The pink swirled deeper when she set it on the counter.

Stupid, stupid, stupid, a little voice buried deep within—neither distinctly Red nor Yellow, but a melding, not a blending, of the two—said, but the pink swallowed it up.

Her hands didn't shake. In slow motion, she spread her fingers wide and lowered them onto George's picture, breathing slow and easy while the second-hand on the wall clock tick-tick-ticked away the time.

"Please," she said, her voice a rasp of sandpaper.

The clock ticked. A car raced down the alley, prompting a slew of barking from several dogs. Alison leaned her hips against the counter and flexed her left knee. The ache in the joint was too big to ignore, but too small to cause worry.

Stupid. This was so stupid. She flipped the cover shut, and left it on the counter.

CHAPTER 5

When Alison unlatched her door for the grocery deliveryman, an unfamiliar face stared at hers. Chubby cheeks instead of sharp cheekbones, lank hair instead of a bald head. His eyes widened. She shook her hair forward, covering as much of her face as possible, and fought to keep her hands by her sides.

"Where's Sam?" she asked, holding the door halfway open.

"He has the day off."

"Will he be back next week?"

"They changed our schedules around, so I'll be the one delivering to you. Least until they change it again. Can I bring these bags in?"

Alison nodded and stepped out of the way, wincing at the stiffness in her knee, and crossed her arms over her chest. He left the first set of bags on the floor next to the coffee table, and went back out for more.

When he returned, he added the bags to the pile, and handed her the delivery form. His gaze lingered on her face as she scrawled her name. She thrust the paper toward him, turning her right side away.

"I'm Tyler, by the way. Were you in a fire?"

"Thank you for carrying all the bags inside," Alison said. Each word tasted like gravel in her mouth.

"My sister was, too. It took her a long time before she could leave the house, but once she did, it got easier. Just saying," he said.

As soon as he was gone, she shut the door hard enough to send an echo through the room, but his words persisted.

"It got easier."

Sam never said anything but hello and goodbye. Sam never asked questions or offered advice. Tyler was wrong.

It didn't get easier. Not for her.

She put her head in her hands and grimaced. She should've met his eyes. She should've at least tried instead of cowering like a kicked puppy. How was she ever going to move forward if she didn't keep taking steps, even if they hurt? It wouldn't be easy, she knew that, so why in the hell didn't she try harder? Next time, she'd look him in the eyes. She would.

She held the words tight, hoping she'd be strong enough to keep their promise.

● ● ●

The last of the groceries put away, Alison sat down with her laptop. Her fingers pecked at the keyboard and black text filled the screen, each ugly phrase a nail from her casket of living death. She lifted her hands from the keyboard with a heavy sigh and flexed her fingers. Tiny cramping pains stabbed her from the inside out, her muscles twitched, and her fingers reflexively curled inward. Before the fire, she'd kept all her poetry in notebooks; after, she'd torn them all up, hating the inherent shape of her words even more than the careful, neat handwriting.

Maybe one day she'd write out all the rage and the pity and find some peace. She skimmed the page.

Or maybe not.

She hit delete until the cursor ate all the words away. Inside, a cold ache twisted, a strange, trembling hurt without the black and grey of real pain in its depths.

She opened a browser and scanned the job listings. She suspected many of the work from home options were scams but found a few that appeared legitimate. None of the jobs meant anything, though.

The world didn't need another telemarketer and the job she wanted, she couldn't have. Not now. She could finish the three semesters needed to get her degree online, but becoming a teacher was a once-was dream. She'd send the children screaming out into the hall and plague their nightmares. Or she'd be the teacher whose name children dreaded seeing on their schedule. She doubted she could find a school that would hire her anyway, even with her two years of experience as a teacher's assistant.

Miss Reese, Miss Reese, come see what I made! Come see!

She curled in a ball on the sofa, her hands tucked under her good cheek. When tears slipped from her left eye, she made no move to wipe them away, too lost in the ebb and flow of the storm within.

Her eyelids grew heavy, slipping down over one real eye and the other, crafted from some sort of plastic, as hard as glass, yet more durable. She'd opted for the eye and all the reconstructive surgery when she still thought they held the power to turn her into something else, something close to a normal girl. The doctors never lied, but their ideas of improvement and repair ended up a far cry from her own. She didn't need to be beautiful; she wanted people to be able to look at her without fear or cringes. She wanted to be able to look at herself the same way.

She smelled something sweet and sharp. Not a phantom, but real. And too close by far. She stumbled into the kitchen (Half-asleep? Half-awake? Half-away in a Monstergirl fugue?), her hands limp at her sides.

George's album still lay open on the counter, amid a haze of bluish-grey smoke. She heard laughter, low and enigmatic. Then another laugh, higher-pitched, a feminine trill of blonde perfection. More voices, hushed and distant. Murmurs of conversation. Music in the background.

"She plays beautifully, doesn't she?"

The clink of glasses.

"Not yet, but soon, I think."

A whisk of rustling skirts.

"Always nice to have a new guest, don't you think?"

Another laugh, George's laugh. Softer, meant for no one else to hear.

"Won't you join us?"

Goosebumps pebbled Alison's left arm as she waved her right hand through the smoke. Tendrils of grey curled around her fingers and thumb. She exhaled and the smoke dispersed, taking away the laughter and the voices. Another plume of smoke crept from the picture—a semi-transparent snake that coiled in a spiral below her palm. Thin wisps encircled first her thumb, then her index and middle fingers. They touched the air where her ring finger and pinkie should be and created gauzy finger shaped outlines in the air.

"We're waiting…"

Alison jerked her hand back. The smoke held the shape, then puffed away. Her mother's words echoed in her mind. *"It doesn't feel right."*

But she reached for the album again, stopping when the shape of her hand fell across the page. A shadow with five fingers. She took several deep breaths. Two of her fingers were gone, gone, gone, burned away to useless char for the snipping.

Her vision clouded with the color of plums. She knew this Muse well. Purple screamed hello when the fire began its heated kiss. Shrieked when the doctors descended with their scalpels and needles. Purple trembled and shook with fear. Purple's voice was never quite as loud as the others, but far more insistent. Purple kept her from meeting eyes, from taking steps, from trying.

Alison grabbed the photo album without pause (no need to linger for shadows and shade, for waiting imaginary voices) and threw it in the trash can.

Gone, gone, gone.

PAPER TIGERS / 47

"Photo albums don't talk," she said, her voice too loud.

Lonely in isolation—what her make-believe George wrote in his journal. Lonely enough to dream up lives for dead faces, yes, but lonely enough to hear them speak? More proof her isolation wasn't healthy. She knew she was hiding (it wasn't a crime and surely anyone would understand the why), but she wasn't strong enough yet to face the world, and she was too afraid. Knowing was half the battle, though. She simply needed to find the armor to help her withstand the fight.

● ● ●

Before she went to bed, she took the photo album out of the trash can, dusted it off, and put it back on the shelf. An overactive imagination was no reason to throw it away.

PART II

THE TIGER BITES

She sits in her prison alone and the time ticks slowly by. Hours into days into months. She waits for the sun to set then emerges like a moth to wander through her neighborhood cloaked in shadows and scarves. She doesn't see many people, but when she does, she hides her face, turning her chin down.

She walks and walks, remembering what it felt like to walk in the sun, to walk into the stores instead of looking through dark windows. She remembers when she wasn't afraid of people looking, of their eyes, when she could meet their gazes with her own. She remembers forever and ever instead of ugly, love instead of solitude. The memories hurt more than the scars and when she returns to her house, she locks the doors, encases herself in pity and loneliness, and wishes for something more.

How she wishes...

CHAPTER 6

Alison sat in the examination room, wrapped in a soft gown, with her hands folded in her lap. The door swung open and Dr. Simon came in, all white coat and perfect teeth. Her stomach twisted. She put on her careful smile.

"Hello, hello," he said, his voice bouncing off the walls and ceiling. "How are we today?"

"Fine."

"Fine is not as good as good, but better than bad, I guess. Have you had any problems or abnormal discomfort? Noticed any tightening or more constricted movements?"

Alison shook her head and stared over Dr. Simon's shoulder. A long, thin crack in the wall marred the yellow with a jagged line of white. He parted the back of her robe, tracing his fingers along her skin; when his hands traveled from scars to real flesh, Alison twitched away with a hiss.

"Sorry, my hands are cold," he said. "Now bend forward slightly and lift your arm please."

The top of the crack, an exclamation point of drywall stress, almost met the ceiling; the bottom disappeared behind a small clock with a round face and a red second hand moving with tiny, staccato ticks.

"Mmm-hmm, okay, you can drop your arm."

His shoes made tiny squeaks on the tiled floor as he rounded the table, blocking her view of the clock and the wall crack. She closed her eyes when he folded down the robe. Fingers poked and prodded, moving across with even, gentle pressure—her upper arm, her shoulder, collarbone, then down, down where her body curved in instead of out, where she appeared neither feminine nor masculine, but a thing. Alison turned her head to the side.

"Lift your arm again, please," Dr. Simon said. He lowered her arm. Placed his hand under her chin, turning her face in his direction. "Any problems with the eye?"

"Not at all."

"Good, good." He stroked his hand along her jawline. "I'm noticing some tightening here. Can you open your mouth?"

The skin stretched, like taffy at the tearing point.

"A little more. Have you had any problems?"

"No."

"Hmmm." His fingers rubbed back and forth. "I want to keep an eye on this. Please call me right away if you notice any change at all, no matter how minor, to your facial movements, okay?"

"I will."

"Okay. Even if you don't notice anything, I'd like you to come back in a month, as well, so I can take a look."

"A month? Do you think—"

"Yes, a month."

Alison nodded and stared down at her hands.

"Okay, jump down and walk for me."

Alison limped across the room, then back to the table. Dr. Simon nodded. "Good." When Alison sat back down, he linked his fingers together and rested them on his abdomen. "I ran into Dr. Rothmann the other day. He said you're not seeing him anymore?"

Alison gripped the gown in both hands. "No, I'm not."

Dr. Simon leaned back against the sink counter. "Alison, I'll be blunt. I'm not sure if that's a wise decision. With injuries such as yours, it helps to have someone like Dr. Rothmann. Now, if you'd like to see someone else, I can give you a referral. Dr. Rothmann is considered one of the best when it comes to helping burn patients, but there are several others I know and trust to give the same level of care."

Alison focused her eyes on the lines across his forehead—three of them, with an even deeper furrow between his brows.

"With injuries such as yours."

Her fingers clenched even tighter. Dr. Rothmann, he of the bushy eyebrows and calm, gentle voice, wore the same expression when she'd told him she intended to stop the sessions, but the fault didn't belong to her. *He* broached the topic she told him she didn't want to discuss. From the beginning, she'd been clear, and he said he understood, but he lied. He lied and brought it up anyway when he decided it was time to discuss it, forcing her to think about it for one brief moment before she shoved it back down in the deepest, darkest part under the scars.

"Face it, acknowledge it, and move past," he said. But he didn't see the look. The revulsion. He didn't see *any* of it, but most important, he didn't follow the rule, the simple rule. She didn't need help dealing with an old ghost; she needed help figuring out how to live.

"That would be fine," she said to Dr. Simon, giving him the careful smile again; when he turned around for his pad and pen, she let the smile go.

"I also wanted to ask if you've given any more thought to the surgery we talked about," he said, over his shoulder. "I do think we can improve the appearance of the facial scarring."

"No. I mean, yes, I've thought about it. I'm not interested."

He turned back around and handed her the paper, meeting and holding her gaze.

"Okay," he finally said. "I'll respect your decision. You can go ahead and get dressed."

After he left the room, Alison sat with her arms wrapped around her body. Reconstruction meant scalpels, stitches, stretching skin, and *pain* with no guarantee of improvement, and what if something went wrong and they made her worse? She shuddered. They couldn't make her whole again no matter how many times they tried. The hope wasn't worth the suffering.

On her way out, she crumpled the list of psychologists penned in Dr. Simon's looping scrawl and threw it in the trashcan below a mound of paper towels. They couldn't help her. Only she could do that.

● ● ●

Arms crossed over her chest, she huddled in the back corner of the hospital shuttle van. Two women with grey, cotton candy hair and tissue paper skin spoke in quiet tones several rows ahead. The van bounced over potholes, its wheels thrumming not far beneath Alison's feet, a hypnotic sound lulling her into a hazy half-awake state.

It slowed down for a light and a bright yellow school bus stopped alongside it. Alison turned her face away from the window and sank down even further in her seat. Even through the windows, she heard laughter, but it was safe, not mocking. She closed her eyes as a memory rushed in. Standing at the edge of the playground while the class ran around. Seeing Olivia struggling to climb the jungle gym. Offering to help. Then biting back a laugh as Olivia stomped one foot and said, "No, Miss Reese, I can do it myself." Olivia hadn't done it that day, or the next, or the next, and she'd rebuffed every offer of help. Even a first grader knew that sometimes no one else could help you find your way.

When the van arrived at her house, Alison exited quickly, avoiding the driver's eyes. Once inside, she stripped off her scarf, sunglasses, gloves, and coat and fetched George's photo album before she sat down on the sofa with a soft sigh. She stretched out her hand, nodding at the truth in the shadow—three fingers and a hand with an odd, sloping edge.

With the edge of the paper held between the tip of her index finger and thumb, she flipped the page back to the inscription and traced her fingers over the letters.

"Paper tiger, paper tiger, swallow me whole," she said, her voice a soft near-whisper.

Her vision blurred. The ink smudges turned into amorphous blobs of violet. High-pitched music notes trilled, like the tinny sound from a child's wind-up jewelry box. Phantom music. Smoke music. Dusty music motes floating in the air, bereft of a sunbeam.

Her shoulders slumped. The tune played on and on, soft and sweet. A spinning ballerina, moving round and round. And in between the notes, a soft murmur of voices. Children's voices—a nursery rhyme.

"One, two, three, tigers at a time."

Little girls twirling, their pink-yellow-white-lavender skirts flying up and out, all ruffles and eyelet.

"Four, five, six, tigers in a line."

Chubby hands linked together and the children sang and laughed and sang.

"Seven, eight nine, stripes in the night."

Hair like spun silk, gold and dark. Cookies and talcum powder.

"And when it's ten, the tigers bite!"

Laughter, laughter. Rising.

Alison turned the page, her hand a heavy weight, and the laughter slipped back into the page. George's eyes stared at hers, good humor in the dark depths. A teasing sort of humor. A *feline* sort of humor. She blinked. Once. Twice. The music shifted and changed. Piano notes replaced jewel-box. A mournful song of love and loss and empty rooms. Tree branches rattled against glass windowpanes; the sound of bones tap-tap-tapping "let us in."

"Let me in," Alison said.

The notes paused.

"Let me in and make me whole."

The notes resumed, laced with melancholy. They slipped in be-tween her thoughts and hovered in her ears. She held out her right hand, covered George's face with her palm, and closed her eyes. The song vibrated through her bones and prickled her skin.

Voices again. Speaking, not singing. Adult voices engaged in quiet conversation, their words slurred at the edges. Glasses clinked together. Footsteps. Sturdy men's shoes on a dark wood floor, their soles clicking in-between the music notes. Pins and needles explod-ed into life beneath her skin. The warmth traced spirals in the places where fingerprints used to hold their shape. The music swelled to a crescendo, all the notes blending one into another. Her hand lifted, pushed by the secret heat, and then dropped back down.

A cool breeze wafted over her fingertips and palm, and rough callused fingers curled around her own, stroking and tugging.

"Come in," a husky voice said.

The hand tugged harder, pulling her in? Down? A thumb stroked her palm, a soft, tiny arc of movement. The edge of a fingernail scraped against the side of her pinkie finger.

She opened her eyes.

Her hand no longer rested on George's photo. Her hand no lon-ger rested on anything, but in. Inside the photo. Inside the album. In with the laughter and the music and the nursery rhymes. Inside with a hand wrapped round her fingers. She yelped, jerked back her arm, but neither the album nor her hand budged. Her skin held no indentations. It sat atop the photo as though severed at the wrist and glued to the surface of the paper.

She wiggled her fingers—five fingers, not three, magicked into existence in a paper world. The hand around hers tightened, pulled, and the album swallowed another inch of her arm.

"No, oh no," she said.

Her forearm slipped in even more; she yanked as hard as she could and the unseen fingers let go. Her arm came up and out of the album, away from the paper, into the real. As she fell back against the sofa cushions, her teeth snapped together with an audible click. A narrow band of smoke rose in the air. Every bit of moisture in her mouth vanished.

With a wordless shout, she frantically waved her hands to disperse the smoke, seized the album with both hands and hurled it across the room, severing the music in mid-note. The album hit the wall with a dull thud and a ruffle of pages, and fell, landing with the cover and pages open. She squeezed her eyes shut tight. A single note, one piano key pressed down for a final goodbye, so long, sorry we have to go, broke free from the paper. She covered her ears.

"Stop. Just go away. You aren't real."

A thin trail of low laughter...

She stumbled from the sofa, her socks slipping on the wood floor as she gave the album a wide berth, and lurched up the stairs to her bedroom. Slammed the door behind her and sank down to the floor with her back pressed against the wood and her face in her hands.

Had it been a hallucination or a daydream? A ghost in the pages? A *tiger* in the pages to swallow her whole?

She dropped her hands onto her thighs. The scars on her right arm ran down in stripes of pink and red—too pale to be normal skin, all the way down to three inches above the lines on her wrist. And below? Healthy skin. Whole skin, with not a scar in sight. Delicate blue veins peeked through the skin, lines crossed her palm, and prints whorled and looped on her fingertips, visible even in the dim light. She turned her hand (still two fingers short of normal) over. Her fingernails gleamed pink.

Something is wrong. Something so very wrong.

She flipped her hand again and traced the lines on her palm. Then she tightened her fist. The flesh didn't pull, like ill-sewn fabric, but gave and flexed. A skin glove of perfect.

"What could possibly be wrong with this?" she said.

She splayed her fingers. The fragile bones rose and fell under the thin veil of skin.

How was this even possible?

She smiled. It didn't matter how. It didn't matter at all.

A tiny patch of skin near the base of her thumb pebbled and turned dusky. Then another, on the back of her wrist. And below the fingernail on her index finger. More spots appeared, polka-dots of melted wax, expanding and replacing the healthy and whole with ugly.

"Please, no."

Her fingers curved, forced into arcs by the tightening skin. On her palm, the scar tissue swallowed the lines, recreating familiar patterns. The changing skin made its way up her arm, a dreadful film running backward to ruin. On her forearm, pink edges rose like strips of ragged leather and joined together with the old, leaving no trace of a seam. She moaned low in her throat.

The prickle of pins and needles under her flesh returned, and then disappeared. She thumped back down the stairs, sockfeet whispering discordant madness on the wood, and grabbed the photo album. She dropped it on the coffee table, sank to her knees, and flipped open the cover. Placed her trembling hand flat on George's picture.

"Please."

Nothing happened. Tears fell from her eye, blurring her vision. She pressed her hand harder. Still nothing. She slapped her hand down once, twice, three times, each thud a painless meeting of unfeeling flesh and old paper. The album skittered across the coffee table and hung over the edge, wobbling slightly.

"Give it back," she sobbed, reaching for the album. It toppled over and landed on the floor between the sofa and coffee table with a dull thud. A wisp of smoke curled up from the pages, followed by a faint laugh, then the cover slammed shut.

Alison scrambled back, breathing hard.

Crazy girl. Seeing things makes you crazy.

"I. Am. Not. Crazy. I know what I saw."

A magic photo album that heals scars, crazy girl?

"It did. It took them away. I saw it. And when I touched it before, it gave me feeling. Real feeling."

Then touch it again.

"Not yet."

Why not? Are you afraid?

Holding the wall with one hand, she made her way into the kitchen. She called information and wrote down the number for the shop, her hands shaking. A sick feeling nestled in the pit of her stomach when she dialed the number. The phone rang once, twice, ten times. A young voice with the barest trace of an accent picked up on the twelfth ring. "Elena's Antiques."

"Hello, I purchased a photo album a few days ago and wanted to find out more about it. Maybe who brought it in?"

"Elena isn't here. She's the one you'll have to ask. Call back later."

"When do—"

Click.

"Hello?"

Alison sat down on a kitchen chair and rested her head on her forearms. Which was worse, crazy or afraid?

■ ■ ■

The second time she called the shop, several hours later, the phone simply rang. Alison lost count after fifteen. After the sun set, she slipped out of the house, walking with her head down. A car roared by, its speakers pushing out loud bass-heavy music, its engine trailing a stink of burning oil.

It's too early, too early.

She approached a group of teenagers smoking cigarettes next to a darkened window; laughter, high and derisive, pierced the night.

Her heart beat a chaotic tattoo and she turned her face away. One, two, three steps, and she was past.

"You're such a freak, Justin, you know that?" a young male voice piped up.

"I'm so not…"

Alison rounded the corner, and a light gust of wind gathered their voices and carried them away. She exhaled and a weight on her shoulders lifted. She hadn't been trying to hide. Not completely.

A solitary set of footsteps clicked on the pavement to her right. She stiffened. Too many people, despite the dark sky. She pressed closer to the buildings, into the shadows created by the awnings.

Go home where it's safe. Call them again tomorrow. You don't even know if they'll be open.

She shoved the voice down and away, and forced her feet into a short, clipped rhythm. Maybe she was pushing herself too hard. Maybe this counted as too big of a step, but she wanted, needed, to take it. As she drew close to the shop, where golden light spilled from the front window onto the pavement, she smiled.

"Sometime close, sometime open." Maybe-Elena's words.

She tugged on the door, met resistance, and her smile fell into a flat, compressed line. The interior of the shop gleamed bright, cluttered with even more items. Old furniture, several large cardboard boxes with the top flaps hanging open, and several large black plastic bags with their tops tied into knots. Cast-offs, no doubt, delivered by people going through their attics or a deceased relative's home. Neither too valuable, nor too sentimental.

Alison knocked on the front door. The lamp and tricycle no longer sat in the front window, but the small dragon statues had been joined by a larger stone gargoyle, a creature half-cat and half-monkey perched atop a small brass-banded trunk. After a minute or two, she knocked again.

Through the glass she heard a thunk, a low curse (a man's voice, not in English), the slam of an unseen door, and then two voices (one male, one female, neither in English) raised in argument. Alison knocked a third time, and the lights in the shop went out. The voices lowered in tone but not ferocity, and a face appeared, a quick, pallid flash in the gloom.

"Dammit," Alison muttered, knocking louder.

The voices fell silent, and a figure advanced through the shadows of the shop. A man with a prominent nose and thick, unruly hair brought his face close to the glass.

"Closed now," he said, his voice deep and raspy.

"Please, I want to ask a few questions about something I bought the other day."

"Come back tomorrow. Daytime."

"It will only take a minute. Please."

"Tomorrow. Not open now." He gave her his back and disappeared into the shop.

• • •

Alison's fingers trembled as she opened her front door. She nudged the album with the tip of her shoe and took a quick step back. No smoke. No laughter. No nursery rhymes. She left it on the floor, went upstairs with her laptop tucked under her arm, and closed her bedroom door behind her. Searching for online classes was a far better and healthier pursuit.

But she felt the album's presence in her mind, a dark little purr she knew she should ignore, although she suspected it was already too late for that.

CHAPTER 7

Come back tomorrow.

After a restless night spent tossing and turning beneath twisted sheets, Alison crept downstairs and hurried into the kitchen without looking at the album. Sunlight, detestable with its false cheer, was sneaking through the space between window and blinds. She made tea and toast, but after taking the first bite, an itch grew deep in the socket of her right eye. She brushed the crumbs from her hands, tilted her head down, and put pressure on the lower lid to reveal the bottom edge of the prosthetic, then dragged her finger sideways. The eye, a curved bit of plastic shaped to fit her rebuilt socket, slid out, dropping into her palm.

In the beginning, she'd rubbed her eyes without thinking, dislodging the eye on a daily basis. She found it once in the sink, floating in a teacup of soapy water; another time at the top of the stairs, a grim memento resting on the wood. The eye, the iris painted a perfect match to her real one, served no purpose other than to improve her appearance. A token enhancement, at best; a poor joke, at worst. Maybe in a few years they'd develop one that could actually see.

She finished eating and left the eye in the kitchen. Halfway to the stairs, she stopped and turned toward the album, still lying on the floor. She took one hesitant step closer. Then another. She wouldn't retreat to the safety of her bedroom because of a stupid photo album. She stalked over. Picked it up.

"None of it was real," she muttered as she flipped open the cover. "Right, George?"

George's eyes gave a silent, somber stare. With a grunt, she dropped the album on the table. George's page lifted, offering a brief glimpse of the page and the edge of a photograph underneath before it settled back down.

Using the tip of her finger, she turned the page by its corner. All the air rushed out as the page flipped over with ease to reveal the photo. A house, Victorian in style, captured in the same sepia tones, with a curved turret at one end rising high over the roof. The house held a presence, a sense of command, owing more to the long rectangular windows and the peaked roof than to the impressive size. Not quite a mansion, yet more than a mere house.

Treetops heavy with leaves peeked above the roofline, a cluster of rosebushes with open blooms surrounded the porch, and a stone pathway led away from the front steps and disappeared off the picture. Alison inhaled a delicate trace of flowers.

Dark shutters bordered all the windows save those on the top floor of the turret. The windows there had curved tops, half-moon shapes above lacy curtains. Ignoring the shake in her fingers, she held out her hand, lowered it onto the picture, and counted off the seconds in her head. She stopped at forty-five, but kept her hand in place. With a slight shake of her head, she briskly rubbed her upper arms.

Let sleeping tigers lie.

She stalked back into the kitchen and grabbed her phone, punching the number in for the shop with sharp jabs of her finger. After three shrill rings, a deep voice answered.

"I'm not sure if you remember, but I stopped by last night with some questions about an item I purchased," Alison said. "You told me to come back, but I wanted to find out—"

"No returns," the man said.

"I don't want to return it. I wanted to find out if you knew where it came from."

"Where it came from?"

"Yes, I bought an old photo album—"

He chuckled. "People drop things off. They don't want, so we take."

"Yes, I know that, but I have some questions about the album, so I was hoping you could tell me who dropped it off. It's an old album and was in the front window."

"I don't know, maybe wife, she know," he said. The phone gave a loud clunk. After a brief, muffled conversation, he returned. "Bring in, she look and see. Maybe know, maybe not."

The call disconnected. Alison dropped the phone on the table and glared at the eye on the napkin.

■ ■ ■

A storm rolled in, banishing the sun behind a heavy veil of grey. The extreme shift was typical for Baltimore weather. *Don't like it? Wait five minutes, it will change.* A common joke, yet one borne from truth. Late in the afternoon, with an oil slick of panic on her tongue, Alison donned her scarf and gloves and zipped her coat high under her neck. With sunglasses in place, never mind that there wasn't the slightest trace of a glare outside, she stepped into the autumn chill, holding tight to a shopping bag containing the album with one hand and an umbrella with the other.

She paused at the street sign. The tips of her shoes had not made it past.

Go back, go back.

She would not. She needed to know where the album came from. She crossed the street, sidestepping a puddle of scummy water. Despite the hour, she passed only three people, all too busy dodging raindrops to pay attention to her.

Several customers stood inside the shop and her stomach twisted into a tight knot. She waited by the far end of the front window, away from the door. The customers moved to another aisle, their laughter a distant trill through the glass. An ache blossomed in Alison's fingers, and she shifted the bag to her other hand. The umbrella slipped, sending cold rain down her face. When the customers laughed again, she took a deep breath.

They saw you. They're laughing at you. You should leave now. Go home, where it's safe.

She cringed as the bell overhead announced her entrance. Keeping her back to the interior of the store, she closed the umbrella with a wet snap and wiped rain from her face and sunglasses.

The dark lenses coupled with the gloom outside transformed the shop into an indistinct maze. A man near the old desk gave her a quick glance and a second, longer one; two women next to the bookcase did the same, but after they turned away, they began speaking to each other in low tones.

I told you so.

Alison sidestepped still-unpacked boxes and plastic bags, her knuckles white, approached the counter, and took the album from the bag. Slowly, the whispers trailed off.

Conversation drifted out from the half-open door behind the counter. Soft, slurring words punctuated with brief pauses and rolling Rs.

"Did he write this one before or after the one you lent to me? I can never remember," one of the women said, her voice thin and reedy.

"Eeep!" Another voice exclaimed, this one deeper-pitched, and a book thumped to the floor.

Alison hissed air between her teeth.

"Spiders, I hate them." Nervous laughter followed. "I think I'll pick that one up new after all."

Elena, her hair covered with a bright orange scarf, peeked out, saw Alison, and held up an index finger. She said something over her shoulder before stepping out, and her gaze panned the sunglasses, on the visible skin, until recognition flashed in her eyes.

"Help you?"

"I'd like to find out if you know anything about this album's previous owner. I called a few days ago, and the man I spoke with told me to bring it in so you could take a look and see if you remember who dropped it off."

She slid the album across the counter, and Elena waited until she took her hands away before opening the front cover, her brows drawn together and the corners of her mouth downturned.

"The pages are—"

Muttering something not in English, Elena flipped through the album, too fast for Alison to catch anything but a brief glimpse. A yellowed scrap of paper slid out from between two pages and landed on the counter. They both grabbed for it at the same time, and Elena pulled her hand away before their fingers met.

Told you, told you, told you.

The words fluttered inside with the insistence of a caged bird's wings.

"This left in back, I think. No owner. Is old," Elena said, pushing the album back to Alison's side of the counter.

"Please, could you show me the pages again? The pictures?"

Elena gave the album another nudge. "You look and see."

"But when I—"

Behind Alison, a man cleared his throat. "Excuse me. Could I interrupt for a moment? I'm interested in the desk, but I can't find a price."

"Yes, I help you," Elena said.

Go, please.

Alison shoved the album back in the shopping bag and the paper in her pants pocket and wound her way back around the plastic bags and the boxes.

Go away, Monstergirl.
We can't help you with the tiger.

● ● ●

Halfway home, the sky darkened from slate to charcoal, and the rain became a deluge whipped sideways by the wind. In seconds, Alison's pants turned dark and her shoes grew sodden and heavy, and she ducked under the awning of an empty building.

The pages had turned. All of them. Fighting the urge to pull the album from the bag and check it herself, she shifted her weight back and forth as rain tap-danced against the shopping bag.

Maybe they were only stuck together for her.

A jagged bolt of lightning split the sky, filling the air with an ozone stink. Thunder rumbled, long and low. Lightning flashed again. She stepped out from the awning, moving with quick, limping steps, her hip crying out in protest. The piece of paper in her pocket held the weight of a promise, but if she—

A muscle spasm struck near the base of her wrist, white-hot pain flaring below the scar tissue. Her fingers twitched, and the bag slipped from her fingers, landing on the pavement with a wet thump.

With a groan, she shifted the umbrella, pressing the handle close to her chest with her forearm. Her traitorous fingers skittered against the bag's corded handle and once she had it firmly in her grip, the umbrella slid forward. She jolted upright in response, but the umbrella kept its momentum, aided by the wind, and slipped from her grasp. Another gust carried it further away.

She barked a laugh and lurched forward. Rain soaked her scarf, pinning it to her head, and streaked the lenses of her glasses. Footsteps approached. Splashing, squeaking.

A scratchy voice said, "Here, let me help."

Don't look at me. Oh, please, don't look at me.

Clutching the shopping bag tight, she took the umbrella from the stranger's hand. "Thank you," she said.

"Most welcome. Take care now."

Lightning pierced the gloom, turning everything momentarily bright. Alison whirled away, nearly losing the umbrella again in the process. But did he see her face, and she his? And what of the look in his eyes? She hunched her shoulders. It didn't matter what he saw or didn't see. He'd helped her, hadn't he?

The muscles in her wrist relaxed, but her hip continued its steady throb, and when she crossed onto her street, she let out a sound halfway between a sigh and a sob. Her front door loomed close, the promise of warm and dry tucked inside. A tiger of brick, plaster, and glass to swallow her whole—to swallow her away from the world.

The album banged against her leg, and she thought she heard the rustle of pages as she turned the key in the lock. A car door slammed shut, and someone called out her name. Her mother rushed over, shielding her face from the rain with one hand, and Alison laughed, urging her to hurry inside.

"Is everything okay?"

"Everything's fine," Alison said, setting the shopping bag by the door. "Here, let me take your coat."

"Don't worry about me. You need to get out of those clothes. You're soaking wet. What possessed you to go out in weather like this?"

"Trust me. It wasn't raining like this when I went out." Alison peeled off her scarf and gloves. Inside the bag, the photo album beckoned. "But what are you doing here?"

"Don't you remember? We're having dinner tonight."

Alison pressed a hand to her forehead. "That's right. I totally forgot. I'm sorry."

"There's nothing to be sorry about. I'm a little early. Now go, change your clothes before you catch a cold."

"Yes, Mother," she said in a singsong voice.

Alison took the bag in hand again and headed upstairs with careful steps, her hip protesting every movement, her shoes leaving a trail of water. In her room, with a towel draped across her shoulders, she took the photo album from the bag and set it on the foot of the bed.

"Okay," she said, flipping the cover open.

So far, so good. She turned to George's photo, then to the photo of the house, but when she tried to turn that page over, it didn't budge. She held the album on its side and gave it a shake. "Come on," she said. She flipped past George to the house, and once again, the page wouldn't turn. It made no sense. Why would it let Elena look at all the pages and not her? How was that even possible?

She stuck her hand in her pocket, suddenly sure the paper had disappeared, but she found it tucked deep in the corner and breathed a sigh of relief that it was still dry. Holding her lower lip gently between her teeth, she unfolded the paper. It was a newspaper clipping, not nearly as old as she'd expected.

August 4, 1992. *Last night, a four-alarm blaze destroyed the house known to local residents as Pennington House. Originally built in the 1800s by one of the state's wealthiest families, the house had been vacant for years, caught up in a legal battle between distant relatives. Two children, identified as Michelle and Zachary Phillips were rescued from the fire. Arson is suspected.*

The rest of the article was lost beyond a neat tear. Above the article, a photo showed a familiar house with curtained windows and gleaming paint. Another photo, obviously taken many years later, revealed peeling paint, boarded-up windows, and a definite lean on the right side of the porch, but there was no picture of the house post-fire.

Alison read the article twice. There was no indication as to whether or not the clipping was from a local newspaper, and the name of the house didn't sound familiar at all, but both would be easy enough to find out.

Had the house burned down completely? They didn't always. Sometimes only the inside burned, leaving an almost normal façade, save for the scorch marks leading from the windows and doors and a gaping hole where a roof should be—

"Alison?"

"Yes?"

"I'm going to start making the salad, okay?"

"Okay, that's fine," Alison called out.

She put the newspaper clipping in her jewelry box, next to a plastic hospital identification bracelet and a tiny diamond

reminder

ring and changed her clothes.

Maybe the album wasn't magic at all. Maybe it was haunted.

■ ■ ■

Her mother set down her fork. "Am I crazy, or do you smell flowers, too?"

Alison sniffed, shifting in her seat as her hip gave another twinge of pain. "I don't smell anything except the food."

"It smells like roses, lilies, lilacs, and a bunch of others." She gave a small laugh. "Like we're standing inside a garden."

"Nope, no flowers here. Did you wear a new perfume today?"

Her mother's brow creased. "I'm not wearing any at all. It's so strange." She shook her head in dismissal. "So, what prompted you to go out today?"

"It was nothing, really. I went back to that shop, where I got the photo album."

"That's twice now, and today, well, it was during the day. You haven't gone out like that in a long time. I'm proud of you."

Alison nodded. "I know you are."

"It's a big step, I know, and I hope it's the first of many. You need to get out more often. It's good for you. I know if you keep trying—"

"Not now, please. Let it go, okay?"

Her mother's lips pursed as she speared a piece of lettuce with her fork, but she said, "Okay. I'll let it go."

Alison toyed with her own salad, her appetite gone. Even if her mother didn't think she was moving forward fast enough, she *was* trying. She was.

● ● ●

Alison closed and locked the door behind her mom and brought the photo album back downstairs. When she set it on the coffee table, the room filled with the sweetness of roses. Her mother's voice echoed in her ears.

Do you smell flowers?

But the scent vanished in the span of a heartbeat, as though it had never been there at all. Alison sank down on the sofa, grimacing at the knot of pain below her hipbone. After she kicked off her slippers, she traced her fingers over the illegible print.

Leave it alone.

She turned past George's photo and stared at the house, imagining the walls blackened and charred, the wood scorched, the windows shattered, the roof caved in. She tried to turn the page again, but of course it didn't budge.

She pressed her fingertips to her temple. She should throw it out before her

obsession

fascination with it grew any stronger.

But it took the scars away...or maybe she only thought it did. Maybe everything was in her imagination, another way to keep herself from facing what needed to be faced. That was far more like—

The curtain in the top window of the turret twitched. Alison sat back. Took a deep breath. Craned her neck forward, ignoring the pull of scar tissue.

A face peeked out from behind the lace curtain, a sepia flash of eyes and open mouth. The curtain shifted and the face disappeared. Alison pressed both hands to her mouth.

Not real. It couldn't be real. It was some sort of trick, that's all. She needed to leave it alone, to close it up and throw it away.

The face appeared again, a doll-like face with dark eyes and round cheeks—a child, holding the curtain back with one pudgy hand. The little girl lifted her free hand, and opened and closed her fingers. Alison raised her hand and waved back even as the voice shouted alarm inside her head.

"It's just a little girl," she muttered, her voice thick at the edges.

A gust of rose-scented wind carried her voice away. The breeze rifled through her hair. An insect flitted across the page, a quick blur of fluttering wings. The little girl giggled a tiny, musical trill. Piano notes played in the background.

A woman's voice called out, "Mary? Are you in there, Mary?"

Shoes tapped across a wood floor. The little girl peered back over her shoulder and dropped the curtain. The lace edge brushed against the other panel before it fell back into place. The girl's shadow darted behind the lace, a quick flash of dark against light, two sets of clicking footsteps, one lighter and quicker than the other, faded back into the paper, and then all was still.

A silhouette remained, frozen in time, behind the curtain. A flash of color flew past, the vibrant orange and black of a Monarch butterfly. It spiraled down and lit on the rosebush, its wings slowly opening and closing. Then it melted *into* the photograph, growing smaller and smaller, its colors changing from brilliant to dull. Alison bent close until her nose was mere inches away. Yes, there on a rosebush, the butterfly sat motionless. She pressed the tip of her finger on the photo, covering the butterfly.

"Come in," a man's voice said.

Her finger slipped into the picture, disappearing through both butterfly and rosebush. Then her hand, all the way to her wrist. An unseen hand wrapped around hers, the fingers holding tight with an iron grip, hard enough to crush her bones together. She cried out. The hand tugged, pulling her down. Pulling her in. The world turned shades of brown and ivory. A sensation of spinning, of vertigo turned upside down and inside out. Pain. Heat like the kiss of flames against her skin. She shrieked wordless cries and a child's merry laughter filled the spaces in-between. A sense of time standing still as she writhed in sepia-colored nothingness, spiraling down into the heat, into the album, into an absolute dark laced with the smell of flowers and tobacco and time.

PART III

DOORWAYS, SCARS, AND GRANDFATHER CLOCKS

She convinces the night nurse, an older woman with dark eyes and a serious mouth, to bring her a mirror. The doctors, including the psychologist whose words always come out laced with condescension, don't think she's ready for her reflection. It will be too traumatic at this stage, they say.

The nurse hands her a compact, pats her hand, and leaves her alone. She holds the compact for almost an hour. Dust from the face powder within drifts down onto the bedsheets, the scent mixing with the chemical stink of the hospital room.

She doesn't pay attention to the smells. I want to see, I want to see, the words run in her head, around and around in circles. She's felt the scars, oh yes, she has, but she wants—needs—to see. She's seen most of the scars on her body, she's traced her fingers along the shifted planes of her face, and she's seen enough in her mother's (and his and his and his, she can't forget his) eyes to know what to expect.

When she looks, she doesn't scream or cry out. She stares and stares, sure it's a mistake. This isn't her face. This is a stranger, a Monstergirl with overlapping bands of pink skin, white skin, shiny and raised, and an empty socket where an eye should be.

She turns her face from side to side, thinks she looks cleaved in two in some grim horror movie fashion. Her left side, the good side, is all pale skin and whole, the right is nightmarish. *Monstergirl*, she thinks again. She knows she will keep this word to herself—her secret name.

Finally, she cries, silent tears that burn like acid on her ruined face, but she doesn't scream. She wants to leave this place of needles and scalpels. There's too much pain here, and if she screams, they might make her stay longer, or worse—they might never let her go.

Now she knows why there won't be any more weekend trips to the beach, no tipping her face to the sun, no walks down the boardwalk, no teaching, no children, no future—only shadows and dark and hiding.

CHAPTER 8

Alison came to, came *awake*, curled on her side with her arms arced protectively around her head. Her breath caught in her throat as she stood, holding onto the wall for support. A wall not in her living room, not in her house, not anywhere known, yet a wide, darkened foyer that held a strange familiarity. Beneath her bare feet, the floor was cool.

Surrounded by heavy silence, she brushed dust from her hands and clothes. Inside the album. She'd fallen inside the album.

Not possible.

She covered her eyes and counted to ten, but when she peeked through her fingers, the house remained. The air was heavy and stale but with a slight chill, and a taste of old, forgotten things crept into her mouth. An old chandelier missing half its crystals hung overhead, draped in a veil of cobwebs. Scratched and pitted wood peeked through the dust on the floor. Several arched openings led to other rooms, and a staircase stood off to the right, intricate carvings on the banister and newel post apparent even through the grime. She turned to the main door, a structure nearly as tall as it was wide. The brass doorknob was speckled with spots of dark and gave a loud creak when she turned it, the sound echoing off the walls. She twitched, glanced over both shoulders, and tried it again.

Locked.

Locked in a house? Trapped in a photo album? Was it real or merely a phantom? She pinched her left arm and grimaced at the resulting welt. No dream. She took one hesitant step toward an archway then another. There had to be a way out, a way back out into the real world.

The room, a large rectangular space, was devoid of furniture. Cobwebs clung to the corners of the high ceiling, dark curtains sagged over three windows, and dingy wallpaper adorned the walls. She pushed a curtain aside, dislodging a cloud of dust. Beyond the glass, a fine grey mist floated in the space beyond the glass, and past that, a blur of white with a darker blur in one corner. The mist rushed in to hide both the white and dark; the curtain gave a soft swish as it settled into place.

She left the room on quiet feet, tracing new prints on the floor, and stopped past the archway to shift her weight from side to side. Somewhere along the way from her living room to the house, the ache in her hip had vanished. The scars gave their normal pull and tug, but without stiffness or pain. Curious. She crossed the foyer and passed through another archway. Her limp, unfortunately, persisted.

The room, shaped much the same as the first, had two curtained windows with the same grey outside. Several fist-sized holes riddled the plaster on the far wall, next to a tall, narrow closed door. She tried the handle. Dust came off on her hand, revealing a cut-glass knob, but the door didn't open.

If her memory served correctly, the door should lead to the turret room. She set her left shoulder against the door while turning the knob. The frame gave a low groan, but still didn't open.

The rest of the rooms on the first floor contained curtained windows, cobwebs, and quiet. With a tremble in her fingers, she stood at the base of the staircase, unable to see the top third through the gloom.

A sudden sense of being watched washed over her; she whirled around. Held her breath. Willed herself completely still. The skin on the unburned side of her neck prickled. When her chest ached, she exhaled in one long shuddering breath.

She tried the front door again. Still locked.

Of course. It's locked and you'll be locked in here forever. Forgotten forever. Here in this house that's not a house. Forever and ever.

Ignoring the voice, she turned back to the staircase. No one was watching. There was no one else in the house.

No one here but you and I, my dear, a voice said. (Not Purple this time. The voice was far too deep. Inside her head, but not her voice at all. Neither Red, nor Yellow, nor Purple. A George voice.) *You and I and fear, my dear.*

A rough, masculine laugh broke through the silence. Not in her head. Not in her head at all. She backed up until her spine pressed against the wall next to the door. From her position, she could see all the entryways leading off the foyer as well as the staircase. She crossed her arms. Counted off seconds in her head. When three minutes had gone by, she stepped away from the wall.

An icy chill swirled around her ankles, curling up to brush against her left arm. Goosebumps pebbled her skin.

Someone is here. Someone here with you.

A kiss of cold swept across her shoulder then her cheek, the suggestion of fingers stroking. She turned her head, moaning low in her throat.

Welcome, the deep voice said. And the chill vanished.

She staggered forward, hands waving in the spaces where the touch had been. Stomach twisting in knots, she stumbled up the stairs, hair falling into her eyes, to a small landing. Another set of stairs led even higher, and when she cleared the last step, she skidded to a stop in a long hallway, the end swathed in murk. A narrow rug with pale swirls on a faded blue background ran down the center, and the tassels bordering each end of the carpet curled in twisted ropes resembling fat slugs. Embossed paper, stained in some spots and peeling in others, covered the walls. Closed doors lined each side, three on the right wall, two on the left, with sconces, their glass frames coated with soot, hanging on the walls between. Lacy cobwebs dangled from the ceiling.

Brushing her hair back from her forehead, she tiptoed to the first door on her right. Locked. She tried the next door on her left. The knob gave a high-pitched squeak, but the door didn't open. She watched the top of the stairs with her jaw clenched tight as she waited for the echo to fade.

Once it did, she walked to the next door. When her hand hovered over the doorknob, the sound of tiny pattering feet trailed down the hall, first heading toward her, then away. A child's footsteps, light and teasing. A soft giggle, muffled. Pinching the inside of her cheek between her teeth, Alison took two more steps, pushing away a long tendril of dusty web.

A door slammed. One loud bang then a creaking shudder of wood. In the distance, not close. She clamped both hands over her mouth to hold in a shriek, spun around, and her foot caught on the rug. As her upper body pitched to the right, her knees bent and canted to the left. The skin on her hip and back pulled. With a moan, she swayed, one hand questing for the wall. She didn't find it in time to stop her descent, only to slow it down into a semi-controlled tumble. She landed hard on her hands and knees, her left hand resting on a hard patch of carpet, the fibers matted and dark with a stain.

She scrambled to her feet. Lumbered down the hallway, back toward the stairs. A sob caught in her throat. She had nowhere to run, nowhere to go. Maybe the front door had opened. Maybe she'd find the way out. She hobbled down the steps, her mouth dry, and paused at the second floor landing. Peered around the corner.

Another long hallway, twice as wide as the one she'd left; another thick layer of dust on the floor. Doors lined each side of the hall, all of them closed. She turned back to the staircase. Gripping the railing tight enough to make her fingers ache, she descended.

A low rhythmic squeal slid through the air. She gripped the railing tight and kept moving, each step slow and careful. Violet chaos twisted inside her mind, a feverish babble of nonsense. Her brow glistened with a thin sheen of sweat, despite the chill.

The foyer appeared exactly the same. There was another squeak, the raspy squeal of old metal. The door leading into the turret stood open, but it had been locked. She'd tried it. On tiptoe, she headed for the open door, her mouth dry, pulse skittering.

Maybe it's a trap.

She shoved the voice away. The entire house held her trapped. What difference did one room make? Five feet from the door, a cold chill skimmed her arm then vanished. She recoiled. Footprints appeared on the floor, tiny footprints, not her own, heading through the doorway.

The circular room was larger than she expected. The tiny footprints curved past the doorway, over to the back wall, and disappeared inches shy of the baseboard molding. And standing in-between the side windows, a grandfather clock with carved, elegant wood in a deep, burnished shade of mahogany, with not a speck of dust anywhere. A long oval of glass revealed a brass pendulum below the ornate face. Black scrollwork hands stood frozen at a minute after twelve. The pendulum hung motionless. A spindle-thin second hand with a tip shaped like the sharp end of an iron gate sat atop the hand marking the hour.

A tiny tick sounded from inside the cabinet, and the pendulum swung in a slow arc from right to left. A sonorous chime rang out; she cried out and jerked back.

The pendulum swung back and forth. The second hand ticked counter-clockwise, its pointed tip skimming across the Roman numerals. "No," she said. The clock chimed again. She held her hands over her ears. The second hand continued to move, giving time back instead of stealing it away.

She extended her hand. Her fingertips grazed the glass. Heat flared through her palm, a deep heat, but that wasn't right because her fingers were dead and numb and she couldn't

no air

breathe. Grey mist swirled in place of air, creeping down into her throat. Heat pressed from the inside. The grey took her in, pulling her down. Her arms flailed as she tried to grab onto something. Anything. The clock chimed, the second hand ticked wrong, so wrong, and she, and she—

● ● ●

—reeled forward, her shin bumping against something unseen, and she fell to her knees. The quiet fading chime of the clock echoed away.

Trembling, Alison stood in the middle of her living room. The photo album lay face down on the coffee table. She took two steps forward before the strength left her legs, and she sank to the floor like a balloon full of empty.

When the rubbery sensation left her limbs, she raked cobwebs from her hair. A thin glimmer of dust coated her arms and legs.

"This isn't possible," she said, her voice paper thin.

She wiped her hands on her pants and stiffened, staring at her hands. At her fingers. Ten finger-piggies, all lined up in a row, healthy and whole, with pink nails and the half-moon of white tucked against the cuticles. She flipped her hands over. The skin of her palms gleamed pale and lined.

She closed her eyes. A haunted photo album, a haunted house inside the album, a little ghost that left footprints in the dust, and a clock that ran backward. Yes, she could almost bring herself to believe in those things, but she had eight fingers, not ten. Ghosts and clocks could not bring back what doctors cut away. Using the tip of her left index finger, she poked her right eyelid and felt the hard plastic beneath the lid. If she wasn't wearing her eye, would the album have replaced that, too?

Beneath her right sleeve, she found smooth skin with a layer of fine hairs. She clutched her chest and exhaled sharply. In a flash, she removed her shirt and traced her fingers around the curve of her breasts—two of them—the nipples hardening beneath her palms.

Perfect skin disappeared into the waistband of her pants. She discarded the rest of her clothing. Warm air from the heat vent caressed her legs.

Then she lifted her hands to her face. Traced her fingertips along her cheekbones, her jawline, her eyelashes, eyelids, and brows. Tears filled her eye.

Go away, Monstergirl. Go away and never come back.

She smiled, running her fingers along the curve of her lips. A real smile. No grimace. No ruined flesh. The Monstergirl had gone to live with the tiger.

She raced into the kitchen, her steps even. Pushed aside the window blind and angled her face until a ghostly image with high cheekbones and wide eyes appeared in the glass. Laughter bubbled up and out. Later, she would think about the how and why. For now, her reflection was enough. So much more than enough. Long, thick tendrils of hair spilled over her forehead, tickling her skin.

"How am I going to explain this?"

The tiger swallowed me up and made me whole.

The explanation didn't matter. She didn't have to hide anymore. She could go out in public. She could get a job, make friends, live.

She could stop being afraid.

CHAPTER 9

Confusion set in as bright sunlight danced across her face and then she remembered she'd opened all the blinds and curtains before going to bed, giggling in schoolgirl fashion. If she'd listened to her mother and thrown out the album, she would never have known. Who would think it possible? How would she even explain it? She wiped the sleep from her eyes and yawned, the skin pulling in a hateful, familiar way.

"No. Oh, please, no."

Eight fingers, not ten. She screamed against her lineless palms. The skin on her cheek pulled again. She knew this sensation. She didn't need a reflection.

A face like homemade sin—something her grandmother had said long, long ago, referring to a neighbor lady with an unfortunate set of features, but the phrase fit, it fit so well, like a smooth leather glove to hide runnels of flesh and scar tissue fingers. Like a scarf tugged down to keep out the eyes with their ever-present questions, their revulsion, their pity. Somebody beat her with a stick full of hideous. Another phrase with cruel perfection in its words, only it hadn't been a stick at all, but it didn't matter. Sticks and stones or flesh and burns. They boiled (and wasn't that a funny choice of words) down to one thing and one thing only: ugly, ugly, UGLY.

Sometime in the night, her old face, her old body, monstrous and scarred, had crept back in and settled into its rightful place. In her mind, Alison could hear its gentle, terrible laughter, feel its smug satisfaction, could taste its triumph on her tongue—a cup full of bitterness and sorrow swallowed too slow.

You can't run away from yourself, you stupid girl. You thought you were whole again, but you're still a walking nightmare. You'll never be anything other than what you are. A Monstergirl. And all the tigers in the world won't help you, won't change you. You are trapped forever.

She put her face in her hands. Nothing but weight against her palms. The same thing she'd felt for years. Not worse than the monstrosity wearing her ruined skin, but it was a final slap in an argument gone too far. The photo album was little more than a trick, a cruel trick designed to tease and hurt. With a shout, she jumped from the bed, stumbled down the stairs, and closed all the blinds and curtains in a frantic rush.

The photo album still sat face down on the coffee table. She lowered herself to the floor and flipped the album open to George's photo.

"Take them back," she shrieked. George's face stared at hers with his somber expression. "Take them all back!" She turned to the photo of the house and pressed both hands flat. "Please, please, take them back." Hot tears ran down her cheek, dripping on the back of her hands, the edges of the photograph.

She slammed her hands up and down on the photo, rage spiraling in a hot coil of scarlet within her.

Not fair. You can't take them away and then give them back. That's. Not. Fair.

With a guttural cry, she hurled the album across the room. It banged into the wall, knocked a vase to the floor in a shatter of glass, the dried flowers within crumbling to bits, and landed with a heavy thump. The pages fluttered down with a soft whisk-whisk, but the cover stayed open. Taunting. Teasing.

The anger slipped away, leaving behind a horrible, hurtful sense of loss.

"Please take them back," she said once more, her voice thick.

She inhaled. Exhaled. Pressed one hand to her chest. Without the distraction of her scars, the truth settled its weight on her. No imagination. No tricks of the light. She'd been inside the album. With the ghosts.

A low moan slipped from her lips. She didn't believe in ghosts. They were movie creations, novel frights, silly explanations for logical occurrences. Yet the footprints she'd seen on the floor, the child's giggle, the slamming door...no one else had been in the house with her. No one real. She was sure of it.

The house...she'd fallen into the photo album. Into the house. She covered her eyes. But it wasn't possible. People couldn't fall into photo albums.

A wave of dizziness struck and on its heels, a rush of exhaustion. The room spun and she swayed on her feet. Her muscles aching with the effort, she staggered toward the couch.

* * *

Her eyes snapped open. Darkness, a dry mouth, and a head that felt stuffed with cotton wool. She fumbled for the light, wincing against the bright. Her muscles felt wrenched out of place and tangled back together. She'd slept the day away. The entire day.

Was this some sort of side-effect of the album? A price to pay for entry? A penalty? She glared at the album. Would that she could conjure an explanation by thought alone.

Some of the indigo smudges of ink above the paper tiger line were darker. She rubbed sleep from her eye. Yes, something was different. The page now held loops and whirls in place of blank space, but more the suggestion of print rather than legible text, as though the words were pushing out of the paper world into the real but had not completed the journey.

The words in their current state only hinted at their hidden meaning, yet goosebumps pebbled her left arm as she tried to make sense of the puzzle within.

"Time, stop, yes, locked, pedal, fast, mental, hear, hour, web," she muttered. "LDS? Mormons?" If the album coughed up another word or two (or ten), she might be able to make some sense out of it, but as it stood now, it was gibberish. Secrets within secrets within secrets. Like her scars and the ghosts.

She yawned, but she refused to go back to sleep. She'd slept enough. Maybe Elena didn't know where the album came from, but someone had to know something. Her scars had been gone. Gone. She had most definitely not imagined that.

She fired up her laptop, typed Pennington House in the search bar, and clicked on the first link, a short article about the fire. It didn't offer much more than the newspaper clipping, save for one salient point—Pennington House was in Towson, Maryland. A local house after all. The second link, on a website listing some of Baltimore County's most notable old houses, offered a bit more:

Edmund Pennington, the son of one of Maryland's most prominent families, had Pennington House built in 1878 as a wedding gift to his wife, Lillian. Two years later, Lillian died giving birth to their son, George.

Edmund remarried two years later, and he and his second wife, Eleanor, had three children. Sadly, none of those children lived to adulthood. One died as an infant, the other two in early childhood. Not long after their deaths, Eleanor passed away in a tragic fall.

Upon Edmund's death in 1899, George Pennington, at nineteen, inherited the family home. As a wealthy man of leisure, George gained a small measure of notoriety for his avid interest in photography. Local families frequently had their portraits taken while attending one of Pennington House's famous soirees and often requested that he take the postmortem photographs of their loved ones, a practice popular during that time.

George Pennington lived in the house alone until his death in 1935, at the age of fifty-five from unknown causes. Pennington House passed into the hands of a cousin, Bernard Landley, who lived in the house with his wife and children for only two years after which time the house exchanged hands several more times until it was caught in a legal dispute between two distant relatives. The house sat vacant for years and eventually fell into disrepair. In 1992, Pennington House burned to the ground. Arson was determined, however, no one was ever charged. The land is now owned by the county.

The website showed the same photos the newspaper article had featured.

The third link offered a different spin. Pennington House was included in their list of haunted places in Baltimore. There were reports of hearing thumps on the stairs, voices, and music. A handful of people had also seen shadows moving on the wall. There was a comments section where a few people had claimed to have gone into the house when they were young. One poster commented that the house was a stupid wreck and wasn't haunted at all and anyone who thought so was a fool. Others disagreed, recounting their experiences—the same thumps and shadows. One comment took the breath from her lungs: *My best friend and I went in it once. We goofed around, jumping out and making creepy noises. When we were about to leave, I heard a door slam from somewhere upstairs and then a clock started to chime, like one of those old-fashioned clocks. My friend couldn't hear it, but it was like it was inside my head. Like I was listening to it with headphones. Then we both saw footprints on the floor. They weren't our footprints. They just appeared, and they were kid footprints, not grownups, and they were coming toward me. We ran like hell out of there and never went back. My friend later said he didn't see anything, but I know he did because he pissed himself when he saw them.*

A notation at the bottom of the page said the house had been torn down after the fire and since then, no reports of anything strange had been reported.

Alison rubbed her hands together. So the house had been haunted even when it was real. She wasn't sure if that made it better or worse, but now she knew she wasn't imagining things.

George's interest in photography explained the album, sort of, but it didn't explain anything at all. How did a haunted house become a haunted photo album? Maybe there was no way to explain it. No rational way. Regardless of the how, George was a ghost inside the paper world and all but forgotten in the real.

She flipped to the photo of the house. Lowered her hand. Waited. No ghostly faces appeared in the window, the pages didn't rustle or turn, and after a time, she took her hand away.

• • •

"So I was watching TV the other night and..."

Dark specks of pain swirled behind Alison's lids, but a darker fog wrapped its arms around her and dragged her down, below the bite of Meredith's hands.

"...it was the most ridiculous thing..."

She floated half-asleep, half-aware, similar to the pharmaceutical haze she'd slept in for months under the hospital lights. Except this time the pain didn't pull her out of the daze screaming and crying.

"...I mean, who comes up with..."

This time, something tugged deep inside and took her under, inside a world of grey shadows and dusty footprints. Ticking clocks, chiming inside out and upside down. Laughter and windows opening to nowhere—

"Alison," a voice said.

—and pipe smoke, drifting around her head, touching her shoulder—

"Alison?"

—shaking her arm.

Her eyes snapped open.

"I can't believe you slept through that," Meredith said. "That's a first."

"Sorry, I didn't sleep well last night," she lied.

"Gotcha. Um, I noticed something...interesting."

"Interesting?"

"Yes. Interesting. Right here." Meredith pressed her fingertips down on an area in the center of Alison's right hipbone. "The scarring feels thinner."

"Thinner?" She propped herself on her elbows, the dark lure of sleep instantly gone.

"Yes, thinner and the tissue here and here," Meredith said, her fingers moving up and down, "is less ridged at the edges. Not a lot, but noticeably smoother. And the color is lighter. When do you go back to see your doctor?"

"Not for another couple of months. I just saw him, though, and he didn't mention anything about any changes."

Meredith helped her sit. "Maybe you should give him a call. I don't want to jump the gun here, but I had to at least tell you about it because it looks like an improvement to me."

"I'll give him a call," Alison said, but she looked past Meredith to the album, still on the coffee table.

"Okay, good." Meredith said. "Time for some stretching."

Alison groaned. "Please, can we skip that today? I'm not feeling up to it. I promise I'll stretch after I take a nap."

"If you didn't have huge circles under your eyes, I'd say no, but I'll let you go this once." Meredith lifted one eyebrow. "Just this once."

"Thank you." She smiled her careful, non-grotesque smile and linked her hands together while Meredith folded up the table.

After Meredith left, she trudged upstairs, wincing with each step. She didn't want to sleep—it was all she'd been doing for the past few days—but she was too tired and sore not to. The clothes she'd worn the other night were still puddled in the corner of her room. Sticky grey dust coated the fabric and several tufts of navy blue fiber were caught in the hem of the pants.

Would she go back into the album if she had the chance? Knowing she'd hurt this much afterward? She traced the scars on her cheek. Heard Meredith's words. The skin tugged as she smiled. If there was even the slightest possibility the album was healing her, of course she would.

CHAPTER 10

The brisk October air stung Alison's unscarred skin, stars glimmered in the sky, and the full moon gave off a brilliant light. Her soft-soled shoes whisked across the pavement with hardly a sound. As soon as she crossed the first street, a deep, relentless throb built in her hip.

Her limp turned into a lurch after she crossed the next street, but she kept going. The walks had been Meredith's idea, and it had taken Alison months to sum up the necessary courage.

Courage, something she'd once taken for granted.

After the fire, her mother had wanted her to move back home, but she'd refused. She knew once there, in the rooms of her childhood, she'd never leave. And her mother would take care of her, never complaining, but how much of her own life would she give up to care for her daughter? Too much. But more than that, Alison had wanted a space where she could forget she'd ever been

anything

anyone other than the Monstergirl.

Her mother had arranged for the house. "Consider it a gift from your father. He was a strong believer in life insurance, and I've been careful with the money," she'd said, when Alison pressed for details.

Of her father, Alison had no memory at all. Growing up, he'd simply been a photograph on the fireplace mantel. The photos all showed the same smiling face and laughing eyes. Her mother told her how he'd read to her every night before tucking her into bed, and how, after she learned to walk, he'd taken her for walks through the neighborhood with her tiny hand in his. When Alison was young, her mother would tell her the stories and she would smile and clap her hands and say, "Yes, yes, I remember," but any memories she'd truly had vanished over time.

Not until much later did she find out her father had been involved in a head-on collision with a drunk driver. She had one memory of a crowd of people with somber faces touching her head and speaking in hushed tones. Whether it was a true memory or a dream plucked from how she knew a funeral to be, she didn't know.

Her feet came to a stop at the elementary school. She didn't even remember making the turn in its direction. No teenagers were on the grounds tonight. Swings swayed in the breeze and a cat, too well-fed to be a stray, loped across the grass. She looped her fingers through the chain-link fence surrounding the playground and closed her eyes. She could almost hear the children laughing, the crunch of wood chips beneath their feet, the squeak of tennis shoes on plastic, and the creak of swings.

She wanted so much to open her eyes and see the children for real, wanted to hear them calling, "Miss Reese, Miss Reese," wanted to turn the clock back and erase what had happened, wanted to be free from the self-pity and the fear.

She scrubbed at her eye with the back of her hand, wiping away the tears before they could fall, and gave the playground one last glance.

When she stepped down from the curb to cross the next street, sharp pain drove from her heel to the middle of her back. She gasped, retreated, and grabbed the street sign, her heart racing. Too much pain.

A tightness shifted in her abdomen, a hard knot of *go-home-now-go-home-now* worse than the pain. A scarf-hidden Monstergirl might pass by someone without being noticed. A hunched-over, limping Monstergirl wouldn't. The quiet streets gave lie to her fear, but the walks never hurt this much. Was this another gift from the album? If so, it was a gift she didn't need, but if it was the price she needed to pay...

With a sigh, she turned around and hobbled home.

■ ■ ■

She carried the album into the living room with hope on her lips. The ache in her muscles had ceased, but the knot in her abdomen remained. Balancing the album on her lap, she opened to the inscription page. The pages rustled as she turned to George's photo, then to the house, and back to George. An odd warmth tingled deep under her skin when she set her hand down on the pages, but nothing else happened.

"Please," she said.

It would let her back in. It would. It *had* to. How many times would she have to go into the paper world before she was healed? Five? A dozen? A hundred?

As many as it takes, a voice piped up. Not the Monstergirl's voice at all, but her voice from before the fire and smoke. A tiny part she'd thought was dead and gone. Like her fingers.

She shouldn't get her hopes up. Maybe it had been a fluke. But Meredith had seen a change in her scars, and scars didn't change on their own. At the very least, she'd get to wear her old face again, and maybe it would stay this time.

She was still staring at George's photograph when her phone rang. (And she should be doing something else, something other than sitting, but what if the album opened its door and she wasn't there?) She jumped, saw her mother's name on the display, and was about to answer when the page holding George's photo lifted of its own accord.

She dropped the phone. The page continued to lift up, up, and over, settling down with a tiny, rustle. Her hand shook as she held it over the photo of the house, but before her skin made contact, that page lifted, too. It brushed against her hand, pushing, insistent. On the edge of the page, tiny depressions appeared—fingertip shaped depressions.

With a jolt, she yanked her hand back. The page hovered, floating half-up and half-down, and then lifted and flipped over. The depressions in the paper disappeared.

The new photo showed a narrow room with flowered paper on the walls, a daybed with tasseled pillows, a tall wardrobe, and a small bedside table holding a glass vase of roses, their full petals glistening with dew, apparent even within the sepia tones. Lace curtains hung at the tall window, slightly parted to reveal the top of a tree. And at the far left edge, a tall, man-shaped shadow hovered, darkening the wallpaper.

"We're waiting..."

Alison brushed a strand of hair off her forehead, closed her eyes, and started to lower her hand. Then she paused, her mouth dry,

Why are you being such a scaredy cat? Footprints in dust and cold ghost hands can't hurt you, you know.

then lowered her hand on the photo.

A low laugh. A distant piano note. One dark and discordant note, droning on. Soft murmurs of conversation, the sound of liquid pouring into a glass, quiet clicking steps, a snick-snick sound she couldn't identify. Laughter again. A child's voice, crying out. Another. And the music note played again and again. A bracelet of cold wrapped around her wrist.

Alison held her breath and her fingers twitched, but when she opened her eyes, her gaze met the walls of her own living room. She groaned, pushing the album off her lap. And one last music note echoed away.

■ ■ ■

Alison carried the album with her upstairs and placed it on the back of the toilet while she showered. Twice she thought she heard a faint whisper, but when she peeked out, only the water bouncing off the porcelain gave reply.

She took it with her into the kitchen when she heated a can of soup. No unexpected sounds broke the quiet. The microwave hummed, the refrigerator kicked on, and somewhere in the neighborhood a dog barked for several long minutes, then fell silent.

With the album on the table an inch away from her elbow, she ate without thinking, without tasting, taking care not to look at the spoon, even though chunks of vegetables and broth concealed the shiny metal. After she emptied her bowl, she sat with her hands in her lap and her head bowed. One little Monstergirl all alone. Hurt and waiting.

■ ■ ■

When she called her mother back, the sun had begun its descent from the sky, draping her living room in shadows. Outside, her next-door neighbors were engaged in loud conversation, their jovial tones punctuated with bright peals of laughter. Alison kept her right hand on the photo album, tucked close to her on the sofa, and held the phone in her left.

"I tried to call earlier to see if you wanted me to bring over dinner."

"I was in the shower when you called. Sorry," Alison said, stroking the open page with her fingertips. Pins and needles crawled beneath her skin.

"Not to worry. I've already eaten dinner, but I bought an amazing Key Lime pie. Do you want me to bring it over and we can at least have dessert together?"

Alison's fingers twitched. The pins and needles intensified.

"I'm not really feeling up to company, Mom. Save me a slice, though, and maybe you can come over tomorrow night?"

"Oh. Okay then. Is everything..."

"Everything's fine. I'm

waiting to be swallowed up, swallowed whole

a little sore and a little cranky. I wouldn't be good company."

"I understand."

Her mother didn't understand. No one stared at her when she went outside, no one whispered behind their hands.

She felt the pins and needles deep in her palm, and she wiggled her fingers. The sensation grew then receded.

The scent, no, the *taste*, of tobacco pushed up and out of the photo, and the dark moved beyond the edge, disappearing from sight. Alison let out a gasp.

"Alison? Is everything okay?"

"Everything is fine, Mom. I'm going to go and take a nap now. I'm tired. I'll talk to you later."

Alison disconnected the call without saying goodbye. The shadow retreated back into the picture, but the smell of tobacco lingered. The music note intoned, low and melancholy. An arm lifted, one sepia-toned finger curled in, out, in. Beckoning. A cold chill ran down her spine.

Don't you dare chicken out now, Red said.

Close it and forget about it, Purple said. *You don't need this.*

One more time to make sure it wasn't a fluke. Wasn't her imagination.

Alison took a deep breath, lowered her hand on the album and stifled a gasp as the tiger wrapped its paws around her and pulled her down once more.

CHAPTER 11

As awareness returned, Alison took a deep breath and exhaled loudly. She was inside the album again and there was nothing here that could hurt her.

She flexed her hands and rose on tiptoe. No trace of pain in her muscles. Once again, she was in the foyer. The air was cool but not quite cold; the silence, a weight. As soon as her eyes adjusted to the lack of light, she headed for the door to the turret room. The *closed* door. She twisted the knob to no avail and pressed her ear to the door. No ticking. No whisk-whisk of a swinging pendulum.

A giggle sounded from behind. She spun around, fingers trembling. A silvery column of dust motes, vaguely child-shaped, shimmered near the archway leading back into the foyer. Then it vanished.

A tiny smudge on the floor was all the ghost-shape had left behind. When she stepped through the space a cold chill wrapped around her ankles, but like the motes, it, too, disappeared. She shivered. Took a step forward. Then another. Both steps were smooth and even. All the scars were in their proper places, but her walk had most definitely changed.

"Tiger, tiger," she murmured.

A long ribbon of cobweb loosened from the chandelier and drifted to the floor. She craned her neck and felt the scar tissue pull, a reminder that the house's magic extended only so far. At least while she was on the inside. One faceted crystal sparkled clean; the others remained dull behind their grey cloaks.

The photograph had shown a long, narrow room with one window. Maybe the door would be open. The wood creaked on the third step and she jumped. Stripes were partially visible beneath the grime on the wallpaper, and she wiped a section clean with the side of her hand. The striping might have been navy blue or black, but it was impossible to tell in the murky light.

Maybe next time, she'd bring a flashlight. She let out a quick laugh. Would the tiger let her bring something into its lair? Halfway up the stairs, she paused. On the stairs below, her shoes had left impressions, but on the stairs she'd yet to climb, the dust obscured the wood with an even, unmarked veil. No trace she'd ever been there at all.

Her shadow on the wall waited patiently. She didn't think the house held enough light, yet there it was. Undeniable. Wrong. Or perhaps not. The house played by its own set of rules.

She continued up, but before she passed beyond the open railing, she cast another look toward the turret room. Until the door opened, she

was trapped

might as well look for the room in the picture. She tiptoed down the hallway on the second floor. No carpet cushioned her steps; each time her foot landed on the wood, a tiny sound echoed back. Four doors lined each side of the hall, directly across from each other with sconces in between; at the end of the hallway, wreathed in dark, another door. All closed.

She stopped before the first set of doors and brushed her hand across the wall, revealing more of the same striped wallpaper, yellow splotches of age resembling sickly flowers. A long strip hung a few feet away. The smoke-darkened glass in the nearest sconce was broken, the pieces scattered on the floor below.

The door on her right was locked, as was the door on her left. The next set of doors, the same.

When she approached the next door on her right, a tiny sound cut through the quiet. A muffled *plink*, like dripping water. She leaned closer until she heard the sound again and confirmed it didn't come from behind the door. In the center of the hallway, she stood facing the door at the end, her head cocked to one side. Waiting.

Soft and distant voices slipped out from under the last door on the left. Alison came to a halt just short of the doorframe.

"So lovely."

A man's voice. George's voice.

A rustle of fabric. A footstep.

"I only wanted to…"

The dripping sound returned. Ignoring the desert in her mouth, Alison opened the door. The room held an old spiderweb hanging in the space between ceiling and wall in the right corner. No furniture. No bright, happy flowers bobbing in a vase. The lace curtains at the window were shreds of torn fabric. She crossed the threshold and the air became an early winter's chill. Goosebumps rose along her left arm, her nipple pebbled hard and hurtful, and her breath turned to a frosty plume. Then the cold rushed past—*through*—her. She sagged back against the doorframe. Neither footprint nor streak marred the floor. The tiny sound of dripping water had gone away with the

ghosts

voices. Beyond the tattered lace at the window, grey mist swirled. Beyond that, formless white.

A flurry of movement flashed past and she spun around, hands to her throat. The room was still empty, the floor marked by only her footprints. Dark spots speckled the wallpaper to the left of the door. The air pressure changed, her chest tightened, and a shadow flickered across the wall. She blinked. Tipped her head. Shapes swam into view, transparent suggestions of a daybed and tall wardrobe, but when she blinked, the illusion vanished and the moving silhouette was closer now.

Purple spirals wound their way around her core. The shadow came closer still, and fingers of cold brushed against her cheek. She smelled pipe tobacco, thick enough to taste.

A voice said, "Alison."

She bolted from the room, feet heavy on the wood, and cold caressed her shoulder and cheek, but once in the hallway, both the cold and the smell of smoke disappeared. She bent, hands on her knees, breathing hard.

I want to go home.

Home, with real light and real warmth and real—

Scars? Red cut in. *Sure, go home and wallow in your self-pity and your ugly. Nothing happened.*

"Leave me alone," she said, turning toward the stairs.

Look and see. There's nothing there.

She paused and gave the room one last look. Darkness and old walls. No smoke. No voices. Wrapping her arms around herself, she left the hallway behind and stood at the stairs.

Go down, go down, Purple urged.

Tiny footsteps pattered overhead and a soft giggle wound its way down the staircase. When Alison's feet met the third floor landing, she heard the giggle again, hidden behind a hand or a door.

The first door on the right, the first door on her left, and the second door on her right were all closed. She stepped deeper into the gloom. Another shadow, this one small and narrow, flitted across the wall on her right, swept along the floor in a puddle of dark up to the wall on her left, and stopped there, staining the wallpaper with its presence. It shimmered and separated from the wall, forming into the shape of a child with shoulders and head down, translucent grey and featureless, save for a deeper shading that suggested eyes, nose, and mouth.

"Please don't be afraid. I won't hurt you," Alison said.

The ghost held out one unsubstantial hand. Alison took a step, close enough now to feel the air change to cold. She held out her own hand. A girl's face came out of the grey, as though she were emerging from a waterfall. Wide-set dark eyes, elfin nose and chin, round cheeks, a tiny rosebud mouth. The girl from the photograph.

"Are you Mary?"

The girl nodded. Her face held no fear, no revulsion, only curiosity. Heavy footsteps sounded in the distance, panicked steps running across wood, thumping down stairs. Voices called out. The ghost's eyes widened, her hand retracted, and she spun around, her features blurring back to grey. She melted back onto the wall, and then she was gone.

"Zack? Where are you?" A young voice called out from somewhere far away, her words wavering.

Alison raced down the hallway to the stairs.

"Here, I'm here." Another voice, even farther away. "Stay where you are."

Alison descended the stairs. On the second floor landing, there were several footprints, too many for her passage alone. In the hallway, there were more, pointing away and toward the staircase, disappearing under locked doors, patterned in circles and wide looping arcs.

"Mitch! I can't see—" The boy's voice turned into a choking cough, nearby, yet muffled.

Then Alison smelled the smoke. Not from a pipe, but the reek of burning wood. She moaned low in her throat.

"Please, no. Not this," she said.

"Zack! Zack?" The girl started to cry.

Despite the stink, despite Purple holding court in her chest, Alison shouted, "Where are you?"

There was no roiling smoke, no red-yellow flames licking at the walls, but the smell was everywhere, a dark promise of destruction. In her nose, her mouth, her throat, burning and hot. Footsteps ran beside her, then a heavy pounding of fists against plaster, a groan of frustration.

"I'm coming, Mitch," a voice yelled. "I'm coming."

The voice was too close, too far away. Alison covered her mouth and nose with a hand and crept down the stairs. The girl's cries grew closer and closer still, but when Alison reached the bottom step, they cut off.

The house remained still and silent, an abandoned statue frozen in time. No fire. No smoke. No little girl, real or ghost. The visible prints belonged solely to her.

She took her hand away from her mouth. All a parlor trick. An illusion. There were no children trapped inside the house. The door to the turret room creaked open, swinging in a wide arc until it slid to a stop. The grandfather clock stood, a sentry or a silent witness, its hands unmoving.

Then it chimed.

Time to go home.

Smiling, she entered the turret room where the clock hands ticked their steady backward pace. She lifted one hand, raised it to the clock, and glanced over her shoulder.

The house shifted and her vision blurred behind a cloud of dark smoke and the creeping orange light of fire. Heat roared into the room, the sound of rumbling thunder or the roar of a hungry beast.

Smoke twisted and coiled on the floor. Alison screamed, tasting char on her tongue, and the clock ticked. A little girl ran into the foyer, her bright blue eyes round with fear, her blonde hair streaked with soot. Blood trickled from a comma-shaped gash above one eyebrow. She stopped, turned toward the turret, and her eyes met Alison's with a mirror of shock and fear. She opened her mouth as Alison did the same, drawing in breath for a shout. The girl's voice rose over the flames.

"Please help me."

"Run away," Alison shrieked.

The girl's eyes widened in abject horror.

"Wait," Alison cried out. "I'll help you. I can help you."

The girl screamed and raised her hands in front of her while her head shook from side to side.

"Run," Alison screamed, tasting the heat, the stink, the smoke. "Run away, get out, you have to get out!"

Alison tried to pull away from the clock.

You can't help her. You have to get away.

The smoke and the fire were so close, she needed to help the girl, but the clock ticked on and on, running backward, and darkness struck the smoke from her eyes as the real world pulled her out and away.

■ ■ ■

Alison banged into the edge of the refrigerator with one shoulder, cried out, spun around, and raced back over to the counter, to the album.

She slammed her hands down, the skin of her palms tingling with the impact, and choked back a shriek. It wouldn't let her back in. Not yet. Her ticket to see the tiger was for one use only, and she had to wait for another photo. She crumpled to the floor, buried her face (and the skin was so soft, so soft and unscarred because it made her whole, like the last time, made her whole and human) in her hands, and broke into tears. The tiger wouldn't let her help the little girl.

"I'm sorry, I'm so sorry," she said.

Was the little girl, Mitch, still trapped inside? Inside a paper fire? Would she die inside, unable to get out, get away? It couldn't. It wouldn't.

The names...

Her sob caught in her throat. Paper and fire and the names. Mitch was sometimes short for Michelle and Zack…she knew those names.

She took the stairs two at a time, her now-perfect legs moving with ease, flipped open her jewelry box, and unfolded the yellowed newspaper clipping. There, halfway down: *Two children, identified as Michelle and Zachary Phillips, were rescued from the fire.*

It had to be the same children and if so, they were safe, both of them. Rescued years ago. She held the clipping to her chest until the last bit of panic subsided, then returned it to the box and held out her hands. Her fingernails shimmered nearly opalescent. Her cheeks were smooth and when she smiled, the skin didn't stretch, didn't pull. No more Monstergirl. She changed her clothes and Yellow came creeping in on tiny, destructive feet.

What are you doing? You can't go out. The people will look, the people will point.

But she *could* go out. She didn't have to be afraid. Nonetheless, her steps were slow as she made her way downstairs. What if it *was* all an illusion? What if she saw unscarred skin but others didn't?

She pushed up her sleeve, lifted her shirt, her pant leg. Ran her fingers through her hair. Touched her face again, reveling in the sensation of skin against skin. It was no illusion. Still, she stood by the front door wringing her hands.

They'll stare and they'll—

"Leave me alone," she muttered.

Still, she put on a scarf, sliding the edge down over her forehead. She paused on her front steps, staring up at the sky. It should've been full dark by now, not twilight. She slipped back inside the house—leaving the door open because she was going back out—to check the time. Gauging by when her mother called, fifteen minutes had passed in the real world since she'd

fallen

stepped inside the

tiger

album, but she'd spent at least five minutes getting dressed, maybe ten, and she'd been inside the album longer than five minutes. She scoffed. House rules, house magic. Why should the time be any different? And did it matter?

She checked her face and arms again and locked the door, but her gaze returned to the sky and her stomach twisted with unease.

Red swept in. *Don't stand here staring at the sky, you can hide in your backyard and do the same thing.*

"Fine," Alison said.

She took long, easy strides, not bothering to check whether or not her toes went past the edge of the street sign, her head full of thoughts of clocks and time running too fast to catch. She wasn't tired at all. Not yet anyway.

She crossed the next street. A dark car drove by, its engine giving off an asthmatic wheeze and the heavy smell of burning oil. Wind scraped the scarf back from her forehead. Her hands fluttered like dying butterflies—she hadn't tied the knot tight enough—but when her fingers met the edge of the fabric, she could feel the silk soft against her skin, the thickness of the stitched hem, the heavy lock of hair that had slipped free. In one even movement, she removed the scarf, and the rest of her hair spilled over her shoulders, its weight unfamiliar.

A dark-haired man exited a shop and Alison cringed, but before she could turn away, he smiled. Her cheeks warmed.

At her. He'd smiled at her.

She walked faster, enjoying the way her muscles worked beneath her skin, the way her clothes brushed against her body, the feel of her sleeves sliding against her arms. Her cheeks tingled as the sky darkened and the temperature dropped. Everything was brighter, more alive—the colors of the window displays in the shops, the voices of the a couple walking into a restaurant, the steady hum of the streetlamps, the rush of the cars.

She caught a glimpse of her reflection in a window—a pretty woman with dark hair, a wide smile, and ten fingers—and stopped, her breath caught in her throat. She touched her chin; the reflection did the same. Her eyes glimmered beneath matching dark eyebrows. A breeze lifted her hair, and she turned her face into the wind, arms swinging freely at her sides.

Not far ahead, a door opened, spilling out a torrent of music and a crowd of people. Four men, standing side by side and taking up the entire width of the sidewalk, coming in her direction.

"Did you see her face?" one said.

"That was messed up. I can't believe you said that."

Another one laughed.

Alison jolted to a stop with her hands clenched tight between her breasts. She knew the flavor, the shape, of that laughter. It was bitter and sharp and cruel.

Go now. Go.

But there was nowhere for her to go. With a taste in her mouth like sawdust, she stumbled to the side, but there wasn't enough room on the sidewalk for all of them. She needed somewhere to hide, somewhere where they couldn't see her, couldn't make fun of her. She backed away. One step. Two. Three. A door. Somewhere to hide.

Without thinking, she darted inside. A moment later, the men passed by, still laughing, still talking. Through the glass panel, she watched until they were out of eyesight and sagged in relief. They hadn't been talking about her. They hadn't even noticed her.

A trickle of sweat ran down the center of her spine, and she dried damp palms on her pants. From behind came the steady rhythm of voices, and the slow realization that she was standing in the vestibule of a drugstore, the lights inside far too bright, washed over her.

Adrenalin sour on her tongue, she shoved open the door and bolted back into the night.

● ● ●

She slammed her front door shut, stood with her back against the wood, and burst into tears. It wasn't supposed to be like that. She didn't have to cringe and hide. She didn't have to run home.

Inside, you're still the Monstergirl, Yellow said.

"Shut up," she said into her palms. "Shut up, shut up, shut up."

She wiped her tears with angry swipes of her hand. It would be easier the next time. She wasn't used to all those people. The voices. The noise. Next time, she wouldn't hide.

And she wasn't a Monstergirl on the inside, no matter what pity said.

● ● ●

Four hours later, her skin was still smooth. She wanted to go upstairs, but instead she had the television on, ignoring it while she paced back and forth. From time to time, her hand slipped up to touch her cheek, holding onto hopeful while waiting for the axe to fall, wondering if Anne Boleyn felt the same on the morning of her execution.

After another hour, she trudged up the stairs, leaning heavily on the railing. She climbed into bed and gathered the sheets to her shoulders, running her hands back and forth across the fabric.

"Please don't bring them back," she said. "Please keep them away for good this time."

● ● ●

Five minutes after she drifted off to sleep, the scars crept back in, slipping back into place. Stealthy soldiers sneaking in behind enemy lines. Alison sighed once, twice, and slumbered on, blissfully unaware when the air thickened with the smell of pipe smoke.

PART IV

NEW HURTS

He walks into the hospital room and stops in mid-smile. She looks up, tries to smile back, but she can't, it hurts too much, and the medicine makes her head foggy, but she sees him and thinks everything is okay, everything is all right because he is here. I'll love you forever, he said. Forever and ever.

Her mother leaves the room, leaves them alone, and she wonders why he won't come closer, she tries to hold out her hand, and he has tears in his eyes, and she wants to speak, wants to tell him how much she loves him, but she can't make her words work. He stands by the door, he whispers her name, and he sounds so sad, but she'll be okay, they tell her she'll be okay, then the medicine takes her down into a trembling darkness that makes the pain disappear, and when she opens her eyes again, he's gone.

CHAPTER 12

She knew the scars were back the moment she woke. She told herself she wouldn't cry, wouldn't get angry and, for a few minutes, she almost believed it.

• • •

The inscription had changed once again. More spidery lettering filled in some of the gaps.

ill chime

Stay

es

locked

ped lik

past

men bri

hear

house

Welco

olds —

A paper tiger to swallow you whole

Alison traced the spaces between the words with her fingers, her brow furrowed. Still not enough to make sense of things, but the words chime, stay, locked, and house were clear enough. Maybe once she unlocked the inscription, she'd unlock the secrets of the album's magic. Maybe once all was revealed, her scars would stay away for good. Somewhere between the words and the spaces, there had to be a key.

She flipped past George's photo and the house to the room. The shadow remained motionless, and when she gave the page a tug, it didn't budge. With the edge of her thumb, she brushed the paper edges and the scent of flowers spilled out. The smell grew in intensity—a cloud of rotting flowers. Coughing, she slammed the cover shut.

Throw it out.

The voice twisted around her ribcage, but reason hid within the corset of fear. Photo albums could not heal, could not be real. Maybe it was a thing best left untouched. A place best left alone.

She rubbed her lower back near the hipbone, where Meredith said the scarring felt thinner. Although Alison couldn't see it, when she rubbed the back of her left arm against the skin, she thought she detected a slight difference there, and the thought was enough. She wasn't afraid of a smell or of a ghost fire, no matter how real it had seemed. And the girl had been saved.

● ● ●

There were nineteen Michelle Phillips listed online as living in Baltimore, and less than half had phone numbers included. The likelihood that one was the girl she'd seen in the house was slim, but Alison couldn't help but wonder. She turned her phone over and over in her hand. What was she going to say? *Did you see a scarred woman in the house that burned down when you were a kid?*

She had to come up with something that made sense. She made a huffing noise deep in her throat. Maybe not sense, but something that seemed *plausible*. She brought up the website that listed Pennington House as haunted and tapped the edge of the laptop.

She yawned for at least the tenth time in spite of sleeping for fourteen hours straight, and rotated her shoulders back and around. A spark of pain flared beneath her right shoulder blade, warning her against doing it a second time.

She typed for a few minutes, reread what she'd written, deleted it, and wrote again. Finally, she had something that, at least on paper, appeared legitimate.

Her voice trembled when the first call was picked up. She read her words, and halfway through, the woman on the line said, "Not interested," and hung up. The second Michelle Phillips at least listened to Alison's halting speech. "Nice," she said. "Did Scott put you up to this?" Then she hung up, too. The third woman didn't let her finish, and the fourth was an elderly woman who couldn't hear what Alison was saying. Alison disconnected the call after shouting, "I'm sorry."

By the sixth call, the speech came easy; the protection of the phone against eyes gave her confidence enough. The seventh went to voice mail, but the woman was older, far older than the Michelle she'd seen would be.

She dialed the eighth number. "Hello, I'm researching strange occurrences in Baltimore for a possible book and wonder if you'd be willing to talk to me about Pennington House?"

There was a sharp intake of breath. A long pause.

"How did you find out about that?"

"I, I found an article about the fire, and since the house was supposedly haunted..."

"This is crazy." The woman laughed. "I was just talking to my husband about the house a few nights ago."

Alison smiled, not caring that the skin twisted. "Did you happen to see anything strange when you were in the house?"

"The whole house was strange. Dusty and creepy as hell. I fell down and cut my forehead while we were exploring, and I still have the scar to show for it. My brother found a secret passageway, but I refused to follow him in."

"A secret passageway?"

"Yep, sounds like a cliché, doesn't it? Scary old house with a hallway behind the walls. Anyway, he went in and while I was waiting for him to come out, I started smelling smoke."

Alison pressed one hand to her chest.

"Whoever started the fire probably didn't know we were inside, or maybe they did and didn't care. But things got really weird. I heard a voice and a clock chimed and it was just weird. Then I saw a man in old-fashioned clothes."

Alison struggled to keep her grip her grip on the phone. "A man?"

"Yep. He was just standing there, looking pissed off, but I could see through him." She laughed again.

"So you think he was a...ghost?"

"I know it sounds crazy, but yeah, I do. My brother yelled my name and when I looked back, the guy was gone, and that was it. After that, all I heard were sirens. Later, my brother said I probably imagined everything, but I don't think so. It was the same guy from the photo album."

Alison's chest tightened and she struggled to find her voice. "The photo album?"

"Yeah, my brother said there was a room under the stairs and it had a bunch of junk in it. Old toys and stuff, and he found a photo album that he brought out with him."

"He..." Alison swallowed hard. "Brought it out?"

"Yeah, he did. My brother was crazy like that. He wouldn't let the firemen take it from him either."

Alison touched the album. "What happened to it?"

"My mother threw it out."

"Did you see it?"

"Yeah, I did, and the first picture in it was the guy I saw. I'm sure of it. The rest of the pictures were of the house and the rooms and some other people. It was weird."

"Do you, do you think your brother would be willing to talk to me, too?"

Another audible breath. Another long pause. Then, "My brother's dead."

"I'm so sorry—"

"It was a long time ago. Is that all you wanted to know?"

"Yes, I think so, unless you've seen a ghost or something strange somewhere else?"

"No, I haven't," she said, her voice clipped and cold. "I have to go. Good luck with your book."

Alison sat with the phone in her hand. So Michelle—Mitch—hadn't seen her in the house at all, but she'd seen George. And when her brother had brought out the album, somehow, as improbable as it seemed, the ghosts must have come along too.

●　●　●

Alison forced her back straight and her mouth to relax. Her mother had a smile on her face and a pie plate topped with tinfoil in her hand, but she stopped as soon as she stepped inside and took Alison's chin with one hand.

"Are you feeling okay?"

"I'm fine. I'm a little tired because I slept too long."

"You have horrible circles under your eyes. And your skin looks pale. Too pale."

"Mom, I *am* pale," Alison said and laughed, pulling away from her mother's hand.

"Why don't you let me check your temperature?"

"I'm fine. Really."

Her mother gave a little nod. "Okay, if you say so." Alison followed her into the kitchen, keeping her steps small. When she sat down at the table, pain radiated out from her hip to the middle of the back, and she stifled a gasp. Her mother frowned but held her tongue, and Alison put on a reassuring smile.

• • •

Wrapped in a towel, Alison left the bathroom, and heard a faint strain of music—piano notes and the soft, mournful tune of a violin. It reminded her of her grandmother, of a song in a snow globe, a delicate treasure of glass and glitter, with a tiny key at the bottom. "Don't touch," her grandmother would say when Alison would visit. "It's fragile." But she'd pick it up and turn the key so Alison could listen to the song.

Alison crept down the steps, holding tight to the railing, humming along with the tune and ignoring the tiny twinges of pain in her hips, back, and shoulder. The notes mixed with a touch of perfume. Lavender, maybe. When she stepped close to the coffee table, the cover of the photo album flipped open with a thump and the music grew louder.

Stay away from it. You don't need it.

The pages fluttered up and over, one by one—George, house, room, and then another. Forgetting the music, forgetting the perfume, Alison lowered herself to her knees and spun the album around.

The new picture revealed an elegant room, all dark wood, heavy draperies, and crystal sconces. A piano stood in one corner with a violin resting on top. In the lower right corner, a swirl of fabric had been caught in mid-motion. A full-skirted woman trapped forever on film despite her best efforts to leave before the flash?

A drop of water fell from the end of Alison's hair, hit the photograph with a small plop, and remained there, a tiny crystal ball glow-ing with colors and light from within. Before she could touch it, it disappeared into the photo, retaining its shape all the while, leaving behind a dry surface and a dark spot on the fabric inside.

A deep, husky voice said, "There's still so much to see."

Her left arm broke out in goosebumps, but she smiled as the words echoed themselves away.

"I want to see everything," Alison said. Her words shattered the music into tiny fragments that vanished with a soft whoosh, taking the scent of lavender with them.

● ● ●

When shadow and hush wrapped the neighborhood, Alison grabbed her scarf, but once she had the fabric knotted under her chin, she paused and glanced at the album. What if the paper world opened when she wasn't home? Would the tiger wait or would it clamp its jaws shut tight? She twined her fingers. Maybe she'd wait another day. Deep below her skin, her muscles still ached, and the streets would be there tomorrow. Her chance to be whole might not.

What if the album never let her back inside? Her hands clenched into fists and a tiny coil of scarlet gathered weight in her chest. It wouldn't do that. George said there was still so much to see.

She stared at a crack in the ceiling of her bedroom for hours with the album open beside her and eventually fell asleep with one hand tucked under her cheek, the other atop the open pages.

● ● ●

The album didn't open its door to her the following night either, but she stayed home. Just in case.

● ● ●

Alison made breakfast and sat down with the photo album open to the new picture. A whisper of voices drifted from the pages. Her spoon clattered to the floor. The swirl of fabric in the corner swished once, twice, and exited the picture, leaving behind a tiny sound of shoes tapping on the floor. Her food forgotten, she lifted her hand. Set it down on the photo.

The tiger opened its mouth; she slid down and down—

CHAPTER 13

—and down.

She was in the foyer once again, crouched with her head down. Music brought her to her feet, soft strains of music flickering through the shadows and the dizziness in her head, and under the music, an odd buzzing reminiscent of cicadas in a summer tree. (But no fire, no smoke, no crying children.) The dust took on a luminous quality, sparkling despite the lack of light. Cold air caressed her cheek. She gasped and an airy laugh broke free. She already knew there were ghosts, but they couldn't hurt her.

A wisp of color flashed in the corner of her eye. She whirled around. Saw translucent figures in the room. Dark suits, full skirts, a figure walking with a cane. The edge of a piano. The shimmer of light bouncing off a crystal sconce. She staggered back. Her eyesight blurred. Then the house shivered, a rumbling of wood beneath her bare feet, and the figures melted into nothing. She blinked. Swallowed hard.

The room was empty of everything but ruin. Dark patches marred the tattered wallpaper at regular intervals. She ran her finger down the nearest one, leaving a lighter trail behind. The sconces from the photo were gone. She stared down at the dark grey mark on her finger. Soot from the candles?

She scrubbed her finger on her pajama pants. Plain blue, no monkeys. She crossed the room to a window, leaving behind a trail of footprints, and pushed the curtain aside. Long strands of pale mist passed by the window; beyond that, darkness. In the corner of the room, a square-shaped smudge, a little larger than a child's wooden block, marked the floor. She traced the shape with her fingertip. Three more shapes marked a wide rectangle. Working her way to the front of the rectangle, she found four smaller marks. She nudged one with her big toe, and the floor shuddered under her feet.

Piano notes swam out of the silence, a crescendo lifting higher and higher. An image flickered in the gloom—a long expanse of black lifted at an angle to reveal the wood and metalwork within. Transparent black and white keys took shape, moving in time with the music. Then a hand, an arm, a shoulder, a head bent over the keys. A long swish of skirts draped on the floor. A pale outline of someone not quite there. Voices gathered behind her back, and she turned, her fingers trembling.

A shoulder here, an arm there, the curve of a cheek, the tailored cut of a jacket, the lace-trimmed edge of a bodice. Three-dimensional paper dolls made of cellophane. Colors swirled past: rose pink, navy blue, black, sea green. The music took a mournful turn, all somber notes and dramatic pauses.

Visible through the shapes and colors, a suggestion of furniture came into view. A low bench with curved feet. An armchair. A crimson settee with tasseled pillows. The sparkle of crystal decanters atop a dark wood cabinet. The amber glow of the liquor within. And the scents: flowery perfume, hair oil, the sharp tang of brandy.

The colors around her intensified. Features and forms sharpened. Three people, no, four. Now five. There, but not there. Could they see her, too?

She stepped forward, into an icy chill, and a strangled moan caught in her throat. A hazy dark mist was gathered around her legs. The ghost of the piano.

She jerked her body free from the cold. Her footprints on the floor were half-hidden beneath a rug with a swirl of flowers along its length. Through it, the floorboards appeared as slashes in the nap, dissecting the flowers mid-bloom. The floor quivered beneath her feet, and the colors sharpened once more. The music changed again. Faster, more insistent.

A woman in a green dress sat on the bench, her hands moving across the keys. Alison touched the space where the woman's shoulder should be, but her hand met only cold air. The woman's hands paused. She gave a small shake of her head and resumed playing.

Alison froze. A few inches above the woman's hem, a dark spot marred the satin fabric of her skirt. Like a water stain. She squeezed her eyes shut and counted to three.

The mark meant nothing.

The spot glared, an eye accusing her of tampering with the paper world. She backed away from the piano, and cold passed over her shoulder and caressed her cheek. Her vision swam with dark and pale. A man's jacket, his cheek above a well-trimmed beard, passed by, *through*, her. She stumbled toward the archway, one hand to her throat.

The music stopped in mid-note, the house trembled under her feet, one quick shudder of wood, and then everything vanished. Alison sagged against the wall outside the room, breathing hard. Then cold grazed her arm again, a finger light touch running from shoulder to elbow.

A masculine voice spoke in her ear. "So much to see."

The cold returned, gentle on her arm.

"Stay and see," George said.

Of course she knew it was George, just as she knew it was his real name, not one of her constructs. The paper world was real and not-real at the same time, but it had secrets to reveal and stories to tell.

"Show me," she said. "Please."

This isn't right. You don't need to see anything. Stay and leave without your scars. Nothing more.

But why shouldn't she stay for a while? What harm could it do? Until the house

let her out

opened the door back to the real world, what else did she have to see other than empty rooms? If it could show her more…

George gave a low chuckle.

The floor lurched and the air cooled. A little girl's laughter flowed by, but the little girl was nowhere in sight. In the foyer, another elegant rug lined the floor, a small table sat in the center, topped with a vase of flowers, and a dark framed mirror hung on the wall. Yet the grime peeked through it all, a hazy afterimage.

Alison took another step into the foyer. The colors deepened, dark green vines twisting into shape on the rug, the wood top of the table gleaming with a mahogany shine, as the flower petals bloomed a deep merlot.

She held out her hand. Wood warmed beneath her hand. The sensation passed and her hand slipped into the table that was no longer there. Children's voices rose in the air, singing numbers and tigers and bites, oh my.

In the next room, shapes overlaid the dust, hiding her prints, hiding the sickly pallor. A long, rectangular table surrounded by chairs, the wood dark and carved. Another chandelier. A sideboard. And on the wall, a large painting of water and trees, but when she extended her hand, her skin met wallpaper, cool and puckered with air bubbles.

She pulled back with a hiss. The scars on her hands were gone. Lines of pink and white on her forearm crept out from under her pajama sleeve, but a line of healthy skin cut across below her wrist, as though her hands had been dipped in a magical healing elixir. She still had eight fingers, but when she curled them toward her palm, the slightest tension in the muscles gave the suggestion of a whole hand. When she touched her face, she winced at the scar tissue pressing against her skin; the wince turned into a smile at the feeling in her fingers and palms, no longer limited to the real world, but somehow part of the paper world as well.

She skirted the table and chair shapes, and cobwebs stuck to her fingers when she fingered the dark curtain at the window. The nap of the fabric in her hand still retained a touch of softness, despite the damage of time. A transparent image of drapes in a deep navy blue sat atop the real curtains, remaining even when she pushed the old fabric aside. Outside, the grey mist swirled and gathered, but beyond...

The hint of a green expanse of lawn bordered by tall trees. Stepping stones. The edge of a white gazebo, the pillars capped with a domed roof. Small figures moving in the distance. Then the grey billowed back in, obscuring everything.

The floor trembled under her feet again; back in the foyer, the table shaped illusion was gone. A single musical note danced in the air before the house swallowed the sound. She wandered in circles through the empty rooms, waiting for a sign, a glimpse of color and shape.

When none surfaced, she took the stairs, her feet tracing new marks in the dust. The house had erased all the signs of her previous passages. On the second floor, the sconces held their places, silent and watchful, and the sound of her footsteps disappeared into the carpet. Something about its scrollwork pattern gave her pause, like a word held on the tip of a tongue, yet refusing to take shape.

The door to the last room on the left stood ajar. Her footsteps had been erased from the floor in this room as well, but a handprint marred the wallpaper next to the window. The dark spots to the left of the doorframe glistened. She touched one finger to a spot the size of a quarter. Under her skin, it felt slick and sticky, but no residue remained on her skin.

Back in the hallway, she rubbed one bare foot back and forth on the rough, matted nap of the carpet. Then her vision twisted. Her stomach gave a lurch. She pressed one hand to her forehead and her knees buckled. She hit the carpet with a small thud, brought her legs to her chest, and closed her eyes. Her toes dug tiny grooves into the rug as she waited for the world to right itself.

There was something about the carpet, something *wrong*, but she couldn't open her eyes to look, she couldn't—

● ● ●

—leave without having a glass of wine. Please, I insist."

Alison touched her chest. "I…"

"Everything all right?" George asked.

"Yes, I think so."

"I'm so glad you joined our little soiree," he said in his husky voice.

Piano notes lifted and fell. Flames danced in the wall sconces; elongated shadows flickered on the walls.

George pressed a glass into her hand, the liquid within deep and dark. She took a small sip. Her mouth flooded with the rich taste of berries. The music stopped and everyone clapped.

"Bravo!" George called out. "Play another song, dear."

The woman at the piano, her pale hair shimmering down her back, flexed her hands, bent over the keys, and began again. The song began with a somber note and spiraled down, each note speaking of sorrow and dread.

George walked away. A woman with high cheekbones and grey streaks at her temples sat on the settee and spread out her rose colored skirts. The toe of one satin shoe peeked out from beneath the sea of fabric. She was elegant and striking with strong arched brows and wide-set eyes.

Next to a liquor cabinet, a bearded man with deep creases cutting across his forehead lifted a monocle and looked Alison up and down, his eye large and owlish through the glass. The woman in the rose dress tittered. Alison trembled and lifted her fingertips to her cheek. Smooth skin welcomed the touch.

The music changed, speeding up to a lively tune and conversation turned to whimsy. Laughter floated into the air. But a steady hum lingered in the room, hidden under the music, under the voices.

"Encore, encore," the man with the monocle called out when the song ended.

"Yes, do give us an encore," George said.

The new song held a sweetness in its solemnity.

Alison headed for the piano, but George stepped in her path, took her arm, and led her over to the liquor cabinet.

"Here, let me refill your glass," he said.

"Oh, no thank you. I should go."

He gave a low chuckle and poured more wine. "But we've been waiting for you for such a long time. Do you want to go back so soon?"

A woman wearing a dress of pale gold entered the room, followed by a tall, clean-shaven man. George clapped him on the back, gesturing toward the liquor cabinet with his other hand. The newcomer poured brandy into a small glass and downed a large swallow, caught Alison's eye, and ambled over.

"I haven't seen you here before. Are you having fun?"

Her fingers tightened around her glass. "Yes, thank you."

He put a hand to his forehead. "Where are my manners? My name is Thomas."

"I'm Alison."

"What a lovely name. I believe Madeline is quite envious of you," he said, nodding to the woman in pink.

"Of me?"

"Quite so. She absolutely despises Josephine. She dislikes any woman younger or prettier than she is, and you are as lovely as your name."

Alison's cheeks warmed.

"Dance with me," Thomas said,

He didn't wait for her reply, simply guided her across the room. Everything became a soft blur as they swayed in time to the music. Thomas spoke close to Alison's ear. "You need to leave."

"What?"

"Shhh. Keep your voice low and a smile on your face. He's watching us."

"George?"

"Yes, now smile, for both our sakes."

She forced her mouth back into shape but her hands were trembling. "I don't understand."

"He doesn't think I remember," Thomas said.

"Remember what?"

"Who I was before. I don't always. It, he, won't let me, but sometimes—"

The music stopped yet again, and the room broke out into applause. She caught George staring. "Before? I'm sorry. I still don't understand." Thomas lifted her hand and pressed a kiss on her skin. She dropped down into a clumsy curtsy.

"He's walking this way. Please leave," he said. "Once he gets hold, he won't let go. And then it will be too late."

"Thomas, you should stop monopolizing our guest. I believe Edmund wishes to speak to you." He nodded his head in the direction of the man with the monocle.

Thomas gave George a small nod. "It was a pleasure to meet you, Alison. Thank you for the pleasure of your company."

"I'm sure you will see her again," George said, reaching for her arm as Thomas walked away. "Here, have more wine."

She took the glass. The floor moved beneath her feet, a gentle tremor that sent the liquid in her glass tipping back and forth. The candles dimmed. The conversation paused. George frowned, and

Thomas turned toward Alison, his eyes grave. The floor trembled again, the glass slipped from her hand, and wine spilled out.

When the drops hit the floor, they remained in perfect spheres, balanced on the wood. The glass followed, striking with a dull thud, but it stayed intact. Then everything reversed. The glass spiraled up, heading back to her hand. The wine dripped up, in search of the glass.

She let out a breathy shout and gasped. George, Thomas, and all the others had faded, their shapes an outline of shimmering air. Like melting reflections. As her fingertips met glass, everything winked out of sight, the air rushing in with a soft whoosh to fill the spaces. A soft brush of fabric tickled her ankles, then that, too, disappeared. She stumbled back, blinking hard, a scarred, barefoot girl in pajamas.

Footprints covered the floor, footprints in circular patterns tracing the line of a dancing couple. But had she been dancing? She rubbed her forehead. No, she'd been upstairs, upstairs, sitting down on the rug. And then, and then...her thoughts were muddled.

Cold kissed her hand. The air wavered into a small child's shape, darker spots marking eyes, nose, and mouth.

"Mary?"

With a giggle, a cool hand curled around hers, pulling somehow, despite missing the warmth and substance of real flesh.

The grandfather clock chimed, a loud peal in the quiet hush of the house. She jumped and the ghost child tugged again.

She can't tug, she's not real. None of it is real.

Alison followed her through the foyer, the room beyond, and into the turret room. The clock chimed again, but the little girl pulled her away from clock toward the wall.

"It's time for me to go," Alison said, twisting her hand away from the chill.

A shadow darkened the wall, as though a portion of the wall had melted away or folded back in on itself. In the darkness, the ghost girl shimmered.

The clock chimed.

The little girl waved and gave another giggle. As Alison disappeared back into the world of the real, the sound changed. Deepened into a growl.

A hungry one.

CHAPTER 14

Alison spilled out onto the kitchen floor, banging her elbow on the counter, and caught herself before her knees hit the floor. The taste of wine lingered on her tongue and a foggy sensation had taken residence in her head. She lurched over to the table, her hip aching, and exhaled sharply as she sat down.

But she wasn't supposed to hurt yet. Not until the scars came back. And the scars were gone. She touched her face and everything faded away except the sensation of flesh touching flesh, smooth skin beneath ten fingertips.

Grey film coated her pajamas; dark streaks marred one leg. She scraped her fingernail over the dried edges, remembering the sticky spot on the wall of the bedroom. She dislodged several loose flakes onto the floor, and held out her hands, turning them from side to side.

Whole again, whole again. But at what price?

She shoved the voice away.

More of the inscription had revealed itself, dark and spidery against the pale paper, another hint of

the secrets

the words it contained.

ch will chime

Stay and

of lies

ose locked

ped like a

drift past

men bring

ver hear

house of s

Welcomes

unfolds —

a paper tiger to swallow you whole

Yet it still made no sense. She rubbed her arms, imagining she could feel the scars hiding under the skin, waiting to slip back in. But for now, she'd shed her Monstergirl skin; she wasn't going to waste the day sitting in her kitchen pining over an old inscription.

Halfway up the stairs she stopped, curling her toes on the wood. Wood and carpet, wood and carpet. She tapped her lower lip with one finger. The carpet in the second floor hallway of the paper house had *not* been there on her previous visit. The floor had been wood, hard under its coating of grey, and one of the sconces had been broken, littering the floor with jagged little glass teeth.

The house had changed. Like her.

Once showered and dressed, she stood by her front door, jingling her keys in the palm of her hand. Daylight peeked around the edges of the window blinds, a harsh reminder that she couldn't hide behind the gloom of night, but she straightened her spine. She could do this, and this time, things would be better.

Something teased in the back of her mind, something about the house and a party, then the taxi arrived, the driver honking the horn three times in rapid succession. After an instant of hesitation, Alison grabbed her coat and scarf.

The inside of the car reeked of stale food and old cigarettes. The driver, a young man with long hair, watery green eyes, and forearms riddled with old tattoos, flipped on the meter and soon enough, her neighborhood lay far behind.

She caught the driver looking at her in the rear view mirror with an odd light in his strange eyes and had a sudden fear that she'd dreamt it all. Photo albums couldn't heal scars, couldn't turn Monstergirls whole, but when she touched her cheek, the skin was smooth.

The driver started to hum, then broke into a song about a girl who was fine, but his deep, gravelly voice turned the words into an unpleasant growl. She dropped her eyes and kept them down until the taxi arrived at her destination.

"Is this the right place?" the driver asked.

"Yes, thank you. I won't be that long."

She clasped her shaking hands together and stepped onto the land where Pennington House once lived. Leaves crunched beneath her feet; the air smelled of the winter to come. Other houses stood not far away, none so large as Pennington House had been, but all with the design and character of houses built long ago. Empty lots lured trash and stray feet as the sun lured an upturned face, but there was neither gum wrapper nor plastic bag and the grass was well-trimmed.

A large rectangular depression on the property revealed where the house had stood. Alison stood at the edge of the space with her hands in her pockets. She took a step forward, holding her breath. She'd expected some residue, some trace of the eerie or strange, but the air didn't change in weight nor were there any odd sounds. Nothing but the chilly air and the grass.

She ignored the ache in her muscles as she walked, bending down here and there to run her fingers through the grass, but neither stone nor sliver of wood had survived the demolition. In the real world, Pennington House was as gone as gone could be.

She wiped her hands on her pants and surveyed the grounds. In the far left corner, near a huge oak tree, she saw a wrought iron fence.

The fence was as high as her shoulders, with ornamental pointed ends to dissuade climbing, the tips sharp enough to injure thigh and groin. A chain and padlock held the gate shut. Inside, seven tombstones stood in two neat rows. The four stones in the back row were tall and ornately carved; the three in front, smaller rectangular slabs of grey stone with slightly curved tops. The lettering on all was weathered but not weathered enough to prevent her reading the names: Lillian, Edmund, Eleanor, and George in the back row; William, Elizabeth, and Mary in the front.

Her knees felt wobbly. She rested her head against the fence, ignoring the bite of cold against her skin. William had died at three months of age, Elizabeth had died before her fourth birthday, and Mary soon after her fifth. Alison knew mortality rates were higher then and it wasn't uncommon for children to die young but seeing it in front of her like this...

"Can I help you?"

Alison jumped, instinctively tucking her chin down. Standing a few feet away was a man with a wrinkled face, a slight stoop to his back, and grey wisps of hair peeking out from a baseball cap emblazoned with the Orioles logo. Even though his face was kind, his expression soft, her stomach twisted and she clutched her hands together.

"I was just reading the gravestones. That's okay, isn't it?"

The old man shrugged. "As long as you're not defacing anything, there's no law against it. I live over there," he nodded toward a stone house, half of which was visible through the trees, "and I saw you walking around and thought I'd come over and check. Sometimes kids try to break in. I like to keep an eye on things."

She unclasped her hands. Forced her breath even. She didn't have to be afraid. She'd managed to keep calm with the strange taxi driver; she could manage the same now.

"I wasn't trying to break in. Just looking. All the kids died so young."

"Lots of kids died young back then. My mother had eight siblings, and only five made it to adulthood. Some families live long and healthy and happy, some get stuck with tragedy. Luck of the draw."

"Did you know them? The Penningtons?"

He gave a dry little chuckle. "By the time I came around in 1939, they were all gone. My parents knew the old man, George, though. I remember hearing my dad talk about him. He was supposedly a cranky old bastard, if you don't mind my speaking such language."

"Not at all, but he was...cranky?"

"That's what my dad used to say anyway. I inherited the house from them, and they bought it in, I guess..." He stared off into the trees, his forehead creased. "1932 or 3, maybe, so yeah, they knew him for a few years. Or knew of him, I should say. They said he rarely left the house. One of them eccentric recluse fellows, I guess. The only way anyone knew he was dead was because he paid people to deliver his food and such and one day he didn't answer the door. Otherwise, he could've been in the house forever without anyone noticing."

Alison shivered.

"Damn shame about the house, though. My mother said it was beautiful, but it was already falling apart when I was a kid. Doesn't take long for a place to fall to pieces if no one's there to take care of it. Family members fighting over or it or some such. Like I said, a shame, and the fire was something else. I hope never to see another one in my life; the sound was like something out of a monster movie."

Alison rubbed her lower lip with the side of a finger. "Did you ever go in it? The house, I mean, before it burned down?"

He grinned. "Sure. A big empty house like that? All the neighborhood kids did."

"Did you ever see anything?"

"What? Like ghosts?" The dry chuckle again. "All I ever saw was mouse droppings and cigarette butts. Once we came across crazy

Mr. Nichols passed out drunk in the upstairs hallway, but he was harmless. Oh, we used to tease each other that we heard voices, and some kids swore they saw things or heard things, but it wasn't anything other than an old house stretching its bones. By that time, there wasn't anything left in the place, just walls and dust."

"And now there's nothing at all," Alison said in a soft voice.

"Maybe it's for the best that the place burned down, though. It brought nothing but bad luck to that family."

"What do you mean?"

"They all died in the house. Not all at once, mind, but they died in the house and then got buried here behind it. Might be why the state's never built anything on the land, on account of the bodies."

"Do you know how they died?"

"They didn't cut people up like they do nowadays. People just died. Anyway, it was nice chatting with you, young lady, but I need to head back over before the wife sends out the cavalry to look for me."

He extended his hand. Alison held the inside of her cheek between her teeth as she did the same. His skin was calloused but warm.

When she turned back to the graves, his words echoed in her mind: *They all died in the house.*

• • •

The playground was small, nestled at the end of a side street. Alison's limbs felt heavy, and the thought of her bed held more appeal that they should this time of day, but she didn't want to go home yet. She was safe; the playground, deserted. The swing, large enough to hold an adult comfortably, creaked as she pumped her legs to get it started. Her hair blew around her face in a tangle of dark. Her neighborhood didn't have a public playground anymore. Often vandalized, it had been paved over for a convenience store.

Enough time had passed for her fingers to start to cramp around the chains when a high-pitched voice carried through the air. A small boy dressed in a bright red coat entered the park with a woman talking on her cell phone.

Alison dragged her feet in the hollow beneath the swing to bring it to a stop, started to get up, then forced herself to stay put. The child didn't pay Alison any attention as he ran over to the monkey bars. When another boy and his mother arrived a few minutes later, the latter joining the first child's mother on a bench off to the side, Alison left the swing behind.

As she crossed the playground on her way out, a little girl came running in her direction and hit her legs with a loud, "Oof." Alison staggered back to keep her balance.

The girl's eyes went wide, her mouth formed a small circle, and Alison blinked rapidly as it triggered a memory. Alison in a wheelchair with a nurse pushing her toward the front door of the hospital, and a little girl walking with her mother, and Alison hid her face too late because for one moment, she'd forgotten about her scars, and the little girl stopped and tugged her mother's hand. "Mommy, what's wrong with the lady?" Her voice like a beacon, drawing more eyes, and Alison felt them crawling over her like insects, and it wasn't the little girl's fault, but they all looked and then they—

A woman with dark hair rushed over. "Becky, say you're sorry. You almost knocked the lady down."

Alison tossed her hair and the memory aside. Everything was fine.

"Sorry, lady," the girl said, her words even and dutiful.

"It's okay," Alison said with a smile. "I'm fine. Honestly."

And she was. If her mouth was dry, if her heart was racing, it was because she'd been on the swing for too long.

■ ■ ■

Alison flipped the dead bolt and paused. A hint of pipe smoke clung to the air, almost faint enough to blame on imagination, but it grew stronger as she walked into the kitchen. The photo album remained where she'd left it, open on the counter. She bent over the pages and inhaled old paper and dust. But no tobacco.

A cool gust of air touched the back of her neck and paper ruffled. When she turned back, the pages were flipping back and forth, too fast to offer anything but a teasing glimpse at the photos within. Alison pressed her fingertips to her lips, holding in a gasp, then the last page turned and the cover slammed shut.

She stepped closer to the album, breathing hard. With the tip of one finger, she opened the cover. Waited. But the pages remained still.

• • •

Alison woke once over the course of the next twenty-four hours—to call Meredith and reschedule her appointment.

• • •

When Alison finally climbed out of bed, she hobbled into the bathroom; each step sent a pinwheel of pain spinning in her hips. She splashed cold water on her face, fumbled for a towel, and sank to the floor, her hands twisted in a semblance of arthritic claws. A strange weight settled in her chest, heavy and liquid. She crawled from the bathroom with her head down, wisps of hair dangling in her face. Right hand, right leg,

This is the price for your vanity, a despicable voice of rational and real said.

left hand, left leg. "Come, Josephine," she sang tunelessly. Her hands left the cool bathroom tile, spidered over the marble threshold and onto the wood. "Going up she goes, up she goes."

Too high...

Right hand, right leg.

...a price, be careful of the tiger.

She used the railing to haul herself up, unfolding like an origami animal crafted in reverse, and touched her right cheek with her misshapen fingers.

"I don't care," she said.

■ ■ ■

Sleep. Wake. Eat.

Hurt.

PART V

INSIDE

Pain. Then white lights. Too bright, but she can't speak, can't tell them they hurt her eye. Yes, only one eye because they've covered the other. She tries to move her hands, to push the dark away, but she's tied down. For your safety, someone says. Jonathan. Jonathan, she tries to say, but her voice won't work.

And the pain, shiny metal pain digs in, tearing the dead flesh away.

CHAPTER 15

Alison turned her face away as Meredith snapped a picture with her camera.

"Did you call the doctor?"

"Yes." The lie slipped from Alison's lips with ease. "He didn't think it was important enough for me to come in."

Another click. Another flash of light.

"Doctors. There is *definitely* a difference and it's bigger now. All the scar tissue in this area is thinner." Meredith used the tip of her finger, pushing down hard enough so Alison could feel the pressure, and in one spot, one tiny spot, there was a kiss of warmth. Skin against skin. "It's not just the way they feel, either. They look different. Better. More like healthy skin and less like scar tissue."

Another flash.

"Okay, I think that's good enough. Here, look." Meredith scrolled through the pictures. "I know it's hard to make out the detail on this small screen. Next time I'll take more and we can compare them, and then you can tell me I'm crazy."

"I didn't say you were crazy. Maybe old fashioned, for using a camera instead of your phone."

"Look who's talking, Miss Don't Have a Cell Phone. And the camera is digital, not old fashioned. But never mind that, you don't believe me, do you?"

"If you say the scars are changing, they're changing."

"Whatever. Come on, climb down. Let's do some stretching."

Alison groaned.

"Nope, don't you dare complain." Meredith tossed the camera back in her bag. "Save that for after I'm gone."

After the stretching, Meredith crossed her arms over her chest. "Are you getting enough sleep?"

"Yes, I am."

"The dark circles under your eyes and you falling asleep on the table again say otherwise, my dear."

"Lots of late night…"

parties

The woman playing the piano. The man with the monocle. The woman in the rose colored dress. The lamplight shining on the wine in her glass. And Thomas's arms, holding her close as they danced, his voice, soft and gentle near her ear.

"Alison?" Meredith's voice was sharp. "Are you okay?"

"Yes, I'm sorry. I'm fine. Just tired."

"Okay, if you say so. You know, you might want to eat more, too, 'cause you're looking a little thin."

"Yes, Mom."

When Meredith ran upstairs to the bathroom, Alison limped over to her bag and grabbed out the camera. She tucked it behind a sofa cushion and wiped the guilt from her face. She wasn't stealing it, just borrowing, and she'd call Meredith when she was done and tell her she'd found it.

She touched the spot of skin on her hip. How many times would she have to go into the paper world? And were there enough photos, enough doorways, to make her whole?

● ● ●

Alison stood in front of the refrigerator with the door open, un-sure when she'd eaten last. She thought she'd made tea and toast earlier or had it been yesterday, before Meredith had arrived? She checked the trash can and found two pieces of toast, one whole, the other with a few bites missing. So this morning then. And yesterday? Maybe not toast, but surely soup or something.

She grabbed a banana, but the first bite tasted like cardboard; the second, not much better. She tossed the rest, uneaten, in the trash can. She wasn't even hungry.

■ ■ ■

When her mother called, Alison was sitting on the sofa with the photo album on her lap. She'd transcribed what little there was of the inscription and played with the empty spaces for an hour, but she wasn't any closer to solving the puzzle.

"I called yesterday," her mother said. "But you didn't answer."

"Meredith was here, and after she left, I took a nap."

"And how is Meredith? I should call her one of these days and say hello."

Alison's fingers dug into the phone. To say hello or to check on her daughter? Meredith would tell her about the scars. Then her mother would insist she go to the doctor.

But she wasn't a child anymore. Her mother couldn't force her to do anything. The pages rustled. She smiled and rubbed her fingers along the edge of the cover.

"Alison?"

"Yes?"

"I thought the phone had disconnected."

"I'm still here. Sorry, I'm still tired from
my trip into the album
yesterday."

"Do you need anything? I can stop over a little later today?"

The pages rustled again, and one tiny music note slipped out.

"No, I'm good."

"Is something wrong?"

Alison traced the bottom line of the inscription. The important word was whole. The tiger was incidental. "Nothing's wrong."

"Are you sure? You seem distracted lately, and you're sleeping a lot."

"I'm fine. Really, I am."

And you can stop questioning me. I'm not a child.

Another music note, faded and forlorn.

"Okay. How about if I come over tomorrow?"

Why? To check up on me? To make sure I'm not moping around crying woe is me?

"Sure, but call first in case I'm napping."

After the goodbyes and the perfunctory "I love you, too" Alison tossed the phone aside and turned to the photo of the parlor. Her breath caught in her throat as the page went up and over on its own, revealing the next photo, the next doorway—the turret room on the first floor. The clock was in its normal position; next to that, two chairs were arranged around a small table, the curtains of the windows behind slightly open to reveal the edge of a rosebush. And to the right of the clock, a rectangular mark on the wall.

Alison bent closer. It appeared to be a crack or an open space. Her lips curved, distorting the scars on her cheek. She touched the photo, imagining she could feel the edge of a door leading inside the walls.

That's where Mary wanted her to go. And where did it lead? A tiny shiver raced up and down her spine. She'd find out soon enough.

■ ■ ■

Twenty-four hours later, the mark vanished. A click broke the quiet, and a tendril of grey crept from beneath the photo's edge, carrying the smell of old, forgotten things: boxes split at the seams, the contents leaking out like disemboweled stuffed animals, old rooms locked for years, books packed away in a grandmother's attic and found three generations later.

Alison slipped the camera's carry strap over her left wrist and lowered her right hand to the photo. Before she left the world of the real, she saw finger-shaped indentations on the photo. Five, not three.

CHAPTER 16

In the house, she ran her fingertips (only eight misshapen finger piggies) across her face. Still a Monstergirl. But the camera had survived the journey. She snapped two pictures of the foyer, cringing at the bright light and the echo of the click. Soon enough, the silence devoured the sound.

Her fingertips tingled. Sensation rushed in. She smiled, despite the scars and the missing fingers. The edges of the camera were still warm.

Footprints marked the floor. Hers, with her toes clearly outlined, larger prints belonging to man's shoes, and a child's. Mary's. Near the turret room, she paused to take another picture and tried the doorknob.

Locked.

She nudged it with her shoulder. No luck. She took a picture of the door and as she turned away, a low creak pierced the air. She whirled around, swallowing a cry of surprise.

The door finished its slow arc, bounced gently off the wall behind it, and came to a stop. A muffled laugh sounded from behind the wood.

"Mary?"

A small, cold hand touched Alison's as she entered the room, tugging her toward the wall. "Yes, I'll go with you."

The fingers tightened in response. Alison cocked her head to the side. The little girl had a pale, shimmery outline that resembled motes caught in a sunbeam.

Together, one real girl and one not, they approached the wall. The cold hand slipped from hers and with a scratch of wood against wood, a section of the wall swung open. A child-sized door.

Alison tucked the camera in her pocket and peered into the darkness, holding on to the edge of the doorway with one hand. She snuck into the hidden space, first her left shoulder, then her left leg, then right shoulder and right leg. The grey light from the house illuminated the first several feet—a narrow but tall hallway lined with dust and dangling spiderwebs. The floor, hard-packed dirt, was cold beneath her socks.

Alison brushed webs away from her face. Keeping her elbows bent because of the width of the passage, she ran her palms over the walls of rough, unfinished wood, feeling pits and hollows and splinters ready for their next victim. The ceiling, made of the same, was a few scant inches above the top of her head.

Mary appeared as a grey waver in the air. Her features darkened into view, taking shape, more visible now in the shadows than in the light of the house.

"Come." Mary's voice was gone before an echo could attach itself to the word, and her footsteps pattered on the floor, deeper into the passage.

Alison walked into another web and gave a breathy laugh as she clawed it away from her cheek. Soft music sounded from far away, the trill of fingers moving across piano keys not in a song but an aimless touch. The door creaked shut, plunging them into darkness. She jumped and half-turned to go back, but Mary grabbed her hand again.

"Come."

Placing her right hand on the wall for security, Alison took another step, then another. Pale light broke through gaps in the wall between the wood; slowly, her eyes adjusted to the gloom. They made a sharp left turn, went straight for ten paces, then made a hard right. Alison paused, ignoring Mary's tug.

"Wait," she said. One music note slipped through the wood on her left. It didn't make sense. The passage wasn't following the dimensions of the house. Were they inside the real walls at all or was this another paper trick?

The passageway narrowed. Alison turned sideways, the wood nearly pressing against her chest and back. She side-stepped five, ten, a dozen times before the passageway opened back up. More cobwebs hung in the air, sliding across her cheeks and sticking to her hair, but the previous inhabitants had all vanished long ago. Nothing living moved in this house, not anymore. Nothing save her, and she only a temporary guest.

The house itself wasn't even real. It was a collection of photographs in an old album, paper memories of something that once was.

Mary pulled her hand once more, and she stepped into a column of air so cold, her lungs ached and goosebumps riddled the skin of her left arm. And then she couldn't move at all. Her heels were anchored to the floor, arms glued in place at her sides, lungs filled but unable to release, heart caught in mid-beat. The cold swirled around her face, stinging her eyes.

Time stretched out, an hourglass tipped on its side, captured inside the cold and—

Can't breathe, can't move, let me go, let me go.

Mary's fingers tugged, and Alison's limbs stuttered into movement. Two staggering steps and the cold vanished with a shift in air pressure she felt in her ears. She leaned against the wall, the wood rough against her cheek. Exhaled and inhaled hard.

"Come."

With another shaking breath, she let the little ghost lead on. They came upon three small steps leading to a small landing, then another three steps, down this time. A turn to the right. A long, straight pathway. Then another turn, to the left. The pale light waxed and waned.

From beyond the wall, a high-pitched, feminine voice said, "I know you're here. I can feel you. Tell me what you want."

A deep voice, a George voice, replied with an echoing laugh, that ended as Alison and Mary made another turn. Another set of stairs, seven this time. Mary stopped and let go of her hand.

They stood in a long, rectangular space with a sloped ceiling. Narrow bands of light filtered into the room, creating starpoints of illumination. The walls, although unfinished, held a certain smoothness the passageway did not. Mary retreated to the far corner. A puddle of old blankets lay in the corner, coated with dust, but when Mary sat down, tucking her legs beneath her, neither blanket nor grime moved. The ghost girl gathered a stuffed bear with a mouth made of black stitching into her lap.

Footsteps sounded above their heads, moving in a staccato rhythm, and Alison knew where they were—under the stairs. Music notes played softly in the distance. More footsteps passed, this time on the right. Mary buried her face in the blankets.

"Mary, where are you hiding now, child?" a scratchy voice called out. "It's time for supper." More footsteps, then the same voice again. "Mrs. Pennington, I've no idea where that child went."

Mary held the bear against her chest. Alison crouched down beside her.

"Is this your hiding place?"

Mary nodded.

"I like it."

"Safe," Mary said.

"Yes, I'm sure it is safe here. Safe and snug."

Mary lifted a hand, extending the teddy bear. Alison took it in her hands. This, at least, felt real. Under her skin, the bear was smooth, most of the fur rubbed away to the silky nap below. The bear smelled of talcum powder and time, a pervasive smell that conjured a sense of sorrow. This button-eyed bear had been loved by a little girl who'd died far too young, yet somehow still lingered here in the house.

"Was George your brother?" she asked.

Mary looked down. Nodded.

"I'd like to try something," Alison said, handing the bear back and readying the camera. "It's okay. Don't be afraid."

When she lifted the camera, Mary's eyes grew wide.

"It's okay."

Alison snapped the picture. Mary recoiled, her hands flailing, as the flash brightened the room.

"See? It's okay. It's safe." She took two more pictures, smiling in-between.

Mary buried her face in the bear's abdomen and pressed against the wall, her mouth a dark circle of alarm.

"What's wrong?"

"Not safe," came the reply.

"It's okay. It's just a camera. It's safe. I promise."

Mary shook her head from side to side, her hair whipping back and forth. The teddy bear dropped from her hands. She stared past Alison to the entrance of the hiding place, and her mouth worked, forming words Alison couldn't hear. The little girl lifted her arms to cover her face, and Alison tried to speak, but a sudden chill morphed her voice into a plume of frosted air.

The air shifted, the cold vanished, and Mary winked out of sight, leaving behind the bear and blankets. Alison rubbed her hands up and down her arms, and bent to retrieve the teddy bear.

The clock chimed. She bolted from the hiding place, back down the seven stairs, but now there was another step after the seventh. She stepped down cautiously, carefully, feeling the space with her toes before descending again, her heart moving faster than her feet, but now there were eight, nine, ten steps, and then her feet hit the floor.

The clock's chime rang out again.

The turn came next, then another and a long straightaway, her feet marking each step with a thud. Had it been this long?

Another chime, and the light peeking through the walls darkened. Alison kept her left hand on the wall. There were steps ahead somewhere. She took careful, halting steps.

"Come, Josephine," she said. "Going up, up, up, where are the steps?"

She snapped a picture. The dirt floor appeared nearly black in places, the walls splintered, but before the light ebbed, she saw the steps. She curled her fingers tight around the camera. Three steps up, she remembered, and three down, but now there were four. And five. Changing shape because it wanted her to stay.

Yet another chime sounded, and Red said, *Stupid girl*, the words laced with venom.

The path straightened, and she batted at the sticky tendrils dangling in her face and tangling in her hair. Why had she thought it a good idea to slip inside the walls?

The clock chimed for the fifth time, and cold stopped her in her tracks with her right leg outstretched, her left hand on the rough wall. Icy bands coiled around her chest, holding her in place.

"Stay with us, Alison." A colorless voice, as flat as a photo in an album, without tone, without sex. The voice of the tiger?

No, it was a paper tiger. And nothing more. She flexed the fingers of her left hand. A splinter dug into the soft pad of her pinkie, but she held in the cry and scraped her hand down the wall.

She wiggled the fingers of her right hand. The edge of the camera dug in her palm. She found the button on top, pressed down, and the flash bounced off the walls, turning dark to day as the clock chimed once more.

"Let me go," she shouted, her voice thick.

Then her left leg was free. Her knee bent, her right foot flexed, and

up she goes

she peeled her left hand from the wall, then her right hand, and she pushed forward. With a lurch, she fell out of the cold onto her knees.

"Stay..."

No thank you. She staggered to her feet, banging her shoulder on the wall. The walls closed in, tightening on each side. Turning sideways, she scuttled through the narrowed section. Another chime reverberated in the air.

The passageway turned to the left, went straight for ten paces, turned to the right. Grey light seeped through the walls. Voices followed, soft and distant.

"And then he told me—"

"Wasn't that funny—"

"Where is that girl now?"

Alison picked up her pace, moving straight now. Soon, the doorway would be on her left. The clock sounded again, closer now. Was that the seventh? Maybe the eighth?

Fool. Why didn't you count them?

She still had time. With steady and even paces, she headed toward the end of the passageway, toward the clock, toward freedom, toward home. Another splinter dug into the fleshy pad of her finger, piercing deep through the scars. She winced but kept moving. Close. She was close now.

She pressed the button on the camera, and the light revealed the dead-end. She stumbled to a stop, her nose inches away from banging into the wall. The clock rang out on her left. Now for the secret door. She flashed the camera, searching for the seam. Her hands swept the wall in wide arcs. No cracks. Only smooth wood. The bitter taste of panic rose in her throat. She swallowed it down and kept searching.

No seam. No hinge. No secret door. No way out.

Impossible.

The clock chimed and it was so loud, so close. "Almost, almost," she said, tracing the wall with her palms. "I know you're here somewhere." She felt the edge of a hinge, carefully concealed in the wood, found the seam and pushed.

Nothing happened.

A man laughed from the other side of the wall. Was he holding the door in place? Keeping her inside? She shrieked in banshee fury and shoved with all her might. The wood creaked. The clock chimed.

She shoved again and the door gave way. Breathless, her heart and lungs a painful weight in her chest, she spilled out into the turret room and propelled her body toward the clock, her left hand out, and then she was falling, falling into, falling down, falling—

• • •

—back home. She collapsed on the floor and wept into her hands. After she was all cried out, she rolled onto her back and stared at the ceiling. She held out her pale, scarless hands. All ten fingers present and accounted for.

A laugh crept from her throat. She'd been trapped inside the walls and it wasn't funny at all, but still, she laughed, a slow, breathy sound that gathered strength, gathered air and mirth and whimsy, and turned into great whoops so loud and hard her stomach ached. When it finally stopped, she wiped tears from her eye.

A stray sunbeam peeked in through the window blind. She rubbed her thumb along two scratches on the side of the camera, two scratches she didn't remember seeing before she'd gone into the album.

The first picture showed a swirl of grey as did the second, third, and fourth.

"Dammit," she said.

So the album would allow her to take the camera in, but it wouldn't allow photographic evidence of its existence.

But why would it? It wasn't real.

Then she saw it—a darker area inside the swirls. The suggestion of a child's face. She held the camera closer. Yes, the darker area showed a child's tiny chin, wide eyes, and round cheeks. Mary's face, in shades of grey.

Mary's face was absent from the fifth photo, but the sixth revealed a bit of an eye, a curl of hair. The seventh photo was a wash, but from the eighth, a face stared back, George's face, his eyes hungry, his mouth open, an expression made all the more malevolent by the lack of color.

The face of the tiger.

She blinked and the face vanished. She squinted. Turned her head.

No face. No face at all.

The ninth photo showed only darkness, but the tenth photo revealed something else—a small rectangle, marked by light around the edges. A child-sized secret door.

Alison grinned. Here then was more proof. She patted her right cheek, now smooth and flawless. As if she needed any more.

Someone knocked on her front door. She jumped, the camera fell from her hands, and she caught it before it hit the floor. With small steps, she crept over to the door. Peered through the peephole. Meredith.

Let her in. Let her in and show her that you're whole again. That your scars aren't simply healing. Sometimes they're completely gone. Let her see you. Please, please, let someone else see you're not just a Monstergirl.

Alison's hands turned to fists, and she shook her head, a tiny movement that sent a thick lock of hair curling down over her face. Meredith wouldn't even believe it. Scars didn't vanish overnight. Not in the real world.

Meredith knocked again then took out her cell phone; a few seconds later, Alison's rang. She grimaced as Meredith leaned closer to the door, listening. After the fifth ring, Meredith turned away from the door, her voice disappearing as she headed back to her car.

Alison's phone gave a small beep, but she waited until Meredith drove away before she listened to the message.

"Alison, it's Meredith. I was in the neighborhood and stopped by, but I guess you're taking a nap or a shower. I think my camera fell out of my bag when I was there. Could you take a look and call me if you find it? It's not end of the world urgent or anything, I've uploaded most of the pictures to my laptop already, but I'd still like to find it. Talk to you soon."

Alison thought of the scratches on the camera. She'd call Meredith later and tell her she found it on the floor. That would explain the damage.

Or I could keep it. For the next time.

She touched her face again. Because of course there'd be a next time. No point in lying to herself about that. And she hadn't been hurt in the house, only a little frightened. A small price to pay.

With a shaking hand, she held the camera at arm's length and pushed the button, but several long minutes passed before she viewed the picture.

Whole. Well and truly whole.

She closed her eyes until the sting of tears was gone, then scrolled through the house pictures once more. Mary's face remained clear, or as clear as a ghost's face shown in grey mist could be. The other face was still gone, not that she'd expected it to return because it wasn't real after all, only a strange illusion.

Liar. Remember the cold? Tell me that wasn't real. Tell me and you're a fool.

"Houses sometimes have cold spots," she said. "Especially old houses."

Fool. That wasn't a cold spot. Someone was there, someone holding you—

She tossed the camera aside and stalked into the kitchen, frowning at the empty counter. She headed back into the living room. No album on the coffee table.

She rechecked the kitchen, scanned the bookcases, and peered under the sofa. A wave of dizziness struck, and she braced herself against the arm of the sofa until it passed. Then she took the stairs two at a time, her dirty socks leaving smudges on the steps. A cold sweat prickled the center of her back.

When she saw the album on the center of her bed, atop the comforter, she smiled.

But how did it get upsta—

It didn't matter. The album was here, safe and sound, and that was all that mattered. Despite the grime on her clothing, she sat down on her bed. The inscription now read:

> *clock will chime*
> *Stay and leave*
> *of lies*
> *ng those locked*
> *Trapped like a*
> *years drift past*
> *men bring forth*
> *will ever hear*
> *row, house of s*
> *Welcomes on*
> *use unfolds —*
> *A paper tiger to swallow you whole*

It still didn't make sense, yet the words *trapped* and *locked* sent another shiver down her spine. Next time she'd be careful. No more trips *inside* the walls.

CHAPTER 17

When Alison opened the door, bright sunlight spilled in. She worried a cuticle between her teeth. She needed to try someplace small. Somewhere close. Next time she could try someplace bigger, more crowded.

She didn't count her steps as she walked, nor did she hesitate when crossing the street and though she pulled off her scarf, she couldn't prevent her chin from tipping down. But maybe that was okay. Baby steps.

There weren't as many people out today; in spite of the sun, the air had shifted from cool to cold. She caught sight of people slipping into and out of stores, but no one looked in her direction. She was another anonymous passerby. Her shoes tapped an even cadence on the pavement, making it easy to ignore the muscle twinges, promises of the hurt to come.

When she passed Elena's Antiques, she spared the window only a brief glance, enough to see that the interior had turned from filled to chaos. She paused at a window display of shoes and jewelry, but instead of filling her with regret, the sight brought to mind a possible future. Buying things she'd need to go to school, to teach, to live.

A small grocery store, not the one where she placed her orders, sat at the end of the block. Although the lights were bright, it was a safe experiment. Still, her heart started to race when she passed through the sliding door.

The first aisle was deserted, and the wheels of her cart gave a soft squeak on the tile floor as she pushed it around the produce bins.

She picked bananas and apples and tomatoes, tracing her fingertips along the smooth surfaces, feeling for bruised spots.

She heard the sound of footsteps and another cart, wheeled sharply into the next aisle, and came to a stop with her face toward the shelf. From the corner of her eye, she watched until the person disappeared out of sight. Exhaling, she pushed her cart toward the soup aisle.

She'd added several cans to her cart when a baby started to cry. Alison stood with one hand outstretched, the other on the cart handle. The cry was high-pitched and mewling. She remembered a baby crying on a night long ago, remembered trying to find it through the smoke. If she hadn't...

A woman walked into the aisle, pushing her cart with one hand and holding a baby against her chest with the other as she made small cooing noises. They drew near and Alison could smell the talcum powder, see the downy hair on the baby's scalp and a lump lodged painfully in her throat.

• • •

With the plastic bag swinging at her side, she stopped in front of a bakery window showing off a display of cupcakes, each one piled high with frosting. She smiled. Something sweet to celebrate her freedom. Moving toward the door, she heard a familiar voice behind her.

"I want to pick something up for my daughter."

Alison came to an abrupt halt.

"How is she doing these days?"

"She's okay. I worry because she keeps herself so isolated, but—"

Her fingers tightened around the bag's handle.

Get away, get away now.

"—I know she has a hard time being out in public."

She moved fast, the bag bouncing hard against her leg, and after a few steps, glanced back over her shoulder. For a split second, she caught her mother's gaze. Alison turned away fast, but not before she registered a complete lack of recognition in her mother's face.

● ● ●

She'd been home for less than an hour when her phone rang. She ignored it. No doubt it was her mother, coming to rescue her from her isolation and loneliness, her poor pathetic daughter locked away alone.

She popped out her prosthetic eye and threw it on the floor, not caring if it cracked. What did it matter? It was a trick, a fake. Like the album. Or the tiny diamond ring tucked away in her jewelry box. Oh, the stone was real enough, but the love behind it wasn't. Not real enough for a Monstergirl, but she didn't blame him. Who would want to be with someone who wore her real face? No one. No one sane and normal and healthy would.

And what would happen when she reached the last photograph? How did she even know there were more? Maybe it was all a game. She was clinging to the hope that she'd keep finding new pages, new photos, until her scars were fully healed, but what if the next page revealed a blank page with no way back into the paper world? Would George be that cruel? She'd be the child allowed to eat half the ice cream cone before it was taken away. The homeless woman dressed in silk and satin, taken to the best restaurant, then tossed back onto the streets. The ash-girl turned into a princess, until the clock struck twelve.

Her phone rang again. She tossed it aside with a snarl. Imprisoned by her scars when broken; trapped without them when whole.

● ● ●

She woke from a dead sleep in the middle of the night. All around her, the house settled in tiny creaks and moans. Her eyelids grew heavy. Then real footsteps, not made of house noise, tapped in the hallway. She sat up, holding the blankets close to her chest. No one could be in the house; she had good locks on all the windows and doors.

Someone is here, Purple said. *Someone wrong.*

Another footstep, hesitant and halting, as though—

They know you're awake.

Or they were unsure of their footing in the real world.

Panic oil-slicking her mouth, she slid her legs from beneath the blankets, feeling the pull in her hips because not only did she have a nocturnal visitor, she had her scars back, too. When she attempted to stand, the best she could do was a feeble hunch because her muscles ached, and all she wanted to do was climb back in bed and sleep it all away, and in the morning she could pretend nothing had happened.

Out in the hallway, there was a tiny thump, the sound a shoulder or arm bumping against the wall would make. Alison shuffled closer to her open bedroom door. Another step and then another until she stood next to the doorway, still hidden inside her room. She'd left the bathroom light on with the door half-closed, enough light to prevent a fall, not enough to turn everything bright.

The hallway was empty. House noise after all.

A shadow, vaguely human shaped, twitched on the wall. Footsteps pressed on the floor, a floorboard gave an answering creak, and the apparition stretched into a long and amorphous darkness. It changed once more, shrinking down and down and down, then melted into the wall and disappeared.

Alison clamped both hands over her mouth. Small sounds crept out between the gaps in her fingers. She shoved her door wide open and staggered out into the hall. One shaking hand touched the wall, but felt nothing.

Stupid girl. Your scars.

She turned her arm, pressed skin that wasn't numb to the wall. It was cool, yet no different from the surface a foot away. Using the side of her hand, she knocked on the wall. Moved a few inches away. Knocked again. Nothing out of the ordinary.

Get rid of the album. Throw it out now!

"I can't," Alison said, her voice small and ineffectual. She curled her misshapen hands into painful fists. "I need it."

● ● ●

Two days later, Alison emerged from a cocoon of blankets with dark circles under her eyes and hollows beneath her cheeks. While waiting for tea to brew, she rummaged through her cabinets. Her stomach rumbled but looking at oatmeal packets and cookies made her queasy.

She slammed the cabinet door shut. It bounced back open. She left it that way and listened to the messages on her phone. Meredith again, asking if Alison had found her *camera*. It wasn't life or death, it was a stupid camera. Couldn't she wait until the next appointment? Couldn't she use her phone instead? And several messages from her mother, of course. Alison deleted them all, her mouth twisted in a frown.

She ate a small container of yogurt while standing next to the refrigerator, not tasting, but eating nonetheless. When finished, she made toast and carried it into the living room. It didn't take long for her to abandon the toast in favor of the pillow on her sofa.

A quiet knock on the door jarred her from a half-sleep. She limped to the door, raising her face to the peephole, and sighed. Her mother. Alison swallowed her irritation.

Her mother gave her a long look. "I've been calling and calling. You look terrible, babygirl. Why didn't you call me? I would've come over."

"I'm fine, Mom. I was trying to take a nap."

"You don't look fine at all. Meredith said she thought you were losing weight—"

"Meredith called you?"

"Yes, she did, but don't worry about that. Sit down, let me fix you something to eat and—"

"I just ate."

Her mother glanced at the plate of toast. "One bite of toast isn't eating."

She reached out to touch Alison's face; Alison stepped back before she made contact. "I'll eat more later."

"Have you called the doctor?"

"No, I haven't. If it was something major, I would, but it isn't. It's just a cold. If you and Meredith don't want to believe that, fine, but don't go running around my back gossiping like fishwives."

"Alison, we didn't gossip."

"Talking about somebody behind their back is gossip."

"We were talking about your health. Your health."

"And I said I was fine. Drop it."

"Meredith also told me some of the scars look like they're healing," her mother said in a small voice.

"That's what she said, yes."

Her mother smiled. "May I look?"

"No."

"But Ali—"

"I said no. I'm not something to be examined under a microscope."

"I never said you were, but she said there's a spot near your hip where the scars have healed. Don't you think that's reason enough to go see Dr. Simon?"

"No. And I don't want to talk it about it anymore."

"I don't understand why you're so angry," her mother said.

"Just leave it alone."

Her mother held her gaze for a long time. Finally, she gave a small sigh. Another wave of dizziness struck, a bigger one this time, and Alison staggered back. The muscles of her hip spasmed. Her face contorted in pain.

"That's it. I'm calling the doctor."

Tell her to leave. Tell her to leave you alone.

"No you are not," Alison said. "It was a muscle spasm. I get them a lot. And I have a cold, a stupid cold. That's why I've been sleeping and not answering the phone. Mom, I'm not a child, okay? I don't need you to come here every time I don't answer the phone quick enough for you. You need to stop spending so much damn time worrying about me."

It was her mother's turn to step back, with her eyes wide, and when she spoke again, her voice was thick with unshed tears. "But I'm your mother. That's what I'm supposed to do."

"Would you do it if I wasn't like this?"

"I know it's hard—"

"You don't know, okay? You don't what it's like. You've never known. How could you?" She pointed to her face. "You don't wake up to this every day. If you did, you'd understand that sometimes I don't want to talk to anyone and sometimes I don't want to see anyone. Not even you."

A long silence stretched out between them.

"I don't know what to say," her mother said.

"There is nothing *to* say. Please, can you just go? I want to take a nap."

"Promise me you'll call the doctor. It might not be a cold. Does your throat hurt at all? You might need antibiotics."

"Mom, please go."

Her mother hovered near the door, one hand on the doorknob, the other worrying the edge of her coat. "I'll call you later, if that's okay."

"Fine."

But it wasn't fine. Not at all.

After her mother left, Alison picked up Meredith's camera and bounced it in her palm. "You had no right to call her. No right at all." She hurled the camera against the wall and smiled when it left a gouge in the plaster and landed on the floor with a crack and a thud.

PART VI

OLD HAUNTS

When the ceiling falls down, the stars sparkle like tiny diamonds. She knows about tiny diamonds and rings and love and soon it will all be over. Sadness reaches in, creeps around the hurt, but she can't cry. The fire and the smoke have taken away her tears.

A voice reaches through the fire, and there are arms lifting her up and pain makes rainbows of color dance in her eyes and she tries to tell them to leave her alone, she wants to see the stars, then she thinks of Jonathan and the ring on her finger and the baby is safe and she smiles in spite of the pain.

Everything will be okay. Everything will be fine. Everything will be—

CHAPTER 18

Two days later, the photo album opened its pages once more. The new photo showed a rounded room, complete with a desk and chair, bookcases, and photographs hanging on the wall in dark frames. The photographs all contained unsmiling, serious faces.

Alison smiled, stroked the edge of the page, and waited.

■ ■ ■

The following afternoon, the smell of tobacco permeated the room. As Alison bent over the album, a photograph fell off the wall, tumbling down to the floor in a slow arc. A faint crunch of wood and a shatter of glass pushed its way out of the paper world into the real. She lowered her hand and smiled as the tiger swallowed her whole.

■ ■ ■

She stood in the foyer, clad in satin skirts the color of a summer sky. Music and voices beckoned from another room. Overhead, a crystal chandelier glimmered, casting light down onto the table in the center and the vase of flowers there. A voice spoke nonsense, something about real and paper and clocks and scars, but it was inconsequential and she pushed it away.

A man with a monocle tapped her arm. He seemed vaguely familiar, but this was her first party at the house, wasn't it?

"Hello, dear," he said. "We're so glad you've arrived."

"Thank you. I hope I'm not too late."

"Not at all, but before you go in with the others, George asked me to give you something."

George. Of course. He'd invited her to the party, hadn't he?

"Is he here?"

"In his office, I imagine. He'll be along shortly, but here," he said, pressing something small and round into her hand. "There's a mirror if you need it." He nodded toward one wall.

On her palm, a marble of glass, painted with iris and pupil.

"I don't..."

"Your eye?"

She lifted her hand to the empty space where an eye should be. "Oh, oh no."

"Not to worry. We all understand, dear. Go ahead now."

She turned her face away, tugged at her lid, and slid the eye in the empty socket. In the mirror, a pretty woman with vibrant eyes stared back.

"George said it would be a perfect match. I think he was right, don't you?

"Yes," she said, touching one smooth cheek. Something was *wrong* odd, but she couldn't quite tell what. It resided on the tip of her tongue, unwilling to spill out.

"Excellent." He gazed over her shoulder. "Ah, it looks as though my wife requires my assistance. It was lovely to see you again."

"Yes, thank you for your help. Wait, please," she said, tugging on his sleeve. "I don't remember your name, I'm sorry."

"Forgive me for being remiss. I'm Edmund, Edmund Pennington." He gave a small bow.

Edmund Pennington? She knew the name, or thought she did, but it was wrong somehow. He couldn't be Edmund because Edmund was—

"But," she said, "who are you?"

"I'm George's father, of course."

"But..." She dropped her voice. "Aren't you dead?"

The words were absurd, but they felt *right*.

He cocked an eyebrow. Smiled. "Dead? No, I'm quite certain I'm not dead. Someone would know a thing like that, wouldn't they? Now, if you'll please excuse me, I need to attend to Eleanor."

Frowning, Alison watched him go. She must've misheard.

In the music room, a woman was seated at the piano, her fingers dancing across the keys. The curtains were tied back, and through the open windows she caught a glimpse of several children, dressed in their Sunday best. They ran past, singing nursery rhymes in sweetly out-of-tune voices. Then a face at the back of the room caught her eye, a young man with brown eyes and a sad smile. She smiled in return. Maybe she'd stay for a little while. It couldn't hurt.

• • •

Every time Alison finished a glass of wine, someone placed another in her hand, yet she didn't feel drunk, simply out of sorts. Faces flitted in and out of her line of sight. The music played on, one song after another.

The lights dimmed, the voices of the partygoers became a subdued hush, and the voices of the children no longer played through the windows. The man with the sad smile had left the music room before she could talk to him; although she kept watching the arched entrance, he hadn't returned.

Somewhere, far off in the distance, a clock chimed, marking the hour. She stepped closer to the sound, and the floor gave a small shudder. The music stopped in mid-note, all conversation ceased, and everyone turned toward her.

Silence pressed down with an uncomfortable weight, like

smothering under a heavy blanket in the sticky heat of August. The air shimmered. The lights dimmed, brightened, and dimmed again. Images flashed in her mind: pavement, a wall, a woman's face, her brow creased in concern.

Edmund cupped her elbow in his hand and steered her back around. The lights flickered back to bright and the music and conversations began again.

"Don't leave," Edmund said. "It's still early."

"I, I wasn't leaving," she said, but she cast a look over her shoulder. The clock chimed again, a sound that seemed to mean something. But what?

"Good. You don't want to make George angry, do you? And you haven't even danced with Thomas yet."

Yes, Thomas, that was his name. But had they met before at another party? This was her first party at the house, wasn't it? A wave of dizziness turned her vision spotty. She touched one hand to her forehead. Swayed on her feet.

"Here," Edmund said, leading her over to a settee. "Sit down for a bit."

She sank down onto the cushion, and the dizziness ebbed away. But her limbs felt heavy, her thoughts, muddled. She couldn't remember how long she'd been at the party, but she should leave soon. As soon as she felt better, she would. She twisted her hands together. Too much wine. Too much wrong. There were spaces in her head where things, memories, should be.

She hid a yawn behind her hand. And why was she so tired, as though she hadn't slept in days?

The woman who'd been playing the piano sat down next to her and smiled. "I'm Rachel. You're Alison, aren't you?"

"Yes, how did you know?"

"We've all heard so much about you. George is quite fond of you."

"What? I don't understand. Fond of me?"

"Oh, not like that. Madeline would kill anyone George thought of in that way." Rachel laughed softly. "Well, maybe not kill. Sorry, that was a poor choice of words."

"Madeline?"

"Don't worry. She isn't here right now."

Rachel brushed her hair back from her forehead, leaving behind a tiny streak of red near her temple.

Alison gasped. "Your fingers..."

Rachel held them up, gazing with disinterest at the swollen flesh. The raw skin of her index fingers were spotted with tiny pearls of blood. Why wasn't she crying or calling out for help?

"Can I help you? Do you need a bandage?"

"Oh, not to worry," Rachel said, but she hid her hands in the folds of her skirt. "It'll go away soon enough."

"But doesn't it hurt?"

"Always," Rachel said with a smile and a small shrug. "But that's the price you pay sometimes for perfection." She turned her face away, toward the piano. A dark spot marred the fabric of her dress, near the hem.

A memory of holding an old book on her lap rushed in. Alison couldn't remember the author or the story, only that it was somehow special. She'd been crying because...because...

A husky laugh pulled her attention away. A woman, all high-cheekbones and upswept hair, stood in the entranceway. Her crimson dress made Alison think of anger, fierce rage laced with poison. The woman gave a slow nod, her eyes sharp with satisfaction. As she approached the settee, Rachel stood and Alison followed suit, but her ankle caught on the fabric of her skirt. Steadying herself on the seat cushion, she bent to pull her foot free. Light from the sconces danced on the wall behind them. Her shadow darkened the wallpaper, hers and hers alone. Still watching the wall, Alison gave Rachel's arm a gentle squeeze, and though her shadow mimicked the movement, it touched nothing. A cold snake coiled the length of her spine.

A throat cleared.

"Rachel, it's time for you to play another song," the woman snapped, turning to Alison. "And you, don't you get any ideas. I was the first."

"I don't understand," Alison said. "The first what?"

"Never you mind. Do your part."

"My part?"

But the woman was already gone.

Rachel walked away, her fingers hanging down at her sides, speckling her dress with blood. Dots of blood flecked the cushion of the settee as well. Despite the animated gestures of the party guests, no shadows marred the wallpaper, save those cast by the lights. But how could they not cast shadows? And why did she?

None of this is real, a soft voice said in her head.

But how could that be? She ran her fingertips across the arm of the settee. Inhaled candlewax and perfume. Tasted wine, rich and sweet, in her mouth.

Music soon filled the room, melancholy notes that lingered in the air and silenced the conversation. Alison crossed her arm beneath her breasts. A thought slipped in—*should there be two?* She didn't understand. Two of what? Something was wrong. Very wrong. She wanted to go home.

But where was home? Not at Pennington House,

not yet

she was sure, but where? The clock chimed for the third time. She turned in the direction of the sound. There was something about the clock, something important that would help her remember.

Forget to remember, remember to forget.

The words rushed in with the force of a jungle cat making its final leap. Her eyes narrowed; her lips pressed into a thin line. She pushed through the crowd, ignoring the looks of surprise. A hand grabbed her arm, but she shied away from the touch. Someone called her name. She didn't look back. A man blocked her path. Thomas. He smiled and held out a hand.

"Dance with me, Alison. Please."

She hesitated. His skin was warm; his touch, gentle.

"Stay here with me," he said.

His fingers curled around hers; she shook them free. They could dance the next time. She was tired and she needed to leave. They had to let her leave.

"Stop her," someone called out.

The clock, the clock, the clock.

Yes, the clock was the key. A flash of red caught her eye. Madeline, moving toward her. Another hand grabbed her shoulder. She staggered back, and said, "Leave me alone," yanking her arm free.

"It doesn't matter," another voice said. "It's too late."

No. She still had time. Her breath came fast and harsh. She heard the clock again. She raced from the room. Through the foyer. The wall sconces sputtered out to wisps of smoke. Everything turned to shadow, but she didn't stop and neither did the clock. Her dress twisted around her ankles; she grabbed the fabric in both hands and lifted it to her knees. Ran through the doorway. And yes, there was the clock, the key to what she'd forgotten.

The pendulum was swinging, the second hand moving wrong, but moving nonetheless. Her answers were close now, so close. The wood gleamed, all dark wood and gilt trim. The clock chimed again, but the sound was distant, muted. The pendulum swung, the filigree hands moved, and her hand passed through it all, as though the clock were mere illusion.

"No," she shouted, clawing at the air, at the clock face that wasn't a face, but a memory of a face. A trick. The clock chimed again and again, each one fading further and further away. And, finally, it stopped. The pendulum paused in mid-swing, the hands froze, and silence fell into place.

"No, please, no."

She held out her hands, fingers splayed. Through her skin—skin turned a translucent shade of pale—the grain of the wood and the glint of the clock peered back.

But that—

A low moan escaped from her throat. She turned her hands from side to side.

—was wrong. Impossible.

Goosebumps broke out on her arms. When they disappeared, a cold chill remained, deep under her skin. She shivered, started to take a step toward the doorway, then turned back to the clock. She'd been so certain it was the key. Was she wrong? She took a deep breath. Her hand slipped into the silent face all the way to her wrist. No smooth wood, no slick glass, no warmth. And all the colors had dimmed, leaving pale imitations in their place. The air tasted flat. Empty.

"I'm afraid you cannot leave yet, my dear. There's still so much to see."

She spun around, but she was alone in the room. From beyond the door, a woman's laughter rose into the air, sharp and hard and cruel. It cut off mid-way, leaving her once more in silence.

The door slammed shut, followed by the thuds of many doors shutting one after another. She jumped, crying out, but her voice emerged as an indistinct hum.

Another voice crept in, tinged with anger that felt both familiar and foreign.

Do something. Don't just stand here.

"Okay," she said, but as she approached the door, her steps were slow.

Her hand passed through the cut-glass doorknob. She tried

again. Hand, wrist, and forearm slipped through the door. Like the clock. Like a *ghost*.

She grimaced. She couldn't be a ghost. She pressed her hand on her chest, comforted by the steady, *living*, beat of her heart. She'd been at the party, she'd heard the clock, and then—

She held out her hands, the dark stripes of the wallpaper visible through them both.

"Then this."

But what about before the party? Why couldn't she remember?

Because they don't want you to.

The floor shook beneath her feet, a quick tremble that vanished just as quickly. The colors brightened back to real. The cold creeping under her skin vanished. She grabbed the doorknob, her fingers dug into the glass and held, and then the floor shivered again. The colors faded. The cold returned. Her hand met only air. She frowned, a movement that felt real and solid. On the inside, she felt

whole

normal, but on the outside, she was anything but.

Stop this. Do something now.

She took a deep breath and stepped through the door. Her vision blurred, as though she were walking through a dense fog, then she passed through to the other side.

And everyone was gone.

She halted, her hands curling into fists. Everyone had been standing in small groups, talking and drinking. Now the rooms stood silent and empty, a tomb of furniture leached of nearly all its color. She took quick steps into the music room, the hem of her dress sweeping along the floor with no sound.

The piano in the corner loomed dark, yet a paler sort of dark, grey instead of deep black. Liquor still shimmered in the glass decanters. The sconces still burned. The air held no smell at all, but surely she should smell perfume or brandy or something leftover from the people who'd been in the room. They couldn't simply disappear.

"Hello?"

The silence stole every trace of her voice. And what had stolen her memories?

Or who?

She needed to remember what she'd forgotten. That was the key to finding the way out.

A strain of music danced in the air, a touch of laughter, and a soft voice spoke near her ear in almost, but not quite words. She turned around with her hands held up palms out.

"George?"

The colors in the room shimmered, then faded back to pale.

"I know you're here."

Another laugh, deep and masculine. Her eyes narrowed. She didn't know what sort of game George was playing, but she'd had enough. She took another step forward. The lights flickered, shadows danced along the wallpaper, and Alison slowly waved one hand. There was no corresponding motion on the wall.

"I am not a ghost. I'm *real*," she said, but her voice quavered.

The other shadows continued to move.

I can't see them, but they're all still here.

But could they see her? Yes, she thought they could. Everything here was a trick. How else could she move through doors and leave nothing behind? The floor trembled beneath her feet. Voices pierced the hush, a gentle susurration of syllables.

"...and then he..."

"...no, she doesn't..."

"...careful..."

Alison tipped her head to the side—colors and shapes blinked into existence. She smelled perfume. Men and women stood shoulder to shoulder with drinks in their hands, mouths moving in con-

CHAPTER 19

Halfway up the staircase to the second floor, she heard voices. A man's voice. George? She raced to the landing and paused in the hallway. The voices vanished, but the first door on the right swung wide.

Edmund, minus his monocle, and a woman with hair the color of honey stood in the middle of the room, deep in conversation. His face was contorted in barely held anger. The woman, her back to the door, put her hand on Edmund's arm. He pulled away. Alison caught sight of her profile—a high cheekbone, strong nose, full lips. Her mouth moved and Edmund responded in kind, yet no sound escaped the room. The

tricklight

candles flickered and their colors washed out, leaving silvery shapes in their place. Then they shimmered back. Still though, at their edges the color was faded, as though it had a tenuous hold in this reality, this *time*.

Because it had run backward. Edmund's beard wore no strands of grey and the lines on his forehead were mere promises of the aging to come. The woman spoke again, wringing her hands. Edmund shook his head. The woman turned, offering Alison a view of her face, all swollen, red-rimmed eyes and cheeks wet with tears.

She heard conversation, not whole, but in snippets.

"...we have no choice..."

"...Eleanor, he would not..."

"...cannot stay..."

"…what would you have me…"

Eleanor put her hand on Edmund's arm again. He yanked it free, stalked over to the window.

"…I don't know…"

"…not safe…"

"…George would not…"

Eleanor turned, her hands fluttering to her throat, and her gaze locked with Alison's.

She's looking at the Monstergirl.

Alison jumped back. Edmund swung around, his eyes narrowed, his mouth set in a grim line. A wave of cold pushed into Alison, the chill pushing deep inside her, cold enough to hurt. From the back of her mind arose a shred of something forgotten, a lightning fast image of hands kneading skin, pushing hard enough to bring tears. And a name—Meredith.

The cold wrenched out of her body, the air rippled, and the door slammed in her face with a dull thud. She rubbed her temples, not caring about their conversation or about George. Meredith and a Monstergirl? She tried to find the rest of it, even a tiny bit more, but the only thing that would come was an image of something striking the wall and falling to pieces on the floor.

A voice drifted down the hallway, deep and throaty. "Still so much to see."

Tightening her hands into fists, she started down the hallway, a ghost-pale woman with one glass eye, a head full of empty, and a handful of hurt.

Then she heard a heavy thud behind her and spun around with a cry. A man, clad in a dark suit, lay face down on the carpet. One arm was extended, the fingers nearly touching the wall, his face turned away from the room. Something glittered, half-hidden by his hand—a monocle.

Alison backed away. Swallowed.

"Edmund?"

Don't be stupid, he can't hear you, a voice said, a voice that was oh so familiar because the voice called her names and—

Edmund turned his head toward her. "Hel—" His voice came out in a thick rasp, his breath labored.

This Edmund was older than the one inside the room. A line of drool spilled out from his lips and dripped down to darken the carpet beneath his head. His eyes rolled wildly in all directions, bleary and bloodshot. His hand scrabbled on the carpet, his fingernails scratching at the rug. A long moan slid from between his lips.

"I'll get…" The words died in her throat.

No, she wouldn't get help. She couldn't. Like the conversation in the room, this was something old, something the house remembered.

Edmund groaned, fingers clenching around the monocle as he pulled himself forward with his other arm.

"I'm sorry," she said. "I'm so sorry."

He coughed, expelling a huge glob of pink-flecked phlegm. His breath turned to a shallow wheeze, and his skin took on a greyish cast as he dragged himself another inch and then rolled over onto his back. The monocle dropped from his hand. He tugged at his collar again and again. His heels beat a discordant rhythm on the floor and he gave another gasp.

Somewhere far in the distance someone whistled, and the tune set her teeth on edge. With one last glance at the dying man, she fled for the stairs.

● ● ●

She paused on the landing of the third floor. Closed her eyes.

A small voice hissed inside her head. *Yes, sleep and pretend, like a child hiding under the covers. Do something. Make yourself remember.*

Her eyes snapped open. She wasn't sleeping. She was trying to remember.

Try harder.

A tiny tapping noise broke into her thoughts. Eleanor, clad in a flowered dress, was making her way up the stairs, her hand curled tight around the railing, her eyes no longer swollen but narrowed, her steps slow and labored.

Not real. It isn't real. Go find George. You don't need to see this.

But Alison couldn't move, and Eleanor continued up the stairs, staring through her

Because I'm not really here. Not to her.

with eyes full of sorrow and pain and more than a hint of anger. Carefully controlled, but seething beneath the surface. The look sent a shiver down Alison's spine, not because of its tone, but because of its familiarity.

It's red, and it's hiding inside, waiting to come out. Waiting and waiting.

Eleanor stopped three steps away from the landing and her mouth curved into a smile that did not reach her eyes. Her eyes flash with grim determination, and then she spoke, the words flickering in and out.

"...know what...did..."

"No, I didn't do anything," Alison said.

Fool, she isn't talking to you.

When Eleanor spoke next, her words were clear and heavy with promise.

"You will pay."

Another voice answered, but the words consisted of an unintelligible hum. Dark clad arms reached. Eleanor's eyes widened. The dark arms extended and shoved. Eleanor's face contorted into fear and disbelief. Alison tasted fear on her own tongue, bitter and acrid.

In slow motion, Eleanor's feet left the stair. She grabbed for the railing, but it was too late. She plummeted down in a rustle of fabric and a trailing scream. There was a thud, accompanied by a sharp crack, and then all fell still. Eleanor's head rested against the space where wall met floor, her neck bent at a wrong angle. Footsteps thudded back down the hallway; Alison caught a glimpse of dark hair and dark clothing.

Even knowing she could not help, she took the stairs. Halfway down, a shout of alarm came from deep in the house, footsteps scurried across the floor, and a woman in a white cap rushed over and bent over Eleanor's still form. "Help," she cried out. "Someone help..."

Her voice faded away at the same instant her body did, yet Eleanor's broken body remained visible. Alison fisted her hands. This wasn't real, not now, but it was a long time ago. Somehow, she'd been silent witness to Eleanor's

murder

death.

Eleanor's eyes opened with a tiny little snick. Filled with confusion and stark terror, they fixed on Alison's. Her mouth worked, letting out a strange garble.

"No, oh, no," Alison said.

Eleanor lifted one hand. But how? She was dead.

What had Edmund said? "Someone would know a thing like that, wouldn't they?"

A foul smell made her gag. Covering her mouth, Alison turned and ran back up the stairs, a strange crackling noise following all the way.

She skidded to a stop just past the landing. Darkness shrouded the entire hallway. She blinked several times, but the pitch black remained, as though she stood at the edge of a great abyss. Impossible. She'd been here moments before.

From deep within the darkness, a voice said, "Come and see..."

She took a step back. The strange sounds, the stink, continued to drift up the stairs. Alison covered her face with her hands.

Enough. I want to go home.

She dropped her hands and stepped into the darkness.

● ● ●

No light, no sound, until a door creaked on her left, letting out a band of sunlight into the darkness.

No, don't, it's another trick.

But what if George was in the room? Only one way to find out.

The little girl sitting on the floor did not look up when Alison entered. The smell of talcum powder hung in the air, but another persisted beneath, sickly and wet.

Wisps of pale curls hung over the girl's forehead and shoulders. She held a doll in one hand and a well-loved blanket in the other. Sing-song nonsense words slipped from her lips in tiny murmurs. Alison remained by the door with a smile on her face. The girl stood and spun around with her arms outstretched; the blanket trailed around her, obscuring her face. Her dress, a cheery sunshine yellow, belled out around her thin legs. With a ragged sigh, she dropped to the floor again and stretched out on her back, her narrow chest moving with harsh breaths of exertion.

When the girl turned her head, Alison's mouth dropped open. Shadows marred the skin beneath the girl's eyes, a sickly pallor tinged her cheeks, and her tiny rosebud mouth held a shade of pale instead of blossom.

Alison crossed the room and bent down on one knee. This close, the girl's illness wept from her pores, a nightmare of labored breaths, fever, and sour sweat. In the back of her mind, Alison heard a clock ticking away the minutes.

The sun streaming in the windows offered no warmth. Beyond

the glass, a grey mist moved, long tendrils that pushed against the panes only to slither away.

More tricklight. A fake.

"Elizabeth?" a voice said.

The little girl sat up, a wide smile on her drawn face. The air beneath the doorframe shimmered and took shape in the form of a teenage boy, all smiles and dark hair, with a cup in his hand.

"I thought you might be cold, so I brought you some cocoa," he said, stepping closer. "You should be in bed, resting."

"I don't want to rest. I want to play."

"You can play when you're well," he said. "You don't want to upset your mother, do you?"

She shook her head.

He held out the cup. "Here, little cub. Drink this and be warm."

She took the cup in both hands and lifted it to her lips.

"Good?" the boy asked.

As she nodded and drank more, the boy winked at Alison, and she rocked back on her heels. She knew that wink, knew the man's face masked within the boyish features.

Elizabeth drank the rest and handed the cup back to George, but it was the wrong George, not the George with answers, but a once-George.

"Now, back to bed with you, before I tell your mother you were up."

"Please don't tell," Elizabeth said and scampered over to her bed, a tiny white-framed construction piled high with pastel blankets.

George tucked her in, pulling the blankets high, and kissed her forehead.

"My blankie," Elizabeth cried out.

"Stay there, I'll get it."

When he picked up the blanket, his eyes met Alison's. Without another word, he handed the blanket to Elizabeth and left the room, closing the door behind him.

196 / DAMIEN ANGELICA WALTERS

Elizabeth began to cough, and her face darkened. Her eyelids dropped shut, her lips parted, she exhaled one long, ragged gasp, and her chest went still.

"Help, someone help," Alison cried out.

But it didn't matter how much she yelled or how loud, because no one could hear, no one would come in time. One of Elizabeth's arms slipped from beneath the blanket and dangled off the edge of the bed.

Had there been something more than cocoa in the cup? No, George wouldn't have done something like that, would he?

Bone ground against bone as Elizabeth turned her head, slow, so slow. Alison shrieked and backed away. The blankets slid off the bed and puddled on the floor. The air grew vile with a wet, rotten stink. Elizabeth's flesh turned a dark shade of green, then grey. Her cheeks pitted and her chest collapsed, the ribs apparent even through her nightgown. The skin of her arms and legs shriveled into matchsticks of decay, and her hair sloughed off into a blonde mass above her head as her face turned into that of a wizened crone. Alison wanted to run, but her feet would not move, could not move.

With a whisper-soft rustle of fabric, Elizabeth's nightgown rotted to shreds. Her skin began to flake off, falling to the sheet, first slow, then faster and faster until all that remained was a skeleton draped with desiccated bits of flesh. The bones gave way with a clatter and crumbled to dust.

A slick taste of ash and decay coated the inside of Alison's mouth, and she scrubbed at her lips, gagging. The floor gave a gentle shift, a slight tipping first in one direction, then the other. Everything in the room disappeared, leaving behind peeling wallpaper and the broken frame of a bed. No foul taste, no foul odor.

Alison's shoulders sagged. It hadn't been real at all. But had it been real once? Just as Edmund's collapse in the hallway and Eleanor's fall down the stairs? She thought of the darkly clad hands pushing, the thump of Eleanor's body, and the gasps from Edmund's throat. Was it some sort of trickery, a sick game to frighten her? Or had George killed them all?

She held out her pale hands. Had he killed her, too?

"No," she said. "I am *not* dead."

She stepped out of the room, back into darkness.

Not yet.

Another door opened, letting out a grey light, and from within, a baby cried. Inside a wooden cradle, an infant kicked his feet and waved his arms, his tiny face red.

"Shhh, it's okay. Everything is okay."

Her body went cold as an arm clutching a pillow speared her chest. The arm descended. The cries cut off. Alison tried to grab the pillow, the arm, but she passed through them as the arm had her. She screamed for someone to come and help, for someone to come and stop it because she couldn't help. She couldn't do anything.

No, it's another trick. Just a trick.

But she heard the choking, a terrible lullaby of death, and backed out of the room with her hands fisted against her breastbone.

Stop, please, stop. I don't want to see this.

Shadows claimed the room, and someone whispered her name, freezing her in place.

Don't go. Don't listen to him.

But she knew that voice. It wasn't George. It was someone who shouldn't be here, someone she knew, but his name was buried somewhere deep in her mind.

"Alison?"

She started down the hallway. Maybe he

who?

could help her remember, could help her find the way out.

"Alison, is that you?"

"I'm coming," she said.

She came to a halt just inside the doorway. A figure stood at the window. The light from the sconce played along the length of her green dress.

No, this is wrong. Wrong.

Slowly, Rachel turned around. "I think I'm lost," she said, holding up her arms, arms bound at the ends with thick white bandages. "I only wanted to play the piano again." Roses of red bloomed in misshapen stars on the bandages. "You can understand that, can't you?"

A drop of blood freed itself from the bandage and dangled in the air, gem dark and shimmering in the light, before it let go and fell to the floor with a tiny splash.

Rachel lifted her arms higher. "They couldn't save my hands. My mother said they did all they could."

One after another, pearls of blood dripped onto her dress, turning the green fabric black. As Rachel shuffled forward, she left a trail of red on each side. The blood flow quickened into macabre leaking faucets, and the ends of the bandages fell free, uncoiling in slow motion like barber poles of red and white.

You can't help her. You have to go home.

Rachel watched them uncurl, her mouth slack. Finally, the bandages fell free, floating to the floor, unveiling two raw stumps with hints of white bone beneath the gore. A hot, meaty stench poured from the wounds, strong enough to make Alison's eye water.

Rachel smiled, despite tears in her eyes. "When they stop bleeding, I'll be able to play again. Will you stay with me until then?"

"I'm sorry," Alison said. "I can't."

"Please?"

"I, I..." Alison fled before she could finish. As soon as she ran back into the hallway, the door closed with a definitive click, muffling the sound of Rachel's cries, and plunging her once more into darkness.

"Alison?"

She turned from side to side. The voice was faint, coming from no discernible direction. Then another door opened on her right.

"Hello?"

No response.

Her hands shaking, she peered around the doorframe. Josephine sat on a chair in the corner of the room. She gave Alison a cursory glance before looking back down at her lap. The pale gold gown she wore hung in tatters around her emaciated frame, sores dotting the corners of her mouth, her skin a shade of grey-green. Her hair, the dull color of dishwater, clung to her shoulders in tangled clumps.

As she turned to go, the woman spoke, her voice soft. "I'll eat this time. I promise I will."

Without a word, Alison backed out of the room. The door swung shut. The dark returned. All around her, voices whispered.

Don't listen to them. Don't listen to any of them.

But—

"Ally?"

She pressed one hand to her chest. His name, his name, what was his name? She couldn't leave him. Not in this place.

But he left you, a small voice said.

Another door opened, and soft moans issued forth. Madeline was lying in a canopy bed beneath a nebulous figure. His pants were pushed down to his ankles; her legs were wrapped around his waist. But Madeline was

wrong

a grey husk, her cheeks withered, her eyes dull pits of dark held in hollow sockets, her body twisted. Her lips curved into a smile, a horrorshow of pleasure.

"I told you I was the first," she said. A flake of skin dislodged from her shoulder.

Alison ran. The door slammed shut. She stood in the darkness with her hands over her ears. "Alison."

"Go away, just go away," she said.

But when the door opened, she turned.

No, don't do this. Don't look.

Damn her for a fool, she did.

A man stood in the corner, his face hidden.

"Alison," he said in that terribly familiar voice. "Please help me."

His steps were limping and awkward, his face still a dark blur. A scent of warm bread fresh from the oven made her mouth water, and she took a step inside,

They'd made bread together, that first night in their new apartment, laughing at the misshapen lump they created, pulling it apart with their fingers, eating it with the steam still rising up and butter dripping down on their fingers and then the love, oh the love, and he said forever and she believed him and he gave her the tiny diamond ring.

then another.

Forever, forever, forever.

But why couldn't she remember his name?

He moved into the light. Thomas of the sad eyes smiled. Extended his arms.

"Stay with us, stay with *me*, here."

He lurched forward, his legs and arms hanging at odd angles, as though they'd been badly broken then put back together the wrong way.

She didn't move away as he reached for her hands. The floor shivered and warmth rushed in as his fingers curled around hers. One of her hands appeared real, not grey, all the way to the wrist.

"Stay with me, please."

The real moved to her forearm, filling in the transparent haze with solid pale. His fingers held tight and they were warm, so warm.

"Please stay."

Her skin turned warm and flesh, up, over, her elbow, up to her shoulder as his thumb made a lazy arc on the back of her hand.

It's another trick, a voice said.

The skin of Thomas' cheek changed, rough replacing smooth, and a fragment in the shape of a quarter moon peeled away.

He caught her glance, and smiled. "Don't worry about that, it's just a piece of—"

"No."

Alison wrenched her hand away. The warmth lingered briefly, then all turned grey and cold. Before he could say another word, she ran. The door shut and darkness rushed in, thick with voices begging her to stay, to help.

"No more," she said. "Go away, all of you."

She took a step. Then another. Choked back a sob. Then a hand touched hers.

Before she could scream, another door spilled out pale light, allowing her to see that the hand belonged to a young girl with an elfin face. Translucent, like her own. The little girl smiled, and the scream in Alison's throat vanished. A name flickered in her mind—Mary

Alison took a step toward the open door, but Mary pointed to the end of the hallway. Another trick? Mary gave her hand a gentle squeeze. Her touch was feather-light. Cold. Yet Alison sensed neither malice nor cruelty. When they passed the doorway, Alison caught a glimpse of a dark shape and a flash of light. Heard a sharp pop.

Then Mary tugged her away again. They came to a stop at the last door. Mary nodded.

"Okay," Alison said.

Together, they went through the door. Alison's vision blurred; her bones chilled.

They walk in, their faces indiscernible behind masks, scalpels in their hands, drugs in the bag by the bed. Sleep now, they say. We're here to help you. Straining against the pain. Hold on, just hold on, they say—

On the other side, the voices in Alison's head slipped away. She tried to pull the memory back, but it was slippery

like blood and scar tissue

and fell through her grasp. She groaned. Mary clutched her arm and placed one finger to her lips.

Inside the room, curls of unmoving smoke hung from the ceiling in stalactites. Alison brushed her hand through the nearest one; the smoked swirled then reformed. Mary pointed to the wall, to a series of framed photographs.

Some of the faces behind the glass were familiar: Rachel, Thomas, Josephine, Madeline, and several others she'd seen at the party. But the photos held secrets, too, dark secrets the party concealed: Rachel wearing a sweater with the cuffs pinned over a space where hands should be; Thomas slumped in a wheelchair; Josephine in a dress that couldn't hide the jutting bones and skeletally thin limbs; Madeline hunched over, her spine distorted, her hands lumpy claws.

Alison's fingers slipped through the glass covering Rachel's photo, but she didn't need to worry about broken glass and broken skin, because her fingers went into the picture and it was—

An accident. A terrible accident. It could have happened to anyone, but Rachel had studied at Peabody and everyone knew how well she played. She was a rising star, going up and up, and then the car, the tangled metal, the pain, the quick slip of metal into skin, parting flesh from bone and bone from bone, and there were no more pianos, no more music, no more smiles. Until he took her in and gave her back her hands, gave her back her music, then made her play until her fingers bled, but she played because the pain was worth it, so, so worth it and one day, she didn't come back, but she had her music, she didn't need to come back, there was nothing to come back to.

Alison drew her hand back with a sick feeling in the pit of her stomach. Mary tugged on her skirt, her mouth turned down into a frown, and pointed at the last photo in the bottom row. No, Alison didn't want to look at that photo. Not at all. That photo was a nightmare, a woman, her face heavily scarred, scarred into a sideshow freak, a—

"Monstergirl," she said.

She touched Thomas's instead and—

She was gone for good. His brother had told him she would leave. She loves me, Thomas had told him. It's not enough, his brother had said. And his brother was right. He'd thought she loved him enough and not just his money, but it wasn't enough. There wasn't enough money in the world to make her stay. He tried to make her happy and pretended not to notice the way her eyes moved away.

Then he came and the promise was too good to resist. He could walk again, and if he could walk, then he was whole. He wasn't the enemy. The enemy's name was Multiple Sclerosis, and it was taking Thomas apart a little more each day.

But she left, even after he told her. She didn't believe him and wouldn't wait to see it for herself. A daydream, she called it. But it wasn't a daydream, it was real, and after she left, he had nothing. So he stayed because inside he was whole—

Too much pain. Too much suffering.

He was weak, a voice said. *They were all weak.*

Mary pointed to the nightmare photo, then to Alison and back again. With a sigh, Alison took a closer look. The sorrow and the hurt on the woman's face was

weak

pitiful. And her eyes, something about her eyes, one peeking out from normal, whole skin; the other, sticking out from a nest of scars.

Ugly girl, what an ugly girl.

Alison didn't want to touch the photo. Didn't want to know. But she knew she had to.

Her fingers slipped through the glass.

She walked alone at night, alone so no one would see, because when they saw her, they pointed and murmured behind their hands. She was ugly, yes, an ugly little Monstergirl. Fire and smoke and ugly and broken. In hiding and in pain, with the windows shut and the curtains closed. No sunlight. No friends. No one but her and the faces of strangers to keep her company, and in the dark, she went outside, walking to nowhere. There was nowhere to go, but back in her house, her prison, with her scars and her sorrow and her pity.

And then she went in, inside, he took her and made her whole again with all her finger piggies in a row and a face that anyone would love—

Alison wrenched her hand from the picture, breathing hard, breathing *hurt*. "It was me," she said, her voice the sound of broken glass ground in a fist. And everything rushed back in. Her house, her face, the fire, her mother, her isolation, her fear, the junk shop, the album, George's album, in the front window. All of the real waited for her on the other side of the clock—the doorway. She put her face in her hands.

Mary patted her arm. A whisper caught in the air. "Sorry."

From below, a round of applause broke out, cheers of "Hurrah", then a woman's voice. "Again, again." Piano notes began to play.

The floor shivered beneath her feet, footsteps thumped down the hallway, and Mary's mouth dropped open. In a blur of grey, she grabbed Alison's arm and guided her toward the wall, but Alison shook her head. Mary let go of her hand, slipped into the wall, and disappeared just as the door swung open with a loud creak. George laughed, low and husky.

Alison took a deep breath, armed with her self, and turned to face the tiger.

* * *

George wore a hungry grin on his face.

"You're looking a little...pale, my dear."

"I'm not your dear," Alison said. "I know what you did to them, to Elizabeth and William, Mary and Eleanor...and Edmund. You killed them. You killed them all and trapped them here in the house."

His smile grew wider.

"I'm not staying here. With you, with them," she nodded toward the wall.

"Haven't you realized that it's too late for that? You were so willing to give up everything to be whole. Now you're whole. Eventually you'll forget about everything else, and you'll be far happier here than you could ever be hiding in your house with your scars and your ugliness."

"You call this whole?"

His eyes flashed with mirth. "Whole enough, yes. Your scars are gone. I gave you what you wanted, what you asked for. I gave them all what they asked for. None of them had a real life before. Do you think they'd want what that life would offer?" He waved a hand toward the photos. "Now they have parties and music and dancing. Now they're whole, which was all they wanted. All you wanted. You said, "Let me in and make me whole," did you not? And I've been waiting for someone like you for a very long time."

"Someone like me?"

"Yes. Such exquisite pain, such perfect sorrow. It's quite extraordinary. You truly are special. Every minute of your existence is a tortured one. The fire took so much from you. Your face, your fiancé, everything."

"How do you know about that? How do you know anything at all?"

"I know everything, Monstergirl."

"But that's—"

"You gave it to me when you entered the house. Every bit of it."

"And if I'd been whole?"

"Oh come now, you aren't stupid. Naïve, perhaps, but not stupid. If you'd been whole, the doorway would not have opened. You wouldn't be here."

Because it doesn't let anyone in who isn't *hurt. It doesn't want anyone whole and happy. It can't use them. It can't feed off them. It needs pain and hurt. No flesh for this tiger, but meat nonetheless.*

"But *here* isn't even a house anymore. The house burned down." She let out a hoarse laugh. "It's gone. This is just a bunch of old pictures in an old album."

"But photographs have a special power, don't you agree? They can capture so many things. Sorrow, pain, life. A handful of lives kept and held. A handful of time forever preserved. Unchanging. Perfect in its simplicity, yet absolute in its possibility. Anyone and anything can live forever in a photograph. Even a house. And this house will never die. Never. I gave it far too much. I gave it life."

"No, you gave it *death*. You killed everyone in your family. *Everyone*. And all those people." She waved her hand toward the photos. "You tricked them and you killed them, too."

"No, I did not. They're all still here. You saw them."

"But it's not life. It's all a lie. If they knew, they would've never come."

"Perhaps not." He shrugged. "Choices made, deeds done, prices paid. It will make it so much easier for you if you let it all go. Forget about the Monstergirl. Forget about your pain. Drink and dance and forget. I'm certain Thomas would not be adverse to sharing your bed. Tell me, would anyone ever do so otherwise? You can be happy here, Alison. No one will ever point and laugh at you again."

Her chest tightened. A part of her, a shameful, hateful part wanted to stay, wanted to be whole. It would be so easy to let herself believe him, to believe it was all for her, for their, benefit, and he knew it, but she didn't think that the case at all. No, there was something more hidden in the gleam of his eyes.

"What is it that you really want?"

He merely smiled in reply and nodded toward the door. "Go then. You'll be here a long time, you might as well enjoy yourself."

"No. I won't stay here. I will find the way out."

"There is no way out. You belong to me now. You belong to Pennington House."

"I don't belong to anyone but myself," she said, but her voice trembled.

"No?"

Music notes played, soft and sweet. Then laughter. Voices. She took a step toward the door, toward the party, where she wouldn't have to hide.

"No," she said.

The music faded. The voices vanished. Tricks and games, nothing more.

"You will not keep me here."

She turned to the photographs.

My exquisite pain.

George laughed, but some of the surety was missing.

"You can't have me. You can't have my pain. I take it back."

She willed herself still. Empty. A place where nothing could touch her. She dug deep, under the pity and the anger and the sorrow that lived inside her skin, poisoning her self with every cutting word and thought. And how it all wanted to overflow and spill out, because the house, the tiger, wanted it so.

She searched even deeper and thought of—

Her mother, who always found something she thought Alison would like, a sweater, a book, a piece of Key Lime pie. All the times she called just to say hello and I love you. And her house, her tiny safety net, a perfect place for one.

Dimly, Alison heard a shout, but it came from far away.

She went further down, where the girl who wished on pennies and the first evening star still lived, the girl who loved to read and write poetry, whose favorite color was orange, who wore monkey pajamas and socks with cats and frogs and ladybugs...

Being whole was more than a photograph's image. It was power, strength, will. Inside, the coils that held her prisoner loosened and flickered away—vanishing streamers in a ghost parade. The house gave a gentle shake. The wood solidified under her feet. Her skin warmed, and she opened her eyes. George was gone. Her hands, though still grey, shimmered, as though lit from within. This time, her fingertips tingled, touched glass and wood. It was more than a photograph. It was a key, a tether from paper to real. And all doors had keys.

With all the force she could muster, she lifted the picture over her head and threw it on the floor. The glass shattered into a thousand fragments. The frame bent, cracking and splitting at the seams. Instinct sent her down on one knee. She pried the photo free and ripped it in half.

The house lurched, knocking her off balance. The smoke overhead winked out of sight. Her hand came down hard on the wood, barely missing a jagged splinter of glass, but it didn't matter because the wood beneath her hand was firm and hard. And her skin gleamed, but not grey.

The last of the cold inside her drained away. Long cracks appeared in George's desk, filling with grime. The cushion of his desk chair let out a foul stinking cloud—old sweat, smoke, and mildew. Wallpaper bubbled and peeled, water spots appeared in the corners of the ceiling, and the floorboards warped and lifted. The scent of tobacco was replaced by the heaviness of age and forgotten memories.

From somewhere deep within the house, a voice rose in outrage and then dwindled. Alison smiled and got to her feet; the chime of the clock shook the rafters. Right before her hand met the doorknob, the door swung open.

Dust, cobwebs, and ruin held court in Pennington House now. She ran out into the hallway, the torn photo clutched in one hand. The fabric of her dress swished around her ankles, heavier and heavier with each step. Halfway down, she stopped to lift the satin, but it wouldn't budge. She tugged harder. The fabric slipped through her fingers.

The clock chimed for the second time.

Dropping the photograph, she grabbed two thick handfuls of satin. The fabric clung to her hands, slick yet sticky, not exactly satin anymore. It wrapped around her legs, fastening her in place.

"No," she shrieked, ripping her hands free.

The house would not win. It would *not* keep her prisoner. It would *not*. The edge of the skirt slipped into the floor, melting into the carpet. With a slippery wet sound, the carpet sucked in more of the skirt and pulled her down to her knees. She twisted her body from side to side. A third chime sounded.

"You can't have me!"

She wrenched her body back and forth. The fabric near her hip ripped. She jerked harder, flinging her body in every direction, tearing skin from her knees and straining the muscles of her back. And the rip expanded.

"Can't have me, can't have me, can't have me," she said, the words thin and breathless.

She yanked at the rip until it became an open slit. Her hands worked again, digging in. Now, a gaping mouth. And again. A wide hole. Again.

The clock chimed.

The fabric caught at the seam. The thread held tight as the floor swallowed a torn length. Alison grabbed the seam, one hand on each side, and with a *snick-snick-snick* of popping thread, it came loose. She laughed in triumph.

"I'm free, do you hear me? I don't belong to you."

She stepped from the ruined fabric, a mermaid rising from a silken sea, kicked off the delicate slippers the house had given her, and ran. At the landing, she glanced back, over her shoulder. The tattered remnants of her skirt lay on, not in, the carpet, a heap of shimmering blue against the dusty grey, the discarded shoes on their sides next to the pile. And on the floor, two scraps of torn paper.

She ran back, careful not to touch anything else but the photo. Heard the clock.

The skin of her knees burned and stung. Blood trickled down her legs. But it didn't matter. What were a few more scars? Scraps of torn fabric fluttered around her hips and her bare feet left streak-prints in the grime as she ran down the stairs. She raced across the landing. Down the stairs leading down to the first floor, but she misjudged the distance and her entire body jolted forward. Her foot slid over the edge of the first step; her hands grabbed empty air. The photo fell from her hand, seesawing all the way.

She pinwheeled her arms, yanked herself back, pulling her foot away from the edge as the clock chimed again. Her fingers found the banister and she stopped with a lurch. How many chimes so far? Six or seven, she thought, but she still had plenty of time.

She found the first half of the photo mid-way down the stairs, scooped it up, and tucked it inside the front of her dress. The second half lay in the corner of the landing.

The table in the foyer lay on its side, the wood cracked and gouged, the vase broken, dead flower petals scattered on the floor. As she sidestepped the table, a hand curled around her upper arm. Her scream pierced the quiet, but when she turned, no one was there, and the sensation of fingers digging into her skin vanished.

The clock chimed once more, and breathing hard, she ran. The unseen hand grabbed again, then another, and another, all trying to pull her back. The air thickened. Snippets of color and faces with mouths open, horrible faces drawn and grey and rotting away to the bone beneath, flashed in her peripheral vision. Struggling against the hands, she drew breath to scream, and the taste of decay poured down her throat. Voices flickered in and out.

...stay...

...forever and ever...

...don't go...

...we need you...

...please...

"It's not real!" she shrieked.

But the clock was real, the chime was real, and she had to get there before it stopped, had to get out. Discordant musical notes joined the voices and the grey. Hands batted her arms, her hair, the remnants of her dress. She struck out again and again, her fists meeting the air with liquid thuds.

...no...

...please no...

"Let me go!"

The music built, and she pushed through the thick air, the people. A small, cold hand took hers, pulling as the clock chimed, pulling as she twisted away from the other grasping fingers. The air changed weight, the fog lifted, and once again, she was free.

She ran with Mary at her side. The door to the turret room stood open, and the clock beckoned with its gilded promise of home. George materialized in front of the clock as it chimed again, winking into existence with his eyes narrowed, blocking the way. The tiny fingers tightened around hers, and then they were gone. A dark shadow flitted across the wall before it disappeared inside.

"Where do you think you're going?"

"Home."

He sneered. "And stay inside, locked away from the world, little Monstergirl?"

•

"You can't keep me here anymore."

He grabbed her arm, his fingers digging into her flesh. "You think not?"

"Let me go!"

He laughed. "Never."

Hush, a quiet, still voice whispered inside her head. *It's another trick. A game. He isn't real and he can't keep you here. Not anymore.*

"You're a dead man in a false house, that's all. Nothing more than that."

His grip on her arm intensified. "No one ever dies here. No one."

She yanked away from his grip and pulled out half the photo. He lunged as she tore it again. The floor quivered, the air wavered, and he greyed out.

"Goodbye, George," she said, her voice overpowered by the sound of the clock.

She stepped forward into a column of cold, into George. She held her breath. Moved in and through, the air thick and heavy. His hands were ice against her, but his touch was a wisp of smoke, and she had no cause for worry because there's nothing here my dear, nothing but fear and fear had no face, no hands, fear would keep you prisoner if you let it and she was going home, back to the real world, back to her life. Hickory dickory dock, a Monstergirl for the clock.

The house held only broken dreams, shattered screams, and secret little dirty things. It was a liar's playground, a dead man's last stand.

And with a smile, she left the paper world behind.

PART VII

GO AWAY, MONSTERGIRL

Sparks fly into the air and she runs, but there's nowhere to go because the fire, the smoke, is everywhere. She falls and flames dance against her skin, tiny mouths that want to bite, to eat her away with their sharp little teeth. She screams, but the smoke turns it into a choke, a cough, there's no air, no air, and the flames hit her skin, tearing it away. Heat and pain and she tries to crawl away, but it's everywhere and she can't get free, can't get away from the smell of burnt hair and roasting meat.

Then everything goes fuzzy and grey and she can't crawl or roll or move anymore. And all around her, the fire roars.

Like a tiger.

CHAPTER 20

Home.

Alison staggered into her living room on mermaid feet of pain. Dizziness swirled in her vision but she didn't care because she was home and real.

Her clothes were coated (her real clothes, because the house kept her party dress and good riddance to bad rubbish) with a scum of grey, and her fleece pants were torn at both knees, revealing the bloodied skin below. The socket of her right eye burned. She dropped the torn picture in her hand, rolled her fingertip along the lower lid, and out popped the glass eye. Not her eye. The tiger's eye. She let out a cry and yanked her hand back. The eye landed on the floor and rolled with a tiny skittering sound until it bounced off the baseboard and came to a stop next to the remains of Meredith's camera. It glared at her with its false pupil, a black spot of come back, come back.

"I don't think so," she said.

Inside me. It was inside *me.*

She pressed a hand to her belly and fought the urge to wash out her empty socket with bleach. With pain raging through every muscle, she hobbled into the kitchen, removed a trash bag from under the sink, and donned a pair of rubber gloves.

The pages of the album rustled as she approached the coffee table, and a quick snick of music crept out. The inscription had changed again, all the words filled in for her to see. It didn't need to hide its—*his*—true intent from her anymore.

Twelve times the clock will chime
Stay and leave your freedom behind
House of promises, house of lies
Claiming those locked forever inside
Trapped like a butterfly under glass
Pain and torment as years drift past
Paper men bring forth real tears
And screams no one will ever hear
House of sorrow, house of sin
Welcomes only pain within
Flee before this house unfolds —
A paper tiger to swallow you whole

A warning. Always a warning.

"But you can't have me," she said. "Not now. Not ever."

Using the edge of one gloved finger, she pushed the album over to the edge of the table, then over and down into the bag. Leaving the gloves on (because the tiger was tricky), she tied the carry handles into a double knot and held the bag away from her body as she carried it outside.

The album hit the bottom of the trash can with a heavy thump. She slammed the lid, ignoring the shake in her hands, and stood with the clang echoing in her ears. Although it had been early afternoon when she went into the paper world, the sky overhead was turning to dark. She'd lost several hours instead of minutes. A trill of piano notes took flight into the air, and a pull, a need, tugged deep inside. A long-lost lover calling

one more time

with promised sweetness.

"The scars will come back," the music said. "You know they will. Come back inside, we'll make you whole."

Lies, all of it.

Alison spun on her heel and stormed back inside, away from the tiger. She picked up the photo pieces and tore them into tiny shreds. Dropped them on the floor next to the eye, the pieces falling like confetti, and made her way upstairs, holding onto the railing and the wall. A shower would be good, to wash off the stink of paper and plaster—and George. But everything hurt, and spots flashed in her eye, so she stumbled into her bedroom and climbed under the covers to sleep.

To forget.

■ ■ ■

Two hours later, sleep still wore the face of a stranger. Everything ached from her skinned knees to the muscles in her side and lower back. Darkening marks, the promise of bruises to come, ringed a half-circle around her upper arm.

Her fingers trembled. Chills raced in a frantic line up and down her spine, beads of sweat dotted her forehead, and a headache pounded behind her temples. She held as still as possible, but the steady beat played on. Under her skin, the scars waited, biding their time.

And the album whispered. A soft voice carried by a breeze. It pulled, as though a connection ran between them, a tether from paper to real. And did she want to climb out of bed, hobble outside, and take the album from its plastic bag? Yes, she did. If she kept it on the shelf, as a reminder, it couldn't hurt her.

Don't be a fool, Red said. *You'll keep it on the shelf, yes, but you won't be able to leave it there. Not forever. Not when you look at your hands, your missing fingers, and touch your face.*

Sleep hovered close, yet a music note sounded far in the distance, bringing her back awake with a jolt.

"Come back," the album said. "I'll make you whole."

And from deep inside: *Needwantmusthavenow.*

Alison covered her head with the sheet. The itch under her skin intensified, a creeping, crawling threat. She scratched at her arm, lightly at first, then dug in with her nails, hard and deep. *Go away, go away.* She dug and gouged at the perfect skin and left marks, then scrapes, then bleeding, stinging cuts, but the itch didn't leave. Maybe if she went outside and got the album, kept it close until she slept and then, when the scars came back, she could throw it away again. She pushed off the covers and sat, ignoring the blood underneath her fingernails.

"Come back."

The tether tugged hard.

And inside her head, the steady beat of *NEEDwantmusthavenow.*

Lies, all lies.

With a groan, she covered her ears with her hands. A car door slammed outside, heavy footsteps tapped on the sidewalk. She could walk, walk away from her house and the album, walk until the itch went away,

NEEDWANTmusthavenow

walk until sleep was a heartbeat away, and then come back. If she walked, she wouldn't hear it calling, but everything hurt, from toes to nose and back again, it hurt too much, and her skin crawled and rolled with

NEEDWANTMUSThavenow

the sensation of a thousand insect feet, and Red didn't know a damn thing. The voice was the fool because one small touch of the album would make it all go away. Just one touch. Just one.

NEEDWANTMUSTHAVEnow

But it won't be enough and you know it.

And Red was smiling; Alison felt it in her bones, deep in the marrow. Smug as a bug in a rug. But oh that voice was right, because one touch would lead to

NEEDWANTMUSTHAVENOW

another, then another, and then she'd open it, just to look, just to check and the paper world would take her back and make her whole, but it would eat her away,

NEED

because it needed her, he needed her to make him

WANT

real, but what was real? The itch, the pull,

MUST

the scars and the looks from the strangers, and everyone would point because she was a Monstergirl,

HAVE

and the pain in her head was a dark cloud.

"I can't do this," she said. "Make it go away."

NOW

"Yes," the album said, sending the words along the tether, each syllable a drop of poisonous oil on a narrow thread. "Come back and it will all go away."

Yes, it will all go away—and so will you.

Too many voices in her head. She pushed her face into the pillow—hating, hurting, wanting. The time ticked by until darkness wrapped her in its arms and pulled her down into sleep, into forgetting, into the void.

But when the sun rose and the drone of the garbage truck's engine made its way down the street, Alison woke with panic flooding her mouth. There was still time. She could run outside and get the album. The trash men might shake their heads, but it wouldn't matter. The album would be safe and sound, back in the house, back in her hands, and it would let her back in and give her what had been taken away, what had been stolen—everything.

No. Let it go. Remember, it lies. It doesn't give anything back, not without a price. All shall be well.

"Come!" the album shouted.

And the rope between them yanked her up and out of bed. She crawled on the floor, toward the door because she needed, she wanted, she—

"No," she said, her voice a sandpaper rasp.

She sobbed into her hands. Heard the shouts of the trash men, the heavy clunk of the cans being emptied and tossed back into the yards, the hiss of the hydraulics pressing the trash down, each sound a warning cry of tragedy, doom, and woe.

The album called and sang and begged and pleaded, but Alison kept still, and when the sounds faded, taking the album (and her chance for something close to normal, no, her chance for something worse than death) with them, she gave a heavy, hurtful sigh. The voice of the album slipped away, and hating, hurting, she let it go.

* * *

The next day, she did not get out of bed, not once, not even when her phone rang over and over again. She covered her head with the pillow and, sometimes, she slept.

* * *

In the middle of the night, Alison crept out of bed, wrapped herself in a robe, and began the long, halting trek down to the first floor. Each step drove pain from heel to hip. She wanted to climb back in bed, but her stomach was growling too much to ignore.

Hunched over, she made her way into the kitchen. And if her hands were shaking the entire time, it was okay. The shake reminded her she was real.

* * *

The following night, after the sun set, she donned her scarf and gloves even though they felt like a straightjacket, and walked the familiar streets with her chin down.

Old habits. Old haunts.

A low-grade headache throbbed in time with her passage, and she shoved her hands into her pockets to help control, and conceal, the shaking. Chills pebbled her skin with gooseflesh, chills that had little to do with the night air, but she kept walking until exhaustion forced her to turn around and head home.

The next night, she did the same.

And the next.

The headache vanished on the following day, the shake in her hands lessened a few days later, and the chills left a few more days after that. With her skin safe inside rubber gloves, she picked up the torn photo, the glass eye, and the broken camera, and tossed them all into the trash can, but even through the glove, a tiny voice said, "Come back."

"Go to hell," she said.

She gathered her thoughts of photographs, parties, and false promises, tucked them away in a box, and locked it tight. Even the steel bands of self-pity she'd grown so accustomed to (and welcomed, if she was going to be truthful, welcomed and hid behind, which was what got her into trouble with the photo album in the first place) finally loosened their grip.

For the first time in a long time, Alison felt something close to normal on the inside.

● ● ●

She invited her mother over for tea, and when she walked in, the first thing she did was take Alison's chin, tip it to one side, and then the other.

"You look wonderful. The circles are gone from under your eyes and your coloring is much, much better. I was getting so worried, and then I—"

Alison couldn't help but smile. "I understand. Everything's okay, I promise. I needed some time to myself."

"Are you sure?"

"I'm positive. I want to apologize, too, for yelling at you about Meredith."

"No, I was in the wrong. I should have asked you first before I spoke to her."

Alison took her mother's hand. "Let's let it go, okay? I've been taking a lot of walks lately and doing a lot of thinking. I know the past few years have been rough for you, too."

Her mother choked back a cry and swallowed convulsively before speaking. "I was so afraid you were falling into another depression, like the one after the fi—I mean, the accident…"

"Mom, it's okay. You can say the word fire."

Her mother blinked away a shimmer of tears. "You still look too skinny. I'll need to bring things over to fatten you up. Pie and cakes and cookies, maybe donuts."

"You know there's a donut shop around the corner, right?"

"Yes. Maybe I should go and get you some right now."

"Why don't we go together?"

They did, and when they passed by a small group of people, Alison didn't drop her chin. A woman did a double take, but her gaze didn't linger.

Of Yellow, there was no sign. In fact, good old Yellow seemed to have gone on permanent holiday. Perhaps Alison had left it behind in Pennington House. If so, good. George could choke on it, for all she cared.

• • •

She took the newspaper clipping, the tiny diamond ring, and the plastic hospital identification bracelet from her jewelry box. She held the ring up to the light, watching the rainbows dance inside. Once, she'd thought of sending it back to Jonathan, but she hadn't wanted him to know how deep his abandonment had cut her, unaware then that she'd cut herself even deeper by keeping the ring.

How much hurt can you hold inside until your soul gives way, crumbling beneath the weight? Too much. Far too much.

She carried everything, along with a pair of scissors, into the bathroom, snipped the bracelet into a hundred tiny pieces, and dropped them into the toilet. With a deep breath, she tossed in the clipping and the ring, too. One push of the handle carried them all away.

All shall be well.

PART VIII

NEW HAUNTS

She's in bed when the thunder begins to roar, deep and growling. She can't remember any clouds in the sky, but in Baltimore, the weather changes in an eye blink. She reaches out and touches empty air in the bed. Jonathan isn't home yet. She rolls over, inhaling his scent.

Then she smells the smoke.

She cries out when she touches the doorknob and heat kisses her palm. Dark, oily smoke sneaks in around her feet, creeping into the space between the carpet and the floor.

The walls shudder. Their tiny apartment is on the top floor of the old house. The only way out is through the front door into the hallway and down the stairs. Heat pushes up from the floor and the wood creaks in protest. She touches the door again. Too hot, it's too hot, but she can't stay in the room and the window is too high.

Think, think, she tells herself, but there's no time to think. She has to get out. She wraps herself in a blanket and opens the door.

Smoke stings her eyes and the thunder rolls in.

And then the blanket is on fire and she is on fire because she opened the door and why did she open the door, only a stupid fool would make such a mistake, but she drops the blanket and then she hears the baby crying. The neighbors have two children, one a newborn. Are they trapped?

The baby cries again. Why would they leave the baby? The door to their apartment is open and she runs in, runs through the smoke, pushes through the smoke, toward the crying. Down the hallway and there's so much smoke, but the baby, the baby, the baby.

She follows the cries to the last bedroom and there on the floor, not a baby, but a doll, and there's no one else in the apartment, the baby is safe, they're all safe, and she's close to the front door but the ceiling falls and then everything is on fire, she's on fire, and she smacks away the flames, but there are more and more and she screams, filling with smoke, filling with pain and she can't see because everything is orang-eredorangeredorangered and hurt and screaming shouts that taste like smoke and the wood creaks and groans and the walls shake and she has to get to the door, the front door, the only way out, and then she'll be safe, away from the orangered.

And sparks dance like fireflies in the air...

CHAPTER 21

On a cold February afternoon, with snowmelt dripping from the eaves, Alison curled up with a cup of hot chocolate, a fleece throw, and her homework. She was only taking three classes this semester but planned to take five in the fall; everything she needed for her degree was offered online by a local university.

She rolled away the stiffness in her shoulders. In the months since she'd returned to the real world, returned for good, she'd had several appointments with Meredith. The first, filled with apologies and reparations, but no mention of the camera; Alison couldn't quite bring herself to mention that. The second, with small sighs of disappointment, when Meredith pointed out the improvements in her scars had gone away, and fears that maybe she'd been mistaken.

Yet Alison knew the truth. Once she'd severed ties with the paper world, all glamour and false hope vanished.

She bent forward to set down the mug, and the sharp-sweet scent of tobacco hit her full on. She exhaled with a loud whoosh and dropped the mug on its side, ignoring the tiny chocolate pool that spilled out.

No, no, no.

Closing her eyes, she wrapped herself in white, but the smell crept in, sneaking like dark little fingers into her mind. She refused to believe it anything other than her imagination or maybe from somewhere in the neighborhood.

But all the windows were shut. And the album was gone. The tobacco was strong enough to taste; strong enough to say it was not imagination. The heat clicked off, leaving behind silence. The missing pinkie on her right hand started to itch, and she curled the remaining fingers toward her palm. Purple coils she'd nearly forgotten came to life, and with the fear holding her heart a heavy prisoner inside her chest, she turned her head slowly from left to right and back again, terrified to look, too afraid not to.

No smoke hovered in the air.

A neighbor slammed a door, the sound reverberating through the connecting wall. Alison jumped. Pressed her fingers to her temples.

The sleeve of her shirt slid back, revealing her right arm up to the elbow. In the light, the scars were slashes of sickly color.

Ugly, ugly, ugly.

The words snuck in before she could stop them.

"Knock it off," she said and yanked the sleeve back into place.

She stomped into the kitchen. Refilled her mug and grabbed a handful of paper towels. Then she saw the scrap of paper, a square shape with torn edges, on the floor near the base of a cabinet. She bent close; the ruined side of her own face peered back. Despite its small size, the paper reeked of tobacco.

With a shuddering sigh, she dropped the photo into the trash can. It turned end over end before it landed with the white side down, and a tiny thought burrowed deep. She'd thrown all the pieces away.

It was conceivable that one piece had fallen from her hand in the process, yes, it was *rationally* conceivable. She'd been wearing gloves; she might not have felt it fall, but how many times had she walked through her living room and kitchen since then? Too many to count. Unless the scrap of photo had stuck to her shoe or sock and traveled into the kitchen, but even then...

No. It was over and done with. All of it. The album was gone.

• • •

Alison watched through the peephole as a man in a brown uniform approached her house. She flipped her hair over the side of her face, and if he noticed her shaking hands or her missing fingers when he handed over the package, he gave no sign. She kept her chin tucked, though, and when she closed the door, she grimaced. She should've looked up, not down. Well, there was always a next time.

She carried the box, as long as her forearm in length and half that in width, into the kitchen and split the packing tape carefully with a knife. Inside sat another box, this one wrapped in shiny gold paper and topped with a dark blue bow. Her mother said she'd sent a present, and despite Alison's prodding, refused to give out any details other than that.

A tiny notecard affixed by the bow read:

Alison,

I found these and couldn't resist. I know your birthday is still a month away, but I'd like to take you to dinner that night, if you think you're up to it.

Love,

Mom

Inside the box, beneath a mound of tissue paper, she found a pair of pink flannel pajamas adorned with smiling cat faces. They were completely silly and utterly fantastic. Beneath the pajamas was a dress. She held it against her; the rich blue fabric hung in folds, and the cut would cover most of her scars. Then she spied a smaller box, half-hidden in the paper with another note attached.

I read some good things about this and thought you might want to try it. If not, throw it out and we'll never speak of it again.

She immediately recognized the brand name of the makeup. Her mother had mentioned it once before. She'd snapped back that it wouldn't help and refused to listen to anything else about it, but that was before she understood that being whole meant acceptance, not wallowing in a stinking vat of self-pity. The makeup came with a compact of setting powder. She held it in her hands, turning it over and over. Unhinged the clasp, caught a glimpse of the mirror within, and snapped it shut.

She thought of the girl in the hospital and the nurse with the mirror. She remembered how it felt to see what she'd become; how her world crumbled, how she fell apart.

But she wasn't that girl anymore.

The scars were every bit as terrible as she remembered. She dropped the compact in her lap and cried into her hands. When her tears were spent, she took a deep breath, and tried again. This time, the scars were not nearly as terrible as she feared. She was still human, still of worth, still Alison. Not a Monstergirl. Simply someone who'd been in a terrible accident.

● ● ●

In the picture, the wig was close to her natural hair color, and Alison held her lower lip between her teeth. The wig was expensive, and although synthetic, it resembled real hair far more than the cheaper options. She tapped the edge of her laptop, exhaled through her nose, and placed the order. If it looked terrible, she could always send it back and try another one.

Then she heard the rolling noise overhead. She cocked her head to the side, listening. Sometimes the heating vents rattled, but this sound was oddly rhythmic. It grew louder and as she got up from the sofa, a new noise took its place. An almost metallic tap. Then another. Coming from the stairs, coming *down* the stairs.

She cupped her elbows in her palms and crossed the room. The tap came again. She didn't want to look because it was the sound of something wrong, but she was neither coward nor child, and although she'd run from the ghosts and the tiger, she wouldn't run from a sound in her own house. She would *not*.

The old-fashioned round glass eye traveled up and down in an improbable arc, the same height each time, as it bounced down the steps. With each bounce, it spun to reveal a flash of iris, a glimpse of pupil. Never mind that she threw it away; never mind that it should not be in her house; never mind that it should not *be* at all.

From deep within the tapping sound, the tiger's voice said, "Do you see me? I see you? Come back so we can *all* see you."

She backed away from the stairs as the eye bounced off the last step, rolled in a wide circle, and came to a stop at the edge of the landing, hovering without a wobble with the iris-side facing out. Facing her.

If she picked it up and put it in, would it tease her by taking the scars away? She thought it would. If it held enough glamour to come back, it would hold enough glamour to make her feel whole. At least for a moment or two. A final bite from the tiger to say, "See what you gave up?"

With a snarl twisting her mouth, she put on her snow boots, gloves, a warm coat, and a scarf and grabbed the eye.

"We're still here and we're waiting," it said.

She shoved it deep in her pocket and the voice turned to muffled nonsense.

"Go back wherever you came from and leave me the hell alone," she said.

She trudged out into the slushy snow as the last traces of the day bled into the night. Wind chimes pealed a jangle of music into the growing dark, and her skin broke out in goosebumps.

Her cheeks burned but she kept on, neither counting her steps nor giving the street signs anything but cursory glances. A few people hurried by, but they paid no attention to the

Monstergirl

girl bundled against the cold because they had their own paths to make, their own ways to go.

I have miles to go before I weep. Before I scream.

A knot grew in the center of her chest and the air pushed a cold trail deep into her lungs. Dimly, she heard her mother saying, "Slow down. You'll make yourself sick," but it might have been her own voice playing charades. Either way, she didn't slow down.

Pausing to catch her breath, she wasn't surprised to find herself standing in front of Elena's Antiques. Every ending had a beginning; every beginning had to end.

At the end of the block she turned into an alley awash in weak yellow light from the lamp on the corner. Not bothering to keep her steps quiet, she splashed dirty snow this way and that.

Finally, she reached the back of Elena's stupid store of useless junk. There were no windows, only a wide wall of brick. A row of trash bags sat next to the back door, and she caught a whiff of wet paper and old food. She fished the eye from her pocket.

"Come back and—"

She didn't let it finish, but put all her weight into an overhand throw. The eye whistled through the air, carrying one word along its path.

"...see..."

It struck the brick, and she held her breath, waiting for it to bounce off and land in the snow near the trash bags. And maybe roll back to her feet. Would it be a surprise? No more than it rolling down her stairs had been.

But the eye shattered with a sharp tinkle of glittering glass. The pieces fell down, pattered on the plastic bags, and tumbled into the snow. Alison shoved her hands in her pockets and watched until the muck swallowed every last one.

● ● ●

Covered with makeup, a scarf worn Audrey Hepburn-style, and a turtleneck with sleeves long enough to cover half her fingers (at least she had fingers and hands and not bloody stumps), Alison sat with her mother at a small neighborhood café. They'd come well after the lunch rush, and their table in the back, away from the windows, was one of only three that were occupied.

She held the menu in her hands, but ribbons of violet lashed at her insides and blurred the words. She told herself having lunch in a café, in public, was the reason, and yes, perhaps it held some of the blame, but not all. The bigger reason was the question in her mind, the question she'd avoided last night.

How did the eye come back?

It didn't fall out of the trash bag and roll its way back into her house. It wasn't even real. But the weight of it in her pocket had been real enough along with the way the glass shattered. If it could come back, could something else from the paper world do the same? What about the torn piece of photo? Perhaps it hadn't fallen from her hand. Perhaps it, too, had returned. And if so—

"Alison?"

She put down the menu. "Yes?"

"You didn't even hear what I said, did you?"

"No, sorry, Mom. I was trying to decide what I want."

"Is everything okay?" The skin between her mother's brow creased. "You have circles under your eyes."

There was no need for her mother to ask that question. Of course everything was okay. She'd had a restless night. She was allowed to have a restless night. It was the eye's fault, not hers. And now she'd taken care of that. Broken bits of glass couldn't roll and bounce down her stairs.

Perhaps she should tell her mom what happened and as an aside, add the rest of the story, tigers and all. Then she wouldn't ask if everything was okay. She'd be on the phone calling Dr. Simon and perhaps discussing medication or a lengthy hospital stay because anyone who thought they could go inside a photo album must be delusional.

Tell that to the tiger. Or the eye, for that matter.

Something must have shown on her face, because her mother drew back and offered a tentative smile. "You seem distracted, that's all."

"No, I'm fine."

Her mother gave a small nod. "Are you okay, being here? We can go if you like."

"No. I don't want to go."

The lie left a bad taste in her mouth.

Alison tipped her chin down as a busboy filled their water glasses. After he left, her mother leaned forward.

"The makeup looks very nice. You can barely see it."

Alison smiled on the outside and cringed on the in.

● ● ●

The next night, after a long bath, Alison wrapped herself in pajamas and robe and padded downstairs on slippered feet. When she stepped into the kitchen, the stink of rotting flowers overpowered her, flooding her mouth with the taste of dead petals and rancid water.

And there on the counter sat the photo album with its cover open in an unspoken invitation. She backed into the doorway, both hands over her mouth. Bile rose in her throat.

The album...

no

The album was...

no

The album was back. Tiny hitching moans crept from between her fingers and could she hear it calling her name? Yes, yes, of course.

"Alison, come back," it said. "We're waiting."

Her heart pounding, she moved closer, not wanting to, but unable to resist because it called, oh how it called, and she stepped closer still. She closed her eyes tight. If the album had magicked its way back to her, drawn mothlike to her

pain

flame in the same way she'd been drawn into its false promises, maybe she could send it away again.

"I don't need you anymore," she said. "I don't want you."

She envisioned white calm. White peace. Nothing inside her but white. When she opened her eyes, the album remained.

Tears gathered in the corner of her eye, but only the one, because only one was a good eye, the other was still an empty socket disguised with a painted piece of plastic—

Stop, a voice commanded, all fury and scarlet.

She took a deep breath, then another. She had to get rid of the album. For good, this time.

And what if it comes back again? Purple said.

She laughed, a harsh, brittle sound. "It won't. Not this time." She pulled out her rubber gloves and a pair of scissors, the blades shiny-sharp in the light.

"Please come back," the album said, in Thomas' voice.

"Say all you want. You're a liar like the rest of them," Alison muttered.

The inscription on the first page was a smear of indigo again. She aimed her first cut at the corner, her fingers awkward inside the glove. The paper resisted the scissor's blades, creasing instead of splitting. She stripped off the glove, bit her bottom lip, and gripped the handle of the scissors tighter. The blades met with a small snick and a triangle shaped piece gave way.

"Come back, come back," the album wailed. This time, Mary's voice sang out, innocent and sweet.

Alison snipped off another piece, and the inscription on the album changed, the letters darkening into view.

"Please, Alison, come back," Mary said again, weeping. "I'm scared."

"I can't help you. You're dead."

With her lips pressed together tight, Alison wielded the scissors again. She attacked the paper, the blades flashing and snapping as they ate away the words, and in a few minutes, the page was a small pile of ink-stained scraps on the counter.

Breathing hard, she looked down at George's face. His eyes were no longer somber. Rage hid inside. A fury to match her own. She lifted the scissors high and stabbed his photo. One blade went through his eye, the other his cheek. A grey swirl of smoke stung her eye, and she brushed it away. She cut and cut and cut, absolute destruction her only goal. More smoke curled into the air. A distant roar of anger competed with her harsh breaths. Crimson burned bright within her chest.

A filmy cloud hovered over the page, her fingers and hand aching, but she didn't stop. She cut until George was gone, nudged the pieces out of the way, and started on the next photo—the house. The photo gave off a dead flower stink, the rose bushes in front drooped, the petals withered, and butterflies lay dead on the ground below.

She cut through the tall windows of the top floor turret room first and the sound of breaking glass held a musical trill. *Snip-crack, snip-crack.* A few more cuts and the house appeared a victim of some strange decapitation.

"Come, Josephine," she sang, her voice all rusty nails and rapid breaths.

When she sliced the front door in two, a discordant ring sounded, dying as the paper separated. She set the scissors down. Flexed her stiff fingers.

The pages rustled, lifted, and separated. Color burst forth, the tiger discarding its sepia cloak to show her so much more. Voices swirled. Whispers, pleas, begging, hatred. The growl of the tiger.

And the photos:

Rachel, her arms outstretched, bloody stumps gaping like red mouths with white bone screams tucked inside. The smell of copper bright metallic.

"Please help me."

Thomas on the floor, a crawling, pitiful thing. A reek of human waste, a broken heart, and regret.

"Alison?"

Madeline, curled in a bed, her mouth parted in seduction, her limbs gnarled and twisted. The scent of lust and sweaty flesh.

"I was first."

Josephine, a wraith, her bones clearly defined beneath her skin. A foul odor of vomit.

"I'll eat this time, I promise I will."

And more:

Edmund, on the floor, blood leaking from his mouth, a poisonous stink seeping from his pores.

"I don't know what's wrong with me."

Eleanor in a bundle of mangled limbs at the bottom of the staircase. A woman weeping salt tears of sorrow.

"Someone call the doctor!"

Elizabeth, marble pale and still, in her tiny bed. A dark cloud of illness and despair beneath a powdery hint of talc.

"Mommy?"

William, on his back in a small cradle, his fists making frantic circles in the air.

No words, only the pitiful sounds of choking.

And Mary, a circlet of bruises around her neck, a stuffed bear at her side.

"George, no. Stop. Please stop. You're hurting me."

The house, grey and shadowed. Old boxes in damp rooms.

"Come back."

The house, burned and broken. Charred wood and heavy smoke.

"Come back."

The last photo—the clock. Spiderwebs nearly covering its face. The wood scratched. The glass cracked.

"COME BACK! COME BACK NOW!"

And underneath it all, the stink of mildew, rot, and decay.

A chorus of children's voices rang out, sweetly singing, far off in the distance. "One, two, three, tigers at a time, four, five, six, tigers in a line, seven, eight nine, stripes in the night, and when it's ten, the tigers bite!"

Alison picked up the scissors again, her smile a lunatic's grin. Blisters erupted on her skin. Blood dripped on the counter and the floor and turned the handles of the scissors slick as the blades tore at the pages and cut away the faces, the smells, the voices, the tiger's low, rumbling growl.

And when she finally lifted the scissors away again, the cover lay open. An eviscerated paper corpse, its pages a pile of ruin.

"I got you."

She put the scissors back in the drawer, bloody handles and all, grabbed a knife, and started on the cover, gouging and digging. A tendril of grey rose, hovered in the air, then sputtered out, leaving behind the stink of smoke and char. The knife slid and bit back into her skin, but of course she didn't feel it (no feeling, no feeling at all for the Monstergirl), and she ignored the blood that dripped down onto the paper.

She slashed and stabbed hard enough to leave marks in the counter beneath, raising her hand high and bringing it down and down, over and over again, each movement punctuated with "got you, got you, got you" until she'd reduced the cover to shreds of cracked leather and cardboard. She dropped the knife into the sink and held her aching hand, all swollen and red with a gaping wet mouth in the center of her palm, close to her chest, ignoring the blood spattering her shirt and the stink of sweat pushing out from her skin. She laughed until tears poured down her cheek, and when the laughter wound down to a hiccup, she fought against specks of light dancing in her vision, and wrapped paper towels around her hand. Roses bloomed on the white, and a throbbing sensation, not quite pain, hummed underneath her skin. Another wave of dizziness hit; a sharp stab of nausea sent her leaning over the sink, breathing through her mouth until it passed. She splashed cold water on her face, and the paper towels on her hand became a soggy pink mitten. Then she grinned at the chaos on her counter.

I did it. I really did it. I destroyed it.

You annihilated *it*, Red said. And was Red smiling? Yes, indeed, grinning a cherry ice cream smile with all her might. And useless Purple, the voice of fear?

Gone again.

Alison swept some of the pieces into a trash bag and knotted it tight. More pieces went into another bag and more still into another. She ended up with five bags, all tied tight. Her kitchen reeked of blood, sweat, and vile.

Unwrapping her hand, she poked at the wound. Possibly, probably, deep enough for stitches, but she had peroxide and butterfly bandages. They'd have to do. But later. She had more important things to take care of first.

She shed her robe for a coat, boot, and gloves, knotted a scarf under her chin and headed out her back door with the bags hoisted over one shoulder. She kept her steps light as she went through the back gate. At the end of the alley, she deposited a bag in someone's yard, replacing the trash can's lid as quietly as possible. She crossed into another alley, picked another yard at random, and disposed of the second bag. The third went into a trash can a block away, and as she lowered the lid, a door opened in a nearby house and out darted a small, barking ball of fluff. She dropped the lid and retreated into the shadows.

The fourth went into a dumpster behind the café where she'd lunched with her mother. Cold and tired, with her nose running and eye watering, Alison carried the last at her side until she came upon a pile, some split and leaking their contents of waste and rot, at the end of yet another alley.

"I got you," she said, and a gust of wind carried her voice away, out into the night.

CHAPTER 22

Come cry, child.

Alison pecked out the words on her keyboard and flexed her hands. Dried blood crusted the wound on her palm; butterfly bandages held the edges together. She smiled, not minding the way the skin stretched. Her new poetry held a different flavor. A little more hope. A little less self-pity.

Tick.

Her brow creased. Her fingers hovered over the keys. The tiny noise did not return. She added a few more lines to her poem, her fingers moving far slower than the words in her head. After she wrote the last line, she nodded and stood, rubbing away the stiffness in her lower back. A few stretches later, she took her empty glass into the kitchen, turned on the faucet, and heard the tick again.

It didn't sound like a laptop or house noise. It sounded like a clock, but the only clock in her kitchen was the one on the microwave and it didn't tick. Water spilled over her hand into the sink and she fumbled for the tap while a snippet of rhyme played in her head: Hickory dickory dock. By the tick of the clock.

The heat whooshed on. She crossed her arms over chest and let out a ragged laugh. Nothing but house noise.

■ ■ ■

Alison was reading in bed when she heard the soft thump of footsteps. She dropped the book on her lap. The sound came again, someone in heavy shoes trying to keep his steps light.

She fumbled on her nightstand for her phone, her mouth dry and her hands trembling. Her fingers met only the rounded edge of her alarm clock and the base of the lamp.

The footsteps paced back and forth.

A few months back, there'd been several break-ins in the neighborhood, but those happened during the day when the homeowners were at work. The thief hadn't been caught, but after a time, the break-ins stopped.

She slid out of bed. She wouldn't stay put and wait for the thief to creep into her room. A floorboard creaked under her foot. She froze in place, but the steps didn't change to a shout or a rush up the stairs. With tiny steps, she crept into the hallway, her fingers shaking. The switch operated both the upstairs hallway light and one in the living room.

She didn't own a gun or a baseball bat, didn't know martial arts, and didn't have a phone handy. The fire extinguisher hanging on the wall would work as a weapon, but she doubted she had the necessary strength. The only thing she could do was lock herself in the bathroom or her bedroom and scream, hopefully catching her neighbors' attention. But maybe...

Maybe they didn't think anyone was home. Maybe they'd run away. And if not, she could get in the bathroom and lock the door before anyone could run up the stairs.

She flipped the switch. The footsteps ceased. Then she smelled tobacco. She staggered back, shaking her head, her hand still outstretched. No, no.

Hearing things, I'm only hearing things. No one is downstairs. No one. Not George, not anyone. And he can't be here. He. Isn't. Real.

She glanced over her shoulder, toward her bedroom. No, she

wouldn't run and hide. She headed downstairs, one hand tight on the railing. By the time she hit the landing, the smell was gone.

And her living room was empty.

A grey smudge on the floor near the window caught her eye. An oval at one end, a line at the other. The mark of a man's shoe? And on the windowsill, a dusty handprint, too large to be hers, with five fingers, not three. A hollow cry escaped from her lips.

George was here.

No, it wasn't possible. He was a ghost, trapped inside the album, the ruined album. He could not be in her house. He could not.

Unless he'd escaped from his paper cage. What if, by destroying the album, she'd set him free?

She stood in her living room for a long time, her thoughts chaos and storm. Finally, she removed the marks with the edge of her sleeve.

She could call her mother, stay with her for a few days, but what tale would she spin? She was afraid of ghosts that went bump in the night? And staying there didn't guarantee that he would go away.

If he was even out. Maybe she was hearing things.

"George?" she said, her voice loud in the quiet, and if it held a tremble of fear, it was understandable given the circumstances. "If you're here, I'm not afraid of you. Do you hear me? I'm not afraid."

But her hands wouldn't stop shaking.

* * *

When her mother called three days later, Alison was sitting on the edge of the sofa, putting on her boots. Those three days had been free from the hint of tobacco, the sound of footsteps, and the death-knell of a ticking clock. Those three days also held sleeping with her bedroom door locked, her phone in one hand, jumping at every shadow, and wincing every time the heat turned on or off.

"Hi, babygirl. It isn't too late, is it?"

"Not at all. I was getting ready to go for a walk." Balancing the phone between her cheek and shoulder, Alison fastened the laces into double knots.

"Tonight? But it's freezing outside."

"I'm bundling up. Trust me."

"I wish…"

"Wish what?"

"Well, I wish you'd let me get you a cell phone. It would make—"

"Okay."

"What? You're sure?"

"I'm not going to stop taking walks anytime soon, and while I don't plan on falling, it would be good to have one just in case."

"I'll pick one up this weekend. Is that okay?"

"Of course. And then maybe we can talk about my birthday, if you still want to take me out to dinner, that is."

A long pause, then her mother asked, "Really?"

"Yes, really."

Her mother replied with a quiet sob.

"No crying, okay? Please?"

"I'm just very, very proud of you."

"I know," Alison said, carrying her empty mug into the kitchen. "But…" How to explain that it made it so much harder when she made a big deal out of everything without hurting her feelings?

"I can make a reservation tomorrow. Do you want seafood or maybe steak? There's that nice place near you that renovated and—"

She caught a flash of movement from the corner of her eye and spun around, her mug crashing to the floor in a scatter of porcelain shards.

"Alison, what was that? Are you okay?"

"I'm fine. I just dropped a mug and it broke all over the floor. Let me go and clean up this mess and we can talk more about everything later."

"Okay. I love you."

"Love you, too."

Alison curled her hand tightly around the phone and her boots crunched the porcelain to powder. Nothing moved in her dining room or living room. Nothing smelled out of place, either.

Even with her steps light, her boots made small tapping noises on the stairs. She rifled through the clothes in her bedroom closet with one hand. Checked behind the curtains. Bent on her good knee and peered underneath the bed.

There's no one here, my dear.

Once sure her bedroom was empty, she shut the door. For the spare bedroom, she did the same. The closet in her hallway contained the expected sheets and towels. In the bathroom, the only place someone could hide was the bathtub, concealed behind the shower curtain.

No one here…

Her shower curtain, a dark navy patterned with swirls of coppery-brown, hung perfectly still. One quick glance, that's all it would take and yet, yet, what would she do if George stood behind the curtain, a pipe in one hand, the other reaching out to grab her and take her back? She could scream all she wanted. By the time anyone came to investigate, she'd be back in Pennington House, her memories slowly slipping away, dancing through a false party of promises while her body wasted away, feeding the tiger, turning paper to real.

…but fear, my dear.

With a grunt, she pulled back the curtain, the hooks clattering across the metal bar, and inside, no George, no ghostly hands, only porcelain white, shampoo, and bath gel. She sagged back against the sink, breathing hard, and scrubbed her face with her hands.

She left the shower curtain and bathroom door open when she went back downstairs. Halfway down the steps, a shadow flitted across the wall, darkening the pale paint, and as it overlapped hers, a cold chill worked its way from the back of her neck to the soles of her feet. She let out a breathy cry and held tight to the railing.

The cold ceased as the human shaped silhouette continued further down. Alison thumped down the staircase as it swept a trail across the front wall, through her sofa, across the floor, stretching and elongating along the way.

She took a deep breath and followed as it went into the dining room and stopped in the middle, a blur of darkness on the wood, only a foot away from the tip of her boots. With a gust of cold in its wake, the darkness raced across the floor into the kitchen, over the tile, the face of the cabinets, the edge of the counter, and down into the photo album waiting there.

Alison came to a halt in the doorway, and her jaw went slack.

"No, oh, no. I threw you away."

But there it sat, whole and waiting.

"I *destroyed* you."

The cover flipped open with a heavy thud, a puff of grey rising from the pages. Alison covered her mouth and shrieked behind her hands. And from the album came an answering laugh, a low, rumbling chuckle. Without another thought, Alison put on her coat and fled from her house, leaving the album behind.

● ● ●

The cold turned her breath to icy gasps and reddened her cheeks. She blinked back tears before they could freeze into ice pearls on her lashes. Smoke plumed from chimneys; warm yellow light peeked around curtains and blinds. Her footsteps sloshed and splashed as she limped through snowmelt turned dark from exhaust. No one walked the streets save her. She tucked her gloveless hands deep into her pockets.

With her cheeks burning, she approached the drugstore, the same one where she'd hid in the vestibule. The OPEN sign cast red and blue lights on the pavement. She paused as the lights flashed over her boots, then pushed through the doors. The girl behind the counter didn't even bother to look up from her magazine.

Seeing, but not seeing, Alison wandered through the aisles on heavy feet turned zombie slow until she came upon a display of fireplace matches, faux quick-burning logs, and lighter fluid. Maybe scissors weren't enough. She held out her Monstergirl hands. In the fluorescent lighting, her scars were garish, the crosshatch pattern a grisly reminder of pain, suffering, and destruction.

No, you can't do this. Find another way, anything but this.

She extended a hand.

There is no other way. This way, you'll be sure. Fire destroys.

The matches rattled inside the box. "It destroys everything," she said. She turned the box over in her hand and an orange and black striped cat's face peered back from atop the brand name—Tiger Matches. A portent or random coincidence? She choked back a laugh and took two bottles of lighter fluid from the shelf. It didn't matter. The name was fitting. She smiled.

She could do this. She *would* do this. And then she'd be free.

● ● ●

Her house reeked of tobacco. She dropped her bags on the floor and stripped off her coat and boots, ignoring the pool of scummy water spreading out across the wood. With her mouth set in a thin line, she put the lighter fluid and matches in the center of her coffee table—a tiny shrine of immolation—and after a moment's thought, added the fire extinguisher she kept next to the sofa.

The album still sat on the counter, the cover open.

A tiny voice slipped out. "Alison?"

And another. "Help us."

Then a chorus.

"Please."

"Come back."

"Don't you want to be whole?"

Using the edge of a spoon, she flipped the cover closed, and swirls of grey curled out.

"You can't fool me," she said. "I know what's really inside. And I am whole."

She took a quick trip into the basement and flipped the lid to the small toolbox her mother insisted on buying her so long ago. "You might need it," she'd said. "Every homeowner should have one."

Alison dug out a claw hammer and a pair of heavy duty gloves.

"Please," the album said again when she returned. Alison gave it her middle finger but didn't bother with a glance. It was nothing but a paper mess of tricks and lies, and soon enough it would be nothing in truth.

One dead album. One dead tiger.

In her living room, she took the books off the bookcase in the corner and slid it away from the wall. Only the slate hearth offered proof to what existed behind; both the mantel and surround had been removed. She gave the wall a quick rap of the knuckles. A hollow echo answered.

The gloves were too large for her hands and two of the fingers hung like empty canvas shrouds, but they'd suffice. She hefted the hammer and let it swing. The claw end stuck in the wall. She tugged and a piece of drywall the size of a fist came free with a crumbling, tearing sound and a mess of paint flakes and powder. If her mother had the workmen use brick and mortar, she'd be burning the album in her kitchen sink or her bathtub. Not a pleasant thought. She ripped out another chunk of drywall and laughed. Her mother would call it progress. She lifted the hammer again.

Do you hear that, George? That's the sound of goodbye.

She laughed again.

You will not win. I will not let you have me.

And again, grunting with each swing. The thuds hid the voices creeping out of the kitchen on quiet little insistent feet. Wisps of hair dangled in her eyes, her mouth tasted bitter and dry, and her fingers ached, but she didn't stop, because George wouldn't stop. Not ever. He'd decided she was the prize-winning photograph in his collection and he wanted to keep her forever.

But we won't let that happen, Red said. *Will we?*

"No," she said, tearing away another piece of drywall. "We won't."

Dust spiraled into the air, turning the gloves and the skin of her arms ghostly pale. Bit by bit, the brick fireplace came into view, a gaping mouth still darkened with soot at the edges from the previous owners. She shoved the pile of rubble to the side. Her fingers trembled as she groped in the chimney's dark throat for the lever that operated the flue. She remembered her mother telling her that they'd closed the flue, but hadn't sealed it shut. Another pinch of luck on her part.

The lever didn't budge. She stripped off the glove and tried again. Sweat broke out on the small of her back as she used her body weight, but the flue wouldn't give. She sat back on her heels, her hands on the brick, breath rasping in and out. Her stupid ruined hands weren't strong enough. *She* wasn't strong enough.

Not true. You are stronger than you ever suspected. Don't you dare give up now.

And from the kitchen. "Alison, help us..."

With a groan, she grabbed the lever again and shoved with all her might. "Open up, open up, damn you!"

Metal squealed, the lever moved, and a cold draft raced down the chimney.

She scrubbed her hands on her pants and swiped her arm across her forehead.

And now for the tricky part, she thought as she tiptoed back in the kitchen. She pawed through her kitchen drawer, but forks and spoons would offer no help. She didn't dare pick up the album, not even with the gloves. She picked up a knife and smiled.

"Alison, please…"

"Do me a favor and shut the hell up," she said.

She lifted the knife and swung it down in horror movie villain style. The blade went through the center of the cover and cut off a voice in mid-syllable. Smoke dripped from the album's wound, running over the cover and off the edge of the counter. She grinned. A warrior baring her teeth. Preparing for battle.

With both hands on the handle, she lifted the knife, carrying the album into the living room at arm's length, speared and silent. More smoke poured out, trailing behind like an ashen wedding veil. Or a funeral cerement.

She shook the album into the fireplace, and it landed with a thump, a puff of smoke, and a husky whisper. "We're waiting."

"Wait all you want." The grin on her face pulled hard at the scar tissue.

The cover flipped open, and her grin faltered. "Oh, no you don't," she said, and upended a bottle of lighter fluid on the album, eye watering at the sharp, oily stink. The inscription, the warning, darkened, the lettering almost black; the parchment turned slick and translucent with rainbows of iridescence reflecting from the overhead light. She glanced at the second bottle. No, one should be enough. She could always pour more if she needed to.

"Alison," Mary shouted. "Please help me!"

She rattled the box of matches. Nails for George's coffin. And perhaps the others, but she couldn't help them anymore. Death would be better than their tortured existence. But guilt worked its way into her chest. Mary and Thomas and all the others, even Madeline. She held their ending in her hands, but it wasn't her fault. None of it. She didn't kill them. He did.

Her fingers trembled as she took out a match. When she slid the head across the striker panel, the match skittered from her hand and landed on the floor.

"Come on, you can do this."

She tightened her grip on the second match before flicking it to life with a snick and a sulfur stink. The tiny flame danced and darted, bright yellow with a blue heart. A hungry heart of danger and destruction, blackened skin and pain. She blew it out.

Stop being so afraid. Destroy it. Kill it. And do it fast.

"I'm sorry," she said and lit another match.

She held her breath as she bent down and tossed the match in the fireplace. It flipped end over end, the flame sputtering. A chorus of voices begged and pleaded. Then the fumes caught hold of the flame. With a whoosh, the album disappeared behind a curtain of orange, red, and yellow, a ripple of heat pushing out from the fireplace. She staggered back, her mouth ripe with the taste of burning paper. Clouds of thick black smoke billowed up, accompanied by an overpowering stench of rot and ruin. Alison covered her mouth with her hands and scooted away from the blaze. She heard a laugh, far in the distance.

And the flames stopped. The roar cut off, plunging the room into silence. A cloud of dark smoke hung motionless over the blaze. Even the breath in her lungs paused, as though time had put down its weary head and cried enough. The air smelled not of smoke and charred paper but of nothing at all.

The flames began to shrink, the colors going pale as the roiling mass folded in, folded down, reversing back to small flickering points of blue-orange-red-yellow light. The heat lessened; the smoke surged in instead of up and out and turned from black to charcoal to steel.

The fire retreated until tiny glimmers of heatlight played across the paper. They rolled off the edges, dancing away to evaporate in the air with tiny soap-bubble pops. A trail of pale smoke backtracked, raced back into the album, and vanished with a puff of grey. The last tiny flame danced across the cover before winking out of existence. A faint haze of heat hung in the air, then that, too, vanished, leaving behind the stink of lighter fluid and a low, malevolent rumble of laughter.

Alison put her head in her hands and groaned against her palms. The tiger would never let her go.

PART IX

A PAPER TIGER TO
SWALLOW YOU WHOLE

*Jonathan kisses her mouth, then says against her cheek, "I promise I
won't be long."
She shivers.*

"What's wrong?" he asks.

*"Nothing." She smiles, but suddenly she wants to tell him to stay with
her, forget the friends waiting in the car outside. Then she pushes it
away. He won't be long, after all. She'll read a book while he's out and
when he comes back, there will be time enough for love.*

Time enough and forever.

"I love you," he says.

"I love you, too."

"Forever," he says.

*Then he's gone and tears gather in the corners of her eyes. He'll be
back soon enough, she knows, but a strange, dark little fear gathers in
her heart.*

CHAPTER 23

Alison tucked her knees to her chin, not caring that the skin pulled. He knew he'd won. No matter what she did, no matter what she tried, the album would keep coming back until she gave up, gave in, and went back inside. She stretched out her hands, her scarred fingers broken soldiers in a secret war of shame. Was it such a bad thing, the want, the need, to be something close to normal? When you were whole, no one looked. No one stared.

Fresh tears coursed down her cheek.

Stop it. This is what he wants. Don't give in. There has to be a way to destroy it. There is always a way.

She crawled to the fireplace, her hip aching. Despite the flames and smoke, the album did not have one scorch mark, one stain, anything to show she'd set it afire.

"Come back," it said.

"I hate you," she said.

You have to destroy it from the inside.

"Why me?"

Because you opened the cage and let the tiger out.

She glanced at the bottle of lighter fluid. Could she possibly go in, start a fire, and leave without being trapped inside? No one would come and save her if she couldn't get free. An image darted through her mind: hungry flames inching their way across the floor, screams as the fire touched her skin, burning her up, roasting meat and singed hair—

"No, anything but that."

She scrubbed her face with her hands. Could she go in, pour the lighter fluid on the floor, and wait until the clock chimed before she lit the match? That would—should—give her enough time to leave. But what if she forgot who she was when she went in? Would she remember what to do? And what if the house wouldn't burn from the inside, either?

You have to try something.

"I *have* tried. Nothing works."

So try again.

She stuck the box of matches in the waistband of her pants, grabbed the lighter fluid, and kneeled on the edge of the hearth, the slate cold even through her pants. She extended her hand. Yanked it back with a sharp exhale.

"I can't do this."

Then he's already won.

The air grew heavy. A haze blurred the edges of her vision. Music notes trilled in the air, and a vapor-pale hand reached through the inscription and seized her forearm. Her eyes said ghost, the grip on her arm said real, her head said George. Bone-deep cold traveled through her skin, stealing the scream from her mouth and the scars from her hand, each line, each mark erasing itself, leaving whole in its wake, with a scratching, re-knitting sensation. Five fingers moved where once there had been three. Five desperate fingers twisted to break free, the two newcomers behaving as though they'd been there all along.

The flow of healthy skin didn't stop with her hands. It crept to her wrist, the skin tingling as the scars melted into smooth, then to the elbow, then to her shoulder, down her back, across her chest, curving down to her hips and last, sliding over her neck and chin to her cheek and scalp.

She pulled her arm back with all her weight, but the fingers dug in hard; the cold, harder still. George's fingers darkened, mottled with spots. She reached with her left hand to pry them free, but her fingers passed through the ghost skin, touching her own beneath.

A forearm broke the surface of the paper, a grim periscope, the white of his sleeve a mere suggestion of color.

"You *will* come back," George said.

And inside, the music played, the voices spoke, the tiger beckoned. George's fingers tightened even more.

"You can't have me," she cried out.

"You. Are. Mine."

Her skin prickled with pins and needles, painful and sharp, digging from the inside out. More of his arm broke through the album. A shimmering shape of an arm, but with every hair, pore, and fingernail clearly defined. Dark spots like dead roses painted on canvas moved across his grey skin.

Her knees slid on the slate tile, her fingers only inches away from the paper. The sharp edges of his now-real fingernails made half-moon bruises on her skin. She tugged her arm hard, and one of the marks opened, spilling out a line of red. Another hand broke free from the paper world; the fingertips curved against the page. He wasn't trying to pull her in. He was using her to pry himself out. She shoved against the arm holding hers.

"Oh no you will not," she said.

He laughed in reply. She twisted her arm back and forth, pain raking her skin. The small gash on her arm widened, joined by another. She twisted again. His nails sliced new marks, but his icy fingers slipped on the blood-slick flesh. With a shout, she wrenched her arm back. His hand slipped again, but she was almost free.

Then he renewed his grip. Too strong. He was too strong. Inside her, Purple screamed, Red raged, and Yellow sobbed.

George's fingers grabbed hold of the edge of the fireplace. The top of his head broke free, his dark hair obscuring the inscription. The image blurred and she swayed on her knees. His head rose even more, all the way to the brow line. She smacked at the image, the flat of her palm striking only the album.

The air tightened. Cold gathered weight. She struck out again, and her hand met a hard curve of bone, the slick of hair, not the album. She grabbed for the knife, but her hand hit the handle too hard and it spun away out of reach. She straightened one leg, pressed her foot against the edge of the fireplace for leverage, and shoved her upper body forward then lunged back, and his hand slipped from her arm. Her scars came marching back in, no need for stealth. They slammed back into her flesh, ripping the breath from her lungs.

George's hands paled to an outline of rippling light, slipping back into the album, and he roared, all fury and hatred. The weight of his attempt at freedom had forced the album hard against the fireplace's concrete interior, and her fingers, her stupid, awkward fingers, could not feel, could not pull it free. Her pulse thumped in her ears. Her breath raced in and out.

Footsteps sounded in the distance, heavy with purpose, and a wisp of fragrant smoke rose from the center of the album.

Scraping her skin against the brick, she hooked one finger under the edge of the album cover. It slipped free. With a shriek of frustration, she shoved her finger underneath the corner until she loosened it enough to lift it up and over. The cover crashed down. The album shook with the reverberation.

"Leave me alone," she said. "Just let me go."

And from far away, George's voice came in reply. "Never."

* * *

Alison scooted back several feet (best not to keep your back to a tiger) and sat with her left leg curled beneath her, and her scarred leg straight.

"One, two, three, tigers at a time," she sang under her breath.

Soft voices offered sweet lies disguised as promises. She ignored them all.

"Four, five, six, tigers in a line."

George would never leave her alone, not until he had what he wanted.

"Seven, eight, nine, stripes in the night."

Not until he used her to get what he wanted.

"And when it's ten, the tigers bite."

And he desired what any caged animal wanted: freedom.

"And they bite and bite and bite."

More than that, he wanted to be real, and he had been, for an instant before she broke contact. She'd hit his head and his arm—real flesh, not a paper mirage. She'd done it. She'd made him real.

She fetched the knife and smiled scarlet. If she did it once, she could do it again, and in the real world, tigers could be killed.

● ● ●

She poked the edge of the album with the knife.

"I know you're there, George."

The voices within stilled. A heaviness grew in the air.

"I'm tired of fighting," she said, the weariness in her voice unfeigned.

She hid the knife behind her back and flipped open the cover. Inside, she was white and still and calm, an empty canvas. On her hands and knees in front of the fireplace, she held her left hand over the page.

"Please let this work."

George's arm burst from the center of the page, the tip of one shimmering finger a hair's breadth away from her own. She bridged the gap between them and curled her fingers around his wrist, recoiling as the cold stole her scars away again.

And in that touch, the tricks and the glamour, the lies and the
darkness, peeled back to reveal the truth. He existed only through
an album filled with images of his precious house, now his tomb, a
thing fattened on sorrow, suffering, and woe. Like a caged tiger no
one remembered to feed, he'd withered away to a pathetic nothing,
surrounded by the ghosts of his making. Desperate to break free
from the prison of his paper construct, he needed her far more than
she needed his illusion of magic.

Alison smiled. It was time to close the door forever to Pennington House.

Once her hand was whole, five fingers tightened around the
knife and held it sure and steady. She tightened her hold on his
wrist, pulling, luring, him out. His other hand broke free, grey, hazy
fingers coming to rest on the hearth just past the concrete interior.
His head emerged, neck bisected by the parchment. He opened his
mouth, but all that escaped was a soft push of frigid air. He frowned.
Both hands pushed, and his shoulders materialized, the only sound
a slight rustling of paper. Another push and his chest slipped out.
He leaned forward to pull the rest of his torso free. Halfway out of
the album, halfway out of the fireplace. Voices distorted in pain and
fear slid into the air.

"Don't leave me," Madeline cried.

A choking sob. "I'll play another song. I promise."

"You promised I'd be whole. You said forever."

"Please," Thomas shouted. "Don't leave me like this."

All of them begging and pleading as he left them behind, and if
George heard, he gave no sign.

His pelvis broke the surface and then one leg, his knee rising
until his foot pressed down on the album. Alison stood, still holding
his arm, as he slid the other leg free and crawled from the fireplace,
his mouth in a mocking smile. He settled back on his heels, a di-
aphanous figure with a blurred outline and dark spots marring his

skin, shirt, and pants. Again, a push of cold air from his mouth, and nothing more. He wasn't real. Not yet.

Breathy gasps and wordless cries lifted into the air.

"Will they die?" she asked.

He shrugged one shoulder, took her hand from his arm, and held it between his. Tiny prickles of cold slipped through her fingers to her palm. The tiger creeping in, searching for what he needed.

Soon, very soon.

Her shadow playdanced on the wall, but he cast none at all. She looked at her hand, swallowed in his own, and gripped the knife tighter. Then she lifted her chin and met his gaze head on.

"You wanted my pain. Here, take it."

She let go of the white and willed everything out in a rush: The razor sharp slice of scalpels cutting away dead, charred flesh. "We have to remove her eye. It's too damaged." The glimpse of Jonathan in the doorway, then waking to find him gone. The sorrow reflected in her mother's eyes. "I'm sorry, so sorry." The shame when a stranger looked a little too close. "Did you see that girl?" The face in the mirror. The hiding. The isolation. The fear. The rage.

She gave him everything. She gave him the Monstergirl.

And made him real.

He threw back his head, grinning in triumph, and let go of her hand to brace himself against the wall. He swayed in place. "Exquisite," he said.

With a shout, she whipped her arm forward and shoved the blade, all the way to the handle, into his upper chest. He jerked forward, his mouth working as he roared.

"You wanted to be real," she said, pulling the knife free.

A cascade of blood spilled over his shirt, and the grandfather clock chimed, the sound far in the distance. George swung his arm around and knocked the knife from her hand. It flew across the

266/ DAMIEN ANGELICA WALTERS

room, flipped end over end, and landed with a clatter on the floor near the front door.

"Did you think you could best me?"

She dropped to her knees and scrambled forward in a lunging crawl. Her hand tightened around the handle of the knife. From behind, he wrapped his arm around her and ripped the knife away.

"You little fool."

The clock chimed again. And buried within the sound, the voices swelled thick and fearful. All of them trapped inside, trapped because they believed his lies, too.

She pushed away and lurched to her feet, backing up until the door pressed hard into her spine, trapped by the wall on her right and

the tiger

George on her left. He tossed the knife over his shoulder, his shadow flitting across the wall. She lifted her hand. Waved it back and forth. Yes, his shadow moved, but only his. Hers had vanished.

No, oh no.

He clapped his hands together and laughed. "And now you see." He winked. "Or not."

The clock chimed.

She raised her hand higher. The edges of her flesh blurred, a halo replacing the real; her body, the same, all the way to her toes.

"Without your pain, you are nothing," he said.

"That's not true."

He laughed again, but more blood seeped from his wound and he staggered on his feet. A tiny movement, but there nonetheless. He grabbed her arm. Pins and needles exploded beneath her skin.

"Tell me," he said, as he brought his face close to hers. "What has it felt like here, all alone? You could've had so much more. Thomas was quite fond of you. He was hoping you'd come back."

"It. Wasn't. Real."

"Perhaps not, but it would've felt real. That's more than you feel here, yes?"

Thomas's face flashed in her mind, and then his features melted into Jonathan's. The last time she'd ever seen him—a glimpse in the doorway at the hospital. The hint of a dream, a promise, through the drug-thick haze; a touch of something good despite the hurt. But when she woke, he was gone. Gone because she was ugly, and no one, no one, no one would ever want to be with her again. And all she had were her scars and the tiny diamond ring and the pity.

She swallowed hard. Shoved the memory away.

The rip in George's shirt revealed the gash on his chest. The blood stopped flowing, and then dripped up, back into the wound. The edges of the skin knitted back together, leaving smooth, scarless skin.

"I knew there was more. I will miss that when you're gone," he said. "Such agony and torment you have suffered. I wish I could've been there." He smiled. "Tell me, when you burned, did the flames kiss your skin like a lover?"

She sagged back and—

chime

—the light shifted. Her skin tingled. The walls flickered and changed from plaster and paint to elegance, freshly polished wood, and a gleaming black piano. The scents of brandy and perfume clung to the air. Candle flames danced on the walls.

A party waiting for the guest of honor, but all of it hazy, and within the haze, the suggestion of human shapes moving toward her. The echo of voices raised in fear.

She stumbled forward, her arms outstretched. Both arms translucent and not quite there. A shimmer in the air, a ghost girl.

The light wavered and traces of the ruin hiding below glimmered: a flash of peeling wallpaper, splintered floorboards, a wisp of cobweb. Emptiness and time. A grey palette of forgotten days and disembodies voices. Calling. Crying.

Images flickered. Rot and ruin, glamour and shine, and the shapes winked in and out between the two. And—

chime

—back to her house. Back to George. She stood in the archway between her living room and dining room and blinked away the disorientation. She'd moved in the paper world, not the real, yet somehow the two were tethered together. Because of George? Or because of her?

A pale haze hung in the air, leaching the color from the walls. The edges of her furniture now matched the edges of her body. Smeared and indistinct. There, but fading away.

And her legs were missing from the knee down. She let out a wail, her voice paper-thin. The rest of her was still blurred at the edges, but past the knee, the blur turned to a waver in the air. She took a step. Pins and needles danced beneath her skin again, and the wood beneath her feet felt insubstantial. Wrong.

George stepped toward her, his smile wide and predatory. "Do you understand now?" he said. His shape held tight to the sharp and defined. He laughed and—

chime

—the haze had lightened. Brightened. The edges still murky and dim, but at the center, vibrant and defined. And she was back in Pennington House. But she wasn't alone. Thomas, Rachel, Josephine, Elizabeth, Eleanor, Edmund, Madeline, all of them with their arms outstretched, mouths open, and eyes wide.

Underneath the perfume and hair oil, there was a trace of rot. She backed out into the foyer, and they followed, a slow-moving hint of color and shape. Pale pink drops fell from the stumps of Rachel's arms. Madeline lurched, her body twisted. Thomas fell to the floor and pulled himself toward her, his muscles straining.

Their edges were pale, but solid in the center of limbs, torso, and face. Her own limbs were the same. Turning to real? A small hand touched hers and—

chime

—the real world stole her back. In her dining room now. Yet the colors had faded even more, were fading still, as though someone had turned on a tap to wash them away. The murky air turned her steps heavy and slow and when she looked down, she saw that her legs were gone and her upper body floated above empty space.

"Bring me back!" she cried, her voice muted and dull.

A chimera of not quite real and not quite missing, caught between the paper and real. And when the clock stopped, which would claim her as its own?

"Go away, Monstergirl," George said, and—

chime

—the world exploded with color. Dark wood shimmered. Wallpaper sparkled from the glow of a hundred candles. Glass-covered sconces glittered. And the prisoners of Pennington House advanced.

A river of red ran from Rachel's severed arms, splashing to the floor. Her dress trailed through the gore, and left a fan shaped spread of blood behind. Josephine, a flesh covered bag of bones, clung to one of Edmund's arms; on his other, Eleanor with her head bent in an unnatural direction. Madeline thumped and thudded, her body malformed. A ruined paper doll. Thomas's useless legs dragged behind him. Pitiful monsters dressed in their Sunday best. Mary stood off to the side, the bruises around her neck a mottled purple. Their mouths worked with cries of pain and moans of torment. Their eyes aware, alive and suffering.

The candles went out with a hiss. Wallpaper bubbled and peeled; curtains sagged at the windows; floorboards splintered and warped. A crack spiderwebbed across the lens of Edmund's monocle. Seams split with quick pops of thread, silk moldered, and lace frayed at the edges.

The flesh beneath it all turned grey.

Cheeks hollowed. Fingers curled in. The cries turned liquid, and the stink of putrescence mixed with the mold and mildew. Flakes of skin dislodged, spiraling to the floor in a macabre snowfall. Rachel's stumps oozed thick yellow-green pus. A white shard of bone poked through Eleanor's neck with a brittle crack.

Mary raised one rotting hand. "Help us, please."

Alison gagged and took a step back.

"Please," Thomas said. His fingertips grazed the skin of her ankles; she shuddered at the slick touch. Her perfect skin gleamed pale in the darkening light—

chime

—and she stood in the doorway of her kitchen, amidst a fog. A dull blur replaced walls and floor. Flashes of color sparked here and there—the metallic glint of the faucet in her sink, the white edge of the refrigerator.

And she was gone from the waist down. Light peeked through the gauze of what remained. She stepped forward, felt nothing, and stifled a cry. She had to put an end to it all; George was too dangerous to allow free. She couldn't let him use or hurt anyone else.

But how? There was so little of her left.

She blinked away tears. Hard. No tears. No pity. She had to kill the tiger. It was the only way she'd ever be free, and she had to end it before it was too late—

chime

—and into Pennington House once more, a world of vibrant color and defined shapes. A world of ruin with motionless corpses strewn across the floor. Twisted bones and human wreckage. A small body lay in the corner, half-skin, half-bone. Alison ran, the floor firm and real beneath her feet, bent down, and caressed the right cheek, which still wore a patch of greying skin.

"I'm so sorry," she said.

"Alison," Mary managed from between cracked lips.

Beneath Alison's hand, Mary's skin warmed and changed from grey to pale. Turning whole, turning to real. Alison touched Mary's arm, and the skin reknitted like a film run in reverse, the damage undone. Decay unmade. Tears sparkled in the little girl's eyes as she held out her hands, turning them over, her eyes twin spheres of surprise and disbelief.

With her free hand, Alison touched the nearest body. The skeletal remains fell apart with a clatter of bone on wood. She touched another. It, too, collapsed.

Something hard dug into her waist; she pulled out the matchbox and held it in one hand while she gave Mary's arm a gentle squeeze with the other. "Everything will be okay," she said, choking out each word.

"Please don't leave me here alone."

Alison's apology caught in her throat, and all she could do was slowly shake her head.

"Don't let him hurt you, too," Mary said.

As soon Alison took her hand away, the grey began to creep in again—

chime

—and she was back in her own house, in her kitchen. Everything was soft, wavering like a photograph left too long in the sun. And she, too, was nearly gone, her arms the only thing left. She turned the matchbox over in her hand.

Fire destroys everything.

The lighter fluid...

It wouldn't be enough. She turned toward the stove. Her arms shimmered translucent from the elbows up, but her fingers still held their shapes. And the knobs on the stove felt real beneath her fingers. Real enough. She turned them all.

Mary's pained voice drifted in the air. "Alison, please..."

She stepped through the table, through the wall, while the gas hissed its sulfurous rotten egg stink. George stood in the dining room, running his hands along the spines of the photo albums. Where he touched, the colors bloomed into life. He frowned over his shoulder. "I thought you'd left already. Not much longer, from the look of it."

Her arms vanished above the wrist, leaving disembodied hands glistening in the hazy gloom..

"Not much longer for either one of us. You said you wanted to know what it felt like to burn, remember?" she said, her voice a breathy ripple in the air.

Triumph built inside her chest, and then the matchbox spiraled to the floor, landing with a quiet rattle. Her hands were gone. All of her, gone. George burst into peals of laughter and turned away. She shrieked; he didn't even flinch.

But I'm still here. I am. Please, it can't end this way. I need to make it right.

Another voice, spoke, a voice in triplicate: *That may be true, but what are you prepared to give up?*

Anything. Everything.

Something tugged deep in her chest, a firework of heat and something stronger, something larger. She tipped back her head, felt herself cleave in two—a sensation of unzipping, of undoing. When it ceased, she was staring at a mirror copy of herself. The copy split into three, three women wearing her face, scars and all, draped in long robes of red, yellow, and purple. Narrow strands of ribbon were tied from their wrists to the air where hers should be.

Although their faces were hers, there were subtle differences: Red's mouth was set into a tight line, her eyes flashing. Yellow's shoulders were slumped, but her face was hard, purposeful. Purple was weeping, her hands clenched into fists, yet her back was straight.

They spoke again as one: "Will you finally let us go for good? Will you let go?"

Yes.

"It is done," a voice said. "Done," said another. "Done," a third.

Icy hands touched hers, untied the ribbons. Pain coursed through her body, ebbed slowly as the women stepped away, no longer Muses of Disfigurement, never muses, but Horsewomen of a Private Apocalypse, pieces of her she no longer needed.

Untethered, Alison saw them for who, what, they truly were: Red had pointed teeth and her fingers didn't end in fingernails but in talons; Yellow carried a length of rope in one hand fashioned into a noose, a long strip of fabric in the other; Purple held a scalpel in her hand. Their smiles were radiant and horrible, their eyes alight with the sheen of madness. They were the true Monstergirls.

George's head snapped around, his face contorting at the sight of the women, his eyes awash in shock.

"End it," Red said, her words whips as she pressed the matchbox into Alison's hand. "End him."

"I'm sorry, Mom," Alison said. "I love you."

She struck a match. The tiny flame danced alone for a split second, a tiny scrap of golden light, and in that moment, he saw her again.

"What have you done?" he shouted.

The tiger, *her* tiger, made of heat and destruction, exploded from its cage.

George's mouth opened in a circle, then the beast engulfed his limbs, and inside the flames, the women writhed round him like a tornado. He howled in pain and fury and they laughed in response, the sound of a hundred prowling hyenas, of a thousand madmen locked in windowless cells.

"Now you can't hurt anyone anymore," Alison said, giving him her back. She didn't need to watch it happen. She didn't want to see.

Something hit the floor with a heavy thump and a grunt. She heard the sizzle of flesh, smelled the stink of smoldering skin. There was a wet tear, a choking scream, a sound like teeth crunching into bone.

And then the roar swallowed them whole.

Flames raced up the walls and across the floor, eating the bookcases, the photo albums, everything in its path. She stretched out her arms and moved through the blaze, a woman-shaped column of flame. No heat. No pain.

No fear.

The colors faded. The roar muted. She spared one last glance behind her. A lifeless husk, bloodied and torn, lay on the floor. The tiger was dead. Well and truly dead. For good, this time.

Of the women, there was no sign.

The clock chimed again, for the twelfth and last time, a small hand slipped into hers, and the darkness pulled her down and down and down.

PART X

THE FINAL PAGE

CHAPTER 24

The woman stands on the sidewalk outside the ruin of her daughter's home. Some of the neighbors have placed flowers on the marble steps, which, though singed nearly black, are still intact. Scorch marks darken the brick front, and open spaces live where glass windows used to be. The back of the house, near the kitchen, is much worse, with gaping holes in the brick. Yet the houses on either side are in pristine, perfect condition. A mystery or a miracle, depending on who is asked.

She looks for explanation in the charred remains, knowing she won't find one. She bows her head, sobs quietly, and as she turns to go, she can almost see, through the haze of tears, her daughter standing just inside the front window.

Almost.

■ ■ ■

Elena finds the album leaning against several bags blocking the back door of the shop. She mutters under her breath, grabs the album, and pushes the bags out of the way. She knows the bags will contain mostly trash. People who bring things worthy of resale do so during the day.

The album is scarred and battered, but she carries it inside anyway. If it has old pictures inside it, someone will buy it. People collect strange things.

She brushes a bit of dust off the cover. Inside, the first page holds an inscription written in indigo ink. She chuckles under breath. A silly bit of nonsense about staying away from tigers because they bite. Foolish. Everyone knows tigers are dangerous.

A faint smell of smoke clings to the page, but no matter. She'll put it in the front window anyway. She turns past the inscription to find a blurry photo of a young woman standing hand in hand with a small child in front of a burned-out shell of a house. A scruffy teddy bear dangles at the child's side. Oddly enough, despite the ruin behind them, both the woman and the girl are smiling.

And the rest of the pages are blank.

ACKNOWLEDGMENTS

Thank you to Richard Thomas and Dark House Press for believing in this book, and to Alban Fischer and George Cotronis for their fantastic art.

Thank you to Linda Epstein for helping me when the story was ugly and full of holes.

Thank you to my friends for your support, especially my Wolfpack. Lena, Mike, Katrin, Joe, Justin, Anya, and Scott, I love you all.

Thank you to the writers who inspire me every day—Livia Llewellyn, Helen Marshall, Laird Barron, and John Langan.

Thank you to E. Catherine Tobler and Kristi DeMeester for always being willing to beta read.

Thank you to my family for their love and support.

And to the readers: without you, the words mean nothing at all.

DAMIEN ANGELICA WALTERS' work has appeared or is forthcoming in various anthologies and magazines, including *The Year's Best Dark Fantasy & Horror 2015*, *Year's Best Weird Fiction: Volume One*, *Cassilda's Song*, *The Mammoth Book of Cthulhu: New Lovecraftian Fiction*, *Nightmare Magazine*, *Black Static*, and *Apex Magazine*. She was a finalist for a Bram Stoker Award for "The Floating Girls: A Documentary," originally published in *Jamais Vu*. *Sing Me Your Scars*, a collection of short fiction, was released in 2015 from Apex Publications. Find her on Twitter @DamienAWalters or on the web at http://damienangelicawalters.com.

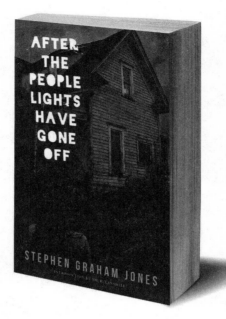

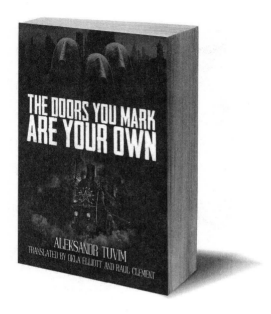